THERE IS NO BODY

THERE IS NO BODY

A Journey Through the Dark Boroughs of a Pedophilic Cannibal's Mind

Eat the Evidence: Part Three

John C. Espy

KARNAC

First published in 2015 by
Karnac Books Ltd
118 Finchley Road
London NW3 5HT

Copyright © 2015 by John C. Espy

The right of John C. Espy to be identified as the author of this work has been asserted in accordance with §§ 77 and 78 of the Copyright Design and Patents Act 1988.

All rights reserved. No part of this publication may be reproduced, stored in a retrieval system, or transmitted, in any form or by any means, electronic, mechanical, photocopying, recording, or otherwise, without the prior written permission of the publisher.

British Library Cataloguing in Publication Data

A C.I.P. for this book is available from the British Library

ISBN-13: 978-1-78220-093-2

Typeset by V Publishing Solutions Pvt Ltd., Chennai, India

Printed in Great Britain by TJ International Ltd, Padstow, Cornwall

www.karnacbooks.com

For Treasa Glinnwater

CHAPTER ONE

Bridgewater and the metamorphosis

Digging through Bar Jonah's stacks of papers seemed never ending. Theisen joked that Bar Jonah's crap reproduced each night after the lights had been turned out. Cameron and Wilson peeled open one of the dusty boxes and found that it was filled with stacks of Bar Jonah's prison records, including his past psychiatric evaluations dating back to the 1975 assault. Bar Jonah had even more reports than Bridgewater had bothered to send when Wilson had made his initial request. The first one that Cameron pulled out of the box was a psychological evaluation by Timothy Sinn, MA, staff psychologist at Bridgewater.

> At the request of the department of mental health and in accordance with the provisions of section 9, chapter 123a, I conducted a psychiatric examination of David Brown at the Massachusetts treatment center. My examination consisted of two interviews on 8/18/83 and 8/25/83, as well as a review of his records at the treatment center. Prior to each interview I informed him as to who I was, the nature and purpose of the examination and the fact

that whatever was said was not confidential and could be used in my report. He indicated that he understood these conditions and agreed to talk with me. Mr. Brown is a 27-year-old single white male who was committed to the treatment center in June, 1979 following a conviction of attempted murder, and kidnapping of two young boys in 1977 for which he received 18–20 years. There has been at least one other similar previous offense for assault and battery on a young boy in which he disrobed him, choked him and then released him. While at the treatment center he has been quite resistant to treatment in any form. He had to be persuaded by other members in his large group to attend group in order not to lose his maximum tier privilege. His participation has been on the minimal side. He has the historical pattern of isolation and passivity, which is played out daily at the treatment center. He has rationalized his unwillingness to participate in group therapy because group therapy would not help him because his offenses are not sexual and he really doesn't belong here. His original willingness to come to the treatment center was because it seemed to be better than serving out a prison sentence. He has been seen by most of the staff as unable or unwilling to participate in therapy. In spite of his resistance to group and therapy he has allegedly been asking for an individual therapist for the past year.

It is not clear what his motivation is for this request. In fact, there is little that is clear regarding any of his motivations. He has no interpersonal relations, minimal job experience; medical defects of double vision, severe headaches, and blackouts, early sexual involvement with peer boys; aggressive assault on a peer girl; active fantasy life consisting of sadistic murderous ideations.

It appears that Mr. Brown's primary aim for these murderous assaults is the aggression, with sexual gratification being secondary. He is preoccupied with violence and unable to identify concurrent sexual feelings; however, he admits to experiencing erections when he thinks or does violent behaviors. Testing results indicate a very disturbed schizoid personality. Mr. Brown is an overweight individual who reports having high blood pressure when he was examined at Bridgewater State Hospital in 1977. He reports frequent "blurred," double and fuzzy vision since he was nine years old along with severe headaches "lasting up to nine days usually." Mr. Brown describes experiencing pounding in his head, which sometimes makes him cry. It should be noted Mr. Brown has one brown eye and one blue eye which, he states, is a result of change when he was a baby ("It makes me different"). He has experienced blackouts "six or seven times" and suggests this may have happened during the current offense.

Timothy L. Sinn, Assistant Staff Psychologist

After Cameron read Sinn's report out loud, Wilson shook his head in disgust that not only Massachusetts but also Montana, in '94, had let Bar Jonah walk. The havoc that Bar Jonah had brought into the lives of children and their families made Wilson sick to his stomach.

Wilson reached into the box and pulled out another evaluation from Bridgewater, this one conducted by psychiatrist Robert Levy, MD, from October 31st, 1983.

To The Presiding Justice
Worcester County Superior Court
Re: David Paul Brown, B. T. #407

Mr. Brown was able to trace back his assaultive behavior to 1963, when as a first grader, he suddenly began to strangle a female playmate. He reports that he has read extensively about multiple murders, and has a long-standing interest in instruments of torture. His fantasies of violence have apparently been the predominant source of sexual excitement for him as he has had no adult heterosexual or homosexual experience. Mr. Brown is a large, almost massive individual weighing close to 375 pounds. His appearance is further notable because of one brown eye and one blue eye. He was able to relate in a comfortable, lucid and cooperative manner and displayed no evidence of either a thought disorder or other active psychotic process. He spoke quite openly about his awareness of the inner anger and rage he has inside of himself and articulated that he still has a lot left which will take a long time to come out. In addition he has some intellectual sense of the origins of this rage as well as the recognition that these feelings have become sexualized making them part of a private inner fantasy life that has been active for years. Mr. Brown also told me that his main purpose in filing this petition was to gain a better sense of what to work on. In this vein he spoke more than once of his persistent efforts to negotiate an individual treatment relationship. He seemed to acknowledge rather neutrally that he has not been able to reveal the kind of material that is therapeutically important in a group setting nor does he feel that this will change. He presents himself as clear that he wants and needs individual treatment and is tenacious in his efforts to obtain it, without being bitter or inappropriate.

I feel that Mr. Brown has made a good adjustment to the treatment center and recognizes that he will need many more years of (hopefully) individual treatment if he is to deal with and resolve the intense, sexualized rage that has led to his offenses and preoccupations with murder and torture. I would be inclined to support his request for an individual treatment relationship especially given the quality and nature of his inner world. At this time Mr. Brown *remains* a sexually dangerous person because he himself is only too aware of the inner anger and fantasies that continue to live within him. Without long-term treatment that would of necessity involve an important human relationship with a therapist(s), the likelihood of repeated offenses outside of the institution would be high.

Respectfully Submitted
Robert D. Levy, M.D., Consultant Psychiatrist

It was clear that Bar Jonah had not been able to fool Sinn and Levy. They saw him as a "sexually dangerous person" and were concerned about his level of sexualized aggression. Each of the two evaluations Cameron and Wilson had looked at so far listed Bar Jonah's name as David Paul Brown. They knew that Bar Jonah had changed his name while he was in Bridgewater. What they didn't know at the time was how it had come about.

* * *

When he was first sent to Wapole State Penitentiary in 1977, he was nothing more than an isolated, fat, puerile, baby-fucker, named David Paul Brown. It didn't take long before he discovered the world of prison pen pals. A network of lonely and frequently desperate people, men and women, looking for friends and sometimes, with more ominous consequences, men and women looking for mates. When David wrote letters, he hoped to get responses from women who were listed in one of the many lonely hearts publications that circulated throughout the prison. He was more often than not unsuccessful. His name was too ordinary. He had not yet begun to rehearse his epic myth about being raped by a gang of marauding neighborhood boys. For David this was a time of confusion and experimentation. He described himself as a chrysalis wanting to become a butterfly.

In August 1983, David began to think about changing his name. Within a few weeks, he had made his decision. Initially he thought about taking the name of "Job." His suffering had been so great, God had tested him, it seemed only right that he should inherit the mantle of the one whose suffering all others is measured by. Since David had gone to prison, he had avoided and resisted almost all treatment, refusing individual and group psychotherapy and medications. But he did attend Bible study. Nothing would get in the way of David going to Bible study. On several occasions David had been disciplined after he dropped his Bible and photographs of young boys tumbled out onto the green scuffed tile floors.

* * *

When Tyra last visited him in August 1983, he told her that he had for sure decided to change his name. He no longer wanted to be known as David Brown. Tyra said she understood; he had to find his own path in life. Maybe changing his name would be a fresh start. Help him rid himself of the anguish of his tortured past. David told Tyra that he was going to take the name of "Job."

On the drive back up to Worchester, Tyra was ecstatic. At some point in time David would probably get out. God knows what he would do when he did. At least this way, she wouldn't have to bear the burden of being identified as his mother. Especially with the name of "Job." A few days later, Tyra got a letter in the mail. He had begun attending Jewish services at Bridgewater. It had made him realize that he wanted to become Jewish. After all, his religious heritage was Jewish, Tyra's maiden name being Bloomquist. He had decided to change his last name from Brown to Bloomquist. Tyra was furious. Rarely had she been so enraged at David. An hour after Tyra opened the letter, she was in her car speeding toward

Bridgewater. She was there so many times during the week that the guards knew her by name. They were always so nice to bend the rules of visiting times. She could pretty much come and go as she pleased.

When she got out of the car, Tyra grabbed the crumpled letter she had received from David that was now lying crumpled on the passenger seat. As Tyra opened her car door, the acrid, humid air came flooding over her. She was an old woman: the dense air made it harder and harder for her to get a good, long-lasting breath. She waited for a moment, wiped the small beads of sweat from her forehead, and struggled to pull herself out of the car. Before she closed the door, Tyra cranked the window a bit to let some of the heat escape while she was inside.

* * *

David's dull eyes lit up when he walked into the visitors' lounge and unexpectedly saw Tyra. She was pacing around and around the green and soft pink Naugahyde chairs that were randomly spread throughout the room. When David walked toward Tyra, he noticed that her eyes were cold, aloof, and angry. As she paced, David saw his wrinkled letter scrunched up in her right hand. He walked over to her and wrapped his right arm around her shoulder and tried to pull her against him. Tyra was stiff as a board. She looked up at him, raised the crumpled letter to his face and said, "What is this crap about you taking my maiden name?" David tried to explain that he wanted to explore his Jewish heritage. Tyra's voice crackled when she yelled, "We have *no* Jewish heritage, I am Swedish." In a rare stand of resistance against David's will Tyra told him flat out, "You will not use my maiden name and if you do I'll file a complaint against you in probate court." David bowed his head, dropped his chastised eyes, and in an even rarer act of compliance, he immediately acquiesced. Tyra turned and began walking out of the visitors' lounge. David stood stunned, listening to Tyra walking away, her tiny heels clicking one after the other against the tile floor, as she scurried toward the guard's station. She stopped suddenly, briefly turned around and said she was sorry but she was just so upset. The guard then heard her say, "How could you even think of doing this to my family?"

* * *

Bar Jonah went back to his cell and prayed. He had been on the wrong path. The pain he had caused Tyra now made it clear to him that changing his name was not just a desire to be closer to his Jewish heritage, but a call from God to present himself to the world for who *he* was. David began studying his Bible more intensely and praying to the Lord God for guidance. In a few short nights, God came to David in his dreams. He was not only sure who he was in God's eyes, but he was now sure of the path that God had laid before him. The name he chose must reflect both. As with all of his decisions, big and small, David began writing. Through God's guidance David was also sure that whatever name he chose, it must point more women with children in his direction. One thing that God had shown David through other inmates was that it was easier to be set free from Bridgewater's bondage if you had the open arms of a spouse-to-be waiting for you on the outside.

During the week of his realization, David barely left his cell. He had come to understand that there would be no discernment on his part. He would not come to choose a name: a name would be chosen for him by the Lord. Everything was out of his control. He had to be patient and let the Lord's hand guide him. David was waking up in the middle of the night, not to the sound of clanging doors, but to the reverberations in his mind, after the Lord spoke to him through his dreams. He had been fervently reading his Bible day and night. For this week, he would give all to God, rarely even going to chow. This was bigger than he was. If he passed the test, God would surely reward him.

David was beginning to understand that he was one of the Lord's disciples, one of His chosen few. One who embodied the message of deliverance. Throughout his life David knew he had caused Tyra immense sorrow. He was sorry but Tyra had to understand that the Lord's plan for him was not a path without pain. Tyra, like the biblical Rachel, mother of Benjamin, must sacrifice herself if her son was to become who the Lord commanded him to be. Pain and suffering were the ways of Israelites. David remembered Deuteronomy 33:27, *The eternal God is thy refuge, and underneath are the everlasting arms: and he shall thrust out the enemy from before thee; and shall say, Destroy them.* The Lord had placed upon David many burdens, one of which was giving him keen powers of seeing the truth in all that he witnessed. This led to wisdom, perhaps the greatest burden of all. But through the granting of the gift of wisdom, David, like the Levites before him, of which he was a direct descendent, could now pass judgment. Two nights before he was to become ordained through God's grace of ascribing him a new name, David had another dream. A dream of Tamar. *I am an Israeli soldier. I am fighting bravely and in the heat of battle I am wounded. My wounds are so bad that my leg must be amputated and I must use a fake limb to get around. There is a nurse, she says her name is Tamar.* Then David dreamed the story of Tamar. *She is a scared woman, a whore in the worst sense of the word. She tricks the good man Judah into making her pregnant while she's working as a whore in Enalm. For payment, Judah offers her a goat. She says no, she only wants the seal of his ring. Judah gives her the seal and goes on his way. Later he hears that a woman has given birth to twins. She is blaspheming the House of Judah with her lies, Judah decries. He orders her to be burnt to death. When Judah's slaves arrive to kill the woman, she says she has the seal of Judah and sends it back to Judah with his slaves. Judah is shamed and calls for the woman, who he knows as Tamar, to come and live in the House of Judah. But in all of the time they are together, Judah will never have sex with her. He will never bring shame into his House again by defiling himself with Tamar*. When David awoke, he knew that he must marry. That he must find a wife. A wife who already has children so he would not have to defile himself and bring shame upon his House.

* * *

David sat in his cell, wrapped in his rough wool blanket, having on nothing underneath, and opened his Bible. He could still feel himself running away from the Lord. He was trying to escape, as all prophets had, before the Lord caught up with them. And He always did. When David looked down at the open Bible lying on his lap, he realized that God had found him again. Like David, Jonah ben Amittai did not want to be a prophet. But God said it shall be so. But Jonah, like a disobedient child ran away from the Lord, his God. Jonah tried to escape from the Lord by boarding a reed boat bound for Tarshish. The Lord was angry and made a violent storm rise up from the sea, causing Jonah to fall into the water. As he was falling, Jonah thought all was lost. He had angered the Lord and death was his punishment. Suddenly, Jonah was swallowed up by a great fish. A fish greater than any other fish had ever been. The Lord made Jonah spend three days and three nights inside the belly of the fish, before it came up out of the water and spat Jonah out onto the land. The Lord sent Jonah out to warn the people of Nineveh to repent, and they did. But Jonah was not pleased that he had fulfilled the command of the Lord. Jonah was angry. Throughout all of his life, Jonah would remain angry. He accepted the burden placed upon him by the Lord and ran away no more. But, even the love of the Lord could never extinguish the fire that burned inside the belly of Jonah. David caressed the onion skin page and felt akin to Jonah.

* * *

David didn't dream that night. He had not tossed and turned on his bed either. Deep into the morning hours, David sat up, leaned back against the cinderblock wall, and opened his Bible again. The time had come. His name would be revealed to him today. It was all there. He had kept copious notes; everything was written on his personal stationery. Stationery that would now need to be changed. When David shoved the covers to the end of the bed, he knocked his Bible onto the cold cement floor. The Good Book fell open to Leviticus, Chapter Seven. David knew Chapter Seven very well. It was one of his favorite books of the Bible. Before he reached down and picked up his Bible, David leaned back, deeply filled his lungs with the cool institutional morning air and exhaled for what seemed to be forever. He was filled with bliss. The Lord was with him now and forever. They were one. David scooted to the edge of the bed. He could feel his bulging belly fold itself in half as he bent down to pick up his Bible. David than sat back and read Leviticus 7:1–9.

Right before David closed his Bible for the day and prepared to bring forth his name, he silently read one final passage from Leviticus. *"This is the law of the burnt offering, of the meat offering, and of the sin offering, and of the trespass offering, and of the consecrations, and of the sacrifice of the peace offerings"* (KJV, Leviticus 7:37). He made a few scribbles on a small white tablet and set it aside. David could feel the depth of the Lord when he pulled a long breath down to the bottom of his lungs. He held it for a moment, wanting to savor the fullness of God in His promise to him. Then he exhaled.

David pulled out a stack of papers from under his mattress and laid them out in chronological order from the first notations of his first realization to the notes he had just made. Then he picked up a loose piece of typing paper and a pencil that he regularly sharpened on the sharp edge of the underside of the metal frame of his bedsprings. He stopped before he went any further, looked up and said, *"To You O Lord I commend My Spirit."* Then David received his transformation from the Lord and wrote *"Nathaneal Benjamin Levi Bar Jonah"* across the paper.

He stood up and walked out of his cell and down to chow. He would never again be known as David Paul Brown.

As Nathaneal Benjamin Levi Bar Jonah sat down to eat, he began to write his first new ad for *Sweetheart* magazine. How was he going to describe himself? It came to him in a flash.

* * *

Cameron read to Wilson and Theisen David Brown's account of how he became Bar Jonah. They sat transfixed. Cameron and Theisen were fascinated with the case. Wilson was fascinated with Bar Jonah. Anything Bar Jonah had written, Wilson was reading. From the tiniest scraps of paper to his voluminous, blue-lined spiral notebooks.

Wilson began to set Bar Jonah's writings out chronologically, looking at his earliest to his latest. There was so much that was written in some kind of code. The FBI cryptographers had begun to look at some of Bar Jonah's writings. One cryptographer told Wilson that he had never seen anyone, outside of Al Qaeda, write more in code than Bar Jonah. After many tries, the FBI was not able to fully unravel his code. It didn't fit any known scientific pattern and was more complex than any code they had ever seen. When the reports came back that Quantico was unable to crack the code, Wilson decided to take it on himself to try to do what he could to understand the sequencing of Bar Jonah's system of moving numbers and letters around. Even though Wilson had opened a file on the Ramsay case, it wasn't considered a high priority by the FBI, especially after four years of going nowhere. There wasn't a strong desire to put many more resources into it than they already had. This was a local matter: let them spend the money.

* * *

Cameron's marriage was now crumbling at a rapid pace. He was never home. The case had taken over his life. Theisen's wife, Laurie, continued to remain steadfast that Bar Jonah was not going to destroy their marriage. Wilson's marriage remained rock solid. The pressure from Groves never seemed to let up. Cameron and Theisen had to defend their work on the case day to day. Cameron would do anything that he could find to justify keeping the case alive. Groves battled him every step of the way. The biggest card Cameron had to draw on was of course that Zach Ramsay was still missing. In the five years since Zach had disappeared, the GFPD had made no progress in solving the case and for the most part had not put any resources into pursuing it. Cameron refused to let the case continue to falter. He knew he had Bar Jonah on the assault of the boys. But he as well as Wilson and Theisen wanted Bar Jonah for the murder of Zach. They were all dedicated to the final resolution of the case; however, they hated going to work every day and dealing with the politics.

* * *

After Brown changed his name to Bar Jonah, responses to his ad in *Sweetheart* magazine dramatically increased. Before he changed his name, he was receiving about ten to twenty responses a month. Most of them were from single women, who didn't have children. Somehow the name David Brown didn't capture the imagination of many of the women scouring the magazine, seeking husbands. Within three months of changing his name, Bar Jonah was receiving more than 600 responses a month. His ad was catchy: *Roses are red, violets are blue, I'm marriage minded, you be too. I desire an already made family. I LOVE kids. I have tutti-fruity eyes, 5' 8" and weigh about 20 stones, have brown hair and have been known to be quite a character at times. I'm a gourmet cook. I LOVE to cook. Send $9.50 to help with my expenses.* He was getting so many answers that he couldn't keep up by sending handwritten responses; Bar Jonah needed a computer.

* * *

Bar Jonah told Tyra that she had to make Bob get him a computer. It was the only way he could keep up with all of his new pen pals. He was sure he was going to be able to find someone to marry through the ads he was placing. At some point, having a fiancée was going to help him get out of prison. Bob was a computer analyst and programmer. Bar Jonah told Tyra that a new computer, the Commodore 64, had just come out on the market. He wanted one. She and Bob could put their money together and get him one. They could afford it. Tyra tried to buck a bit, saying that she was living on a fixed income and that Lois and Bob had to help her out. Bar Jonah didn't care; they had a lot more money than he did and they weren't locked up. Bar Jonah issued an edict to Tyra, get him a computer or don't bother to come back and see him. He pointed out that Bob still had his first nickel. A few weeks later, a large package arrived at Bridgewater; Bar Jonah had got his Commodore 64. Bob even sent him a dot-matrix printer. The guards at Bridgewater were jealous and resentful. They didn't make that much and couldn't afford something like that for their family. Yet Bar Jonah would now be sitting in his cell clicking out hundreds of letters a week and demanding that the guards take them to the mailroom immediately. Every Friday, Bar Jonah called Tyra collect, saying, "I want more stamps." He was meeting a lot of women who wanted to marry him; it was a big plus that they had kids. Bar Jonah said he wanted Tyra to be a grandmother to his kids. Just like the great mom she had always been to him. A thick manila envelope started arriving every Tuesday filled with stamps.

Coming into focus

The wind was howling louder than usual in Great Falls on Saturday morning August 5th. Cameron, Wilson, and Theisen had agreed to meet at the police station to continue going through Bar Jonah's papers. Cameron and Wilson got there on time. Theisen was late and grumpy. A bad dream he had had that night kept him tossing and turning. Cameron and Wilson crossed their legs and sat quietly as Theisen, somewhat embarrassingly, told them his dream.

He was lying on a bed beside Bar Jonah in his jail cell. Bar Jonah reaches over and puts his arm around Theisen, looks into his eyes, and tells him that he beat Zach to death and ate him. Bar Jonah's eyes are looking tenderly into Theisen's when suddenly Bar Jonah's huge hands are wrapped around Theisen's throat, trying to choke him to death. He can't breathe ... then he wakes up.

What Theisen didn't tell Cameron and Wilson was that Laurie sat up in bed and began shaking him. Theisen heard Laurie calling his name like she was at the other end of a tunnel. He heard Laurie saying, "It's okay, it's okay." He felt her hand rubbing his arm. "You're safe," she was saying.

Cameron snottily spoke up and said that at least Theisen got to sleep with Bar Jonah. He'd been sleeping alone most of the time because his wife was getting tired of him screaming in the middle of the night. Wilson said he hadn't had any nightmares; he was only going to let so much of Bar Jonah inside his head.

Wilson had become obsessed with the nine words, *Hasah, Caforum, Minna, Lecourum, Rab, Plumius, Deporum, Alegy,* and *Mackdum* that Bar Jonah carried around with him. Bar Jonah had never been without them and now neither was Wilson. The crypto lab at Quantico said they had no idea what the words meant. Wilson refused to let it go.

* * *

Cameron pulled the lid off of one of the boxes and dumped a pile of papers onto the table. Glancing at the papers, it looked like the heap was mostly recipes. As Cameron fanned out the papers, Wilson quickly reached out and stopped Cameron's hand. Sandwiched in-between the torn out recipes was a thin spiral notebook that was open to a blank page. There was nothing obvious that was written on the white blue lined page. Wilson sat up in his chair and began to move his head around, catching the different ways the light would hit the paper at different angles. Cameron asked him what the hell he was doing.

Wilson didn't say anything. He reached out, picked up the notebook and began turning it around. His sharp eyes set right at the plane of the page, catching the light as it moved over the pad of paper. Like a gentle wave that reveals hidden treasures in the sand as it retreats back into the ocean, the cascading light and shadows were beginning to bring something to the surface of the page. Something someone had tried to hide. Wilson laid the notebook back on the table. He picked up a pencil and in one deft move flipped the eraser end like a baton into the cup of his hand as his index finger slid down to the tan colored sharpened tip. Wilson then began softly stroking the lead over the page.

There, like an image magically appearing in a photographer's developing tray, words began to emanate from the page. Some of the words Wilson could make out; others were lost.

sucked his penis past climax and got him to cum 3 me any trouble then secured him into glass case in the basement I built secretly and put him on the shelf I built. I then told him not to make a sound or I'd leave him down there for good into my second closet I built to hide and keep the light off. I also put the clothes I then left and captured another boy. His name was . He was 10. Once I got him near my home ... put him in a box. I then carried him into the house. I then his clothes we had sex together. I then added him with the boy I brought him some company. His name is and he's 10, too. again and I captured a young boy with a puppy him into my car. His name was into my house him into a box puppy.

Once I was in the house I opened   took the boy out and put the puppy in. I then told him that this is what's going to happen to you if you don't do what I tell you.   then picked up the puppy and took them back into the bedroom. I then fed the puppy to the snake. I then told him that the snake especially loves little boys like him.   his clothes and we had sex together. I   box and added him with the other 2. I then   was cooked. I fed him to the boys   they did eat it   then   I then cooked him. I then cut for at least   hours.   for   It was about 9   boy leaving the school grounds. I picked him up. He was going home because he was late and his mom needed to come back with him.   when we got   the garbage   parked and shut the engine off   shirt. I then grabbed my keys   opened the door   slipped the keys into my pocket. I then closed the door.   the boy. When I got to the house with the boy I pulled out a large knife. I then   off his hat and pushed him down with my hand over his mouth and the knife to his throat. I then asked him if he wanted to die and he said "no". I then told him to undo his pants or I was going to kill him. I watched him undo them. I then told him "Now pull them down" and did as fast as he could. I then said "Good boy". Now, I want you to pull your underwear down and he did as I asked. I then said "Good son", I think your going to be just fine as I played with his penis and held the knife to his throat. He then asked, "Mister, can I ask you a ques I said, "Sure". He then asked, "Are you going to kill me?" I said that depends on you, son if you do what I tell you and don't try to escape. I   you   as I   tell   you   do   what   said, Good   your   clothes   off.   then   took his   He said I   I said I opened the door. I quickly put   I told him if he made a sound I'd kill him. I then took him into the room closed the   him   I then said, "Just relax,   "

17

When Wilson flipped the page and raised the notebook to the light, he saw there was another couple of lines of indentation. *I tied him up and I carried him to the kitchen ... I lay on top of him ... he was going to be my supper tonight.* That night Wilson poured salt all over the steak dinner that his wife had fixed because he had to work on a Saturday. Cameron sweated so much he thought he had pissed the bed. Laurie had to again tell her husband that he was safe. He really wasn't buried underneath Bar Jonah's house and surrounded by packages of rotting meat. That too had just been a bad dream.

The pressure builds

Doc was having troubles with his cats. They seemed to be escaping to the outside more and more and with his leg being bad he couldn't run them down the way he used too. Some new neighbors were starting to complain about the smell coming from around his house. He couldn't understand why though. They were just his precious kitties: why did some people have to be so difficult?

Doc had never met a cop with any sense of style or sophistication. He thought Bellusci was one of the worst, crude and unrefined, especially for a detective. He didn't like the way he dressed either. Typical cheap polyester suits, he would say. You could spot a cop like him a mile away, just by the way he dressed.

Doc knew that at some point Cameron was going to come after him hard. He was the type you could push a bit but then it would get real bad when he pushed back. Maybe he should go on up to Canada like he had planned to with Zach. He hated to go alone though. It would be hard for him to drive so far by himself with the way his leg was. Even if Cameron did come after him or Bar Jonah said something, *he* hadn't done anything wrong. Bar Jonah was the one who made Zach disappear. He had nothing to do with it, except of course, now, how to live with the fact that the love of his life was gone forever. Perhaps by chance, another boy might come to him, who was as beautiful and as sexy as Zach, but Doc could not imagine such wonderment ever occurring. He was now an old man. Youthful boys didn't flock to him the way they had in his heyday. He remembered his time in Colorado and Texas. Those special times that he had shared with so many. The love he was able to bring into the lives of so many lost ones. Doc had so many special gifts. He was handsome, well-educated, and had been given the opportunity to serve his country bravely in the Korean war. He also had a special ability to understand cats. Doc so loved his cats. And, they loved him back.

* * *

A week after Cameron showed up at Doc's, a health inspector and an animal control officer knocked on Doc's door. Doc yelled for them to come in. His leg was so swollen that he just couldn't stand up to get to the door. When the door began to open, the health inspector heard Doc scream for them to be careful not to let any of his cats run out. But three darted out the door before he could stop them. Doc shook his head in exasperation, asking the two men standing in the foyer what they wanted. "Are you detectives too?" Doc asked. When they identified themselves, Doc silently wished they had been detectives.

The health inspector pulled out several complaints that the neighbors had filed and said that just from looking at the place, it was a health hazard and would have to be cleaned up. The animal control officer started to negotiate his way through the house and around the mounds of shit and cats trying to climb up his legs. It wasn't worth the effort. He huffed and told Doc to get rid of the cats. Doc begged him not to take his precious pets. "They are all I have," Doc implored.

Both the health inspector and the animal control officer wrote out a summons for Doc to provide proof to the court in seven days that the cats had been reduced to a "reasonable number" and that the place had been cleaned up. They had Doc sign a carbon-free pink ticket, saying that he had received the summons. When the men left, Doc began to cry uncontrollably. Doc looked down at the tiny black mouse hands on his wristwatch and saw that it had only taken the men ten minutes to make his world begin to crumble down around him.

Smooth talker

Cameron found notes for another ad that Bar Jonah had been working on in early 1990. *Kids are a must from small to 11. I am looking for a long term relationship and am planning on moving to Montana in the next year. So write me and take away my lonely fears. This is a new way for me to find a mate. I have never placed an ad before. I am looking for the right lady with kids to fill my life and make my house a home* What struck Cameron was how sure Bar Jonah seemed to be that he was not only going to be released from prison, but that he was going to be going to Montana. The notes were clipped to a letter from a woman named Pam Coon. Coon said she was twenty-three and had two kids, a two-year-old boy and a three-month-old girl. She was lonely and liked to write poetry. Coon wasn't fat but she wasn't thin either. She had just moved to Billings and was getting ready to go to nursing school. It sounded to her that Bar Jonah was a nice man who the police had pushed around a lot. She would love it if he would consider marrying her and helping her raise her kids. Coon was looking forward to hearing back from Bar Jonah. But she never did. Stapled right behind the letter from Coon were the letters from Sandy.

When Cameron read the letters from Sandy to Bar Jonah he found that she referred to him as "Mr. Romantic". Bar Jonah's letters were effusive with eloquent descriptions of himself. He was also effusive with his desire to devote himself to her and her kids. Bar Jonah wanted to move to Arkansas as soon as he got out of prison. It wouldn't be long, the wheels were in motion. Bar Jonah said that his mother and brother had found a couple of psychologists who understood that he was a Christian man who had dedicated his life to walking with God. The mistakes he had made in the past were long behind him and he had repented for any wrongs he had done. Now he spent most of his time in prison praying for those who had done him wrong. Especially those eight boys who had so savagely attacked him so long ago. It was a scar that he would have to carry with him until the day he died, but with the Lord's help, and He never let him down, he would be able to persevere. Sandy said she wanted to marry Bar Jonah right away. In fact she wanted to come up to Bridgewater and get married. This way her boys would have someone they could call their dad and she would have someone she could call her husband. Bar Jonah had thought it best not to. He wanted to wait and see how things were between them once he got out of prison, which wouldn't be too long. Sandy didn't want to send him any pictures of her boys because she was afraid they might get stolen by some of the other inmates, who weren't like Bar Jonah. She just didn't feel comfortable with her boys' pictures floating around a prison for sex offenders. Bar Jonah said he understood. Sandy wrote that she knew she could count on him for his understanding; he always understood everything. That was just how he was. He wasn't nothing like the other men she'd been married to. Bar Jonah said he didn't want to get married until he met her boys in person. He wanted to make sure that he liked them. Kids, especially boys were a big part of his life. If he didn't like Sandy's boys for some reason, it probably meant that there was something wrong with them. He just wouldn't want to waste his time trying to get to know them. In every letter that Cameron read from Bar Jonah to Sandy, he asked her to give him detailed descriptions of her boys. In every letter she did. She always wrote something different, always something that tried to paint a picture that she had good boys. Her sons knew that Sandy had had it rough and they did everything they could to make things as easy as possible for her. She wrote that she just wanted to find them a good dad.

* * *

Among the papers were Bar Jonah's copies of the pleadings and filings of his release from prison and his ultimate furloughing to Montana. There was also a letter from Oxford chief of police, James Triplett, who was concerned that Bar Jonah was being given a free ride by Judge Walter Steele after assaulting Michael Surprise.

> Date: 8/8/1991
> To: Ms. Rita Ernst, Secretary for the Chief of Police
> Oxford Police Department
> From: William Lochrie
> Title: Lieutenant
> Department of Correction, Fugitive Apprehension Unit
>
> Message: At your request, I am faxing a letter of October 31, 1983 From Robert Levy, M.D., in which he states that David Brown, AKA, Nathaniel Bar Jonah, remains a sexually dangerous person as of that date. I am also forwarding a memorandum of 1 July, 1991 from Leonard Mach in which he states that Justice Steele of the Suffolk County Superior Court found DAVID BROWN no longer to be a sexually dangerous person. This information is regulated and should not be given to anyone outside of law enforcement. Please acknowledge receipt of this fax transmission.

Judge Steele made a note that he had received a correspondence from Triplett. But, he was not going to rescind an order from the bench based upon an evaluation that was conducted in 1983, when he had two current psychologists saying that Bar Jonah wasn't dangerous. When Triplett heard of Steele's decision he contacted the Massachusetts Department of Mental Health. The DPM agreed with Triplett who wrote a letter to the District Attorney's office.

> To: District Attorney
> From: Chief of Police—James B. Triplett
> Address: 450 Main St, Oxford, MA 01540
> Date: 8/16/1991
> Subject: Nathaniel Bar Jonah's request for bail review
>
> Please consider this a request for formal bail review pursuant to Chapter 276, Section 5b. Please find enclosed copies of psychological evaluations performed by the Department of Mental Health that indicates they were quite concerned about his status as a sexual offender. The acting general council for Department of Mental Health has expressed concern that they feel he should not have been released and expressed this concern in a memo to the Attorney General's office. Although it is quite unlikely based on the existing adjudication in Suffolk Superior Court that he is not a sexually dangerous person that we will meet that border, his actions of August 9, 1991 reflect *grave* concerns as to whether this whole issue should be revised once again but more importantly. If this is the case then his bail should be reviewed based on his potential danger in the community. The acting general council for DMH has indicated that if a review of bail is not possible or allowed, then with the assistance of the District Attorney's office, they would be willing to pursue asking Judge Steele, who heard the original petition, to reconsider his original findings. This is not the best of course of action since it will probably require a long-term effort. If you should have any questions or concerns or I can be of any further assistance to you, please feel free to contact me.
>
> *James Triplett, Chief of Police*

Goddamnit

As Cameron read the letters, Wilson and Theisen sat and shook their heads. If Massachusetts had done their job, Zach Ramsay would still be alive. Cameron said he didn't think that Massachusetts was just irresponsible, but criminally liable. He also thought that Bellusci might have at least discovered where Bar Jonah had dumped Zach, if he had bothered to follow up on the afternoon of February 6th, 1996. Cameron thought Bellusci was lazy.

* * *

They continued to go through the boxes, item after item. Each letter or scrap of paper they found dug Bar Jonah's hole deeper. He was a complete psychopath. His ability to manipulate others was like nothing any of them had ever seen. But it wasn't just his ability to manipulate, it was also his uncanny ability to get inside of others. Once Bar Jonah was there, his victims were helpless to do anything but his bidding.

The frustration continued to build for the three investigators. All three were used to getting results. Even though they were sure they had Bar Jonah for the assault and rape of Roland, Stanley, and Stormy, they still had not found Zach's body. Bar Jonah had killed him; they were sure of that. But there had to be parts left over, even if he ate him. He could have done anything with the bones. Cameron hung up a map of Cascade County on the wall of what they were now calling the war room. He plotted out a diameter of 255 miles, half of the 510 miles Bar Jonah had put on the rental car he rented at the time Zach vanished. The investigators sat and contemplated the vast areas of wilderness that the area encompassed. Unless someone saw something or there was compelling evidence to justify a search, the area was just too massive to launch a directionless search. They were coming to the realization that they might *never* find Zach's body.

* * *

Cameron kept in regular contact with Rachel, updating her along the way without revealing anything about the particulars of the case. She was cordial. Rachel told Cameron that she had continued to meet with the Ladies weekly since the day after Zach disappeared. They had now amassed many clues to his disappearance. She thought that Cameron should talk to them. Rachel arranged for a meeting with Darlene and Delores. Cameron stayed open to the idea that the Ladies might be able to provide some kind of leads in the case. The problem was that they did not believe that Zach was dead. Rachel fervently believed that Franz had arranged for Zach to be kidnapped. There had been too many sightings of Zach. She also believed that the cops had never fully investigated the boy in Italy, whom Rachel devoutly believed was her son. Cameron nonetheless tried to convince Rachel and the Ladies that Zach was dead. Bar Jonah had killed him. But they remained steadfast in their belief that he was alive.

Rachel was now getting back into the spotlight and she was enjoying it. There would be interviews with the paper and probably the television networks would want to talk with her again. She told Cameron she might have to go back to New York at any time. Even though it would be inconvenient, she would be willing to if it meant helping to find Zach. Cameron continued to tell Rachel directly that Zach was never coming home. She would never see him again. He wasn't trying to be cruel. He was simply not wanting to give her any false hopes. Rachel was appreciative of all the help the Ladies had given her over the years since Zach disappeared. Sometimes she couldn't even pay her bills and the Ladies unselfishly came through and helped her out. She would repay them some day. Especially if Franz was ever caught for kidnapping Zach and had to pay her the back child support. Cameron seemed like a nice man, Darlene said, but he shouldn't be trusted. There was something about him that she didn't like but she couldn't put it into words. He always had another question; he was never satisfied. If Cameron would just take the leads the Ladies were giving him, Zach would probably be home in a few days. But he wouldn't do it. The likelihood was that Cameron was in on the whole thing too. He was probably getting money from Joan Cook and the other people who were involved in her child-stealing operation. They were sure they already had proof that Wilson was involved. One morning, when they were following Wilson, Rachel and the Ladies were convinced they had seen him dropping off a small boy that they believed Cook had ordered kidnapped. Now with Cameron coming around asking questions, it just confirmed how deep into law enforcement the cover-up went. They were convinced that Cameron's insistence that Zach was dead was nothing more than a ploy to get them to stop their investigation. They knew too much. They were afraid for their lives. But they would not stop until Zach was home.

* * *

Cameron thought Rachel and the Ladies were crazy. It seemed that everyone involved in the case was crazy. Some more than others, but they were all crazy. Cameron told Wilson and Theisen that if they listened to Rachel and the Ladies their time would be spent chasing ghosts.

They were never going to find Zach's body, Cameron said. Theisen followed with the obvious question of how could they charge Bar Jonah with murder if there was no solid evidence. They had Sherri, who said Bar Jonah confessed to her that he had killed Zach. She was crazy. When she had tried to tell Bellusci what Bar Jonah had said, he officially wrote her off as crazy. There was Pam, who could barely string two coherent thoughts together. She was crazy. Rachel even refused to believe that her son was dead, but was in Italy pining for her. She was crazy. From Cameron's standpoint, Doc was one of the most disgusting human beings that he had ever met. He knew that Bar Jonah had killed Zach, but he was crazy. Barry was so pathetic and such a chronic liar that he sounded crazy. Lori, Tanya, and Gerald were seemingly after whatever they could get. They were crazy. And the boys were lost balls in high weeds. When they got them on the stand, the prosecutor was going to have to be very careful to keep them focused and not to let them drift off or else they would exonerate Bar Jonah. Especially Stormy.

After Cameron finished spewing his litany, he grabbed his now cold coffee and threw himself into his chair. He knew they had a good case with the boys, despite his frustration. Cameron also knew it was likely, even without Zach's body, that they could get a conviction on a deliberate homicide charge.

CHAPTER TWO

One surprise after another

At two p.m. one day in early August, Cameron met with Bob, Tyra, Lois, and Lee at Bob's place on 1st Avenue. Bob insisted on serving coffee and cookies. Cameron said he was fine but Bob insisted by pushing the plate of cookies toward Cameron, telling him to "Take one." Then Bob took the porcelain plate and placed it, with a familiar clink, on the speckled granite counter top. Tyra looked up at Bob and told him to get the paper bag for Detective Cameron. Lois and Lee told Cameron that the situation was destroying their lives. The media was constantly following them. Hounding them. They had done nothing wrong and knew nothing. But the media was acting like an insane swarm of bees without a queen. Cameron said he understood. About that time Bob came back, carrying a brown paper bag. Bob handed the bag to Cameron, saying that he had found the bag at Bar Jonah's when he had cleaned out his place in December '99. When Cameron opened the bag he saw a galvanized meat grinder.

Cameron drove directly back to the police station and took the meat grinder apart. The outside was surgically clean. The inside seemed to have some debris caked around the teeth.

Cameron held the serrated edges up to the light and said, under his breath, "I wonder what part of Zach that is." He bagged it and was going to drop by Wilson's office on his way home, whenever that might be.

Before Cameron left for the night, he stopped by the drying room and stood at the door. So many fucking boxes, he thought. Cameron walked over to the stack and reached into box 19. He randomly pulled out a small receipt from Sun Cleaners, dated February 12th, 1996. Six days after Zach disappeared. The receipt was for Bar Jonah's blue nylon police jacket to be cleaned and the zipper replaced. It had cost Bar Jonah $16.50 for the cleaning and repair. Ironically, Cameron had just got the report back from Julie Long at the crime lab early that day saying that no blood was found on the jacket.

* * *

Things had gotten better for Bar Jonah of late. The guards were treating him with respect. A couple of them regularly brought him chocolate bars. He especially liked big bars. This way he could break off a piece and let it melt in his mouth. One of the guards said that he felt guilty giving it to him because of his diabetes but Bar Jonah assured him that it was okay. What other pleasures did he have to look forward to? Typically Bar Jonah would hang his head when he talked to the guards feigning deference, but he would always surreptitiously raise his sneaky eyes to see the guards' reactions to his pantomime. Depending on the guard, some would walk away, while others would express sympathy to the difficulty of his plight. To those guards, Bar Jonah would reveal the trauma he had experienced as a youth at the hands of neighborhood hoodlums. Bar Jonah was sure it had scarred him for life. But he prayed for the boys every day. He had forgiven them. He had heard through friends that they had had a lot of trouble in their lives over the years. It was most likely the Devil at work. But if they accepted Jesus Christ the way he had their burden would be lessened and the Devil would never be able to get a foothold. Bar Jonah had even forgiven the guards who beat and raped him at Bridgewater. He was just that kind of man.

Most of his days were spent in prayer and writing poetry. The guards who became "witnesses" to his revelations rarely failed to be moved by the depth of his rectitude. One of the guards in particular echoed Bar Jonah's angst. He could see, that like him, Bar Jonah had gone through his life with no one to talk to about what had happened to him when he was so young and vulnerable. Yes, Bar Jonah had done some bad things in his past, but his repentance was inspiring. The guard suggested that Bar Jonah write Cameron to see if he would help him get some relief from his suffering. Bar Jonah agreed and as always, thanked the guard for listening to him and for being a friend. He would be sure to see if his brother could find something special from his antique toy collection to bring to his kids. Bar Jonah sat down and began to write Cameron a letter.

* * *

In Montana, there is a saying, "If you don't like the weather, just wait fifteen minutes and it will change." During the first week of September, it seemed like the weather *was* changing every fifteen minutes in Great Falls. Fall was beginning to come earlier than usual. The winds were no longer blowing warm dry air; now there was a cold wetness that folks were beginning to talk about. It's going to be a hard winter, many would say. During that week, Cameron arrived at the station, with his ever-present cup of coffee in hand. He went to his mailbox to see if there were any memos from Lt. Groves issuing another ridiculous mandate. As Cameron fanned through the stack of papers in his box, he felt a sense of relief when he didn't see anything from Groves. He started to turn around without taking the stack out of the box. Then he stopped for a moment and turned back around. Had he seen something, he questioned himself. Cameron pulled the pile of papers from his mailbox and began to look more carefully. He pulled out a letter with his name scrawled across the front written in Bar Jonah's handwriting. Cameron walked down to the drying room. Wilson and Theisen were already there. He walked in waving the letter in the air, saying they weren't going to believe what he had just got in the mail.

The letter from Bar Jonah was short and curt. He made no mention of his lifetime of personal tragedy. It was just a brief note. Bar Jonah had even had it notarized.

> *Dear Detective Cameron*
>
> *1 - I am innocent of all charges against me.*
> *2 - I did not touch Roland, Stormie, or Stanley in any way.*
> *3 - I did not kill Zachery Ramsey or anyone else.*
> *4 - I did not do anything with or to Zachary Ramsey or anybody else.*
>
> *I do agree, that if all charges are dropped against me that I will allow the county or state to commit me to Warm Springs* [Montana's State Hospital] *or to some other mental health facility for a 3 year period of time unless I feel I need to be there longer. This is not a confession or an admission of guilt in anyway but a win, win situation for both of us. I am willing to do this because of my health problems and my lack of funds to be able to pay for the needed medications to keep me healthy. I do hope we can resolve these cases soon. This statement in no way gives up any of my legal rights.*
>
> Sincerely,
Nathan Bar Jonah, 9/15/2000

* * *

Roland was still having problems in Billings. School had just started and he was looking forward to getting back to some kind of routine, seeing some other kids. But he also knew that eventually he was going to have to testify against Bar Jonah. He didn't want to but the cops always got their way, especially against Indians. Roland also really missed Bar Jonah. Yeah, he had done some bad things to him but he was still one of the few men Roland had ever had in his life that made him feel like he was important and not a retard. Even his cousins still called him that sometimes.

Like a flash of bright light, Roland was remembering the night that Bar Jonah had used the stun gun on him. The night in the bedroom. Leaving Stanley to fend for himself. Feeling inadequate and betrayed as he walked out to the old caves. Sitting for hours! Losing track of time. Knowing that things would never be the same between him and Bar Jonah again. Lori was still trying to get Roland to go and see his therapist, but he didn't think much of her. She was a nice lady, especially for a white, but she just wanted to talk about what Bar Jonah had done to him. Roland would open up and talk sometimes. Sometimes he would even cry. He always felt so bad way down inside of his belly, because when he testified in court, Bar Jonah was going to be sent to prison forever and never get out. It was going to be his fault. Lori tried to tell him that he wasn't responsible for what was going to happen to Bar Jonah. He'd brought all that on himself. Roland usually nodded and said he knew. Then he would slink away and be swallowed up by his sadness. Marijuana was easy to get at the high school. Roland hadn't tried it yet, but he was sure getting a lot of offers from his friends.

* * *

Cameron stayed in touch with Roland and Stanley, letting them know how much he needed them to testify. Lori wouldn't let Cameron talk to Stormy unless she was there too. She said she just wanted to make sure that Stormy was going to be okay. Cameron thought it was because Lori always hit him up for cash. "Do you have some money? I need to pay my rent and my check ain't here yet, init?" Lori also wanted to know if she and the kids could be paid for their testimony. It sure would help a lot, she said. Cameron always told her no. The boys were now trying to play on Cameron's sympathy too. Whenever Cameron saw them, they'd always try to get a few dollars out of him. Just a little something, they'd say. Sometimes he'd slip them a dollar or two.

* * *

Cameron and Theisen were building the case now, preparing for a murder indictment against Bar Jonah. It was going to take a few months to get the evidence set out in a sequential way for the prosecutor's office to be able to level charges. But charges were imminent. They were going right for the death penalty too. Cameron, Wilson, and Theisen wanted to know where Bar Jonah had dumped Zach's remains but they wanted to make sure he didn't pull some sleight of hand gesture and end up out on the streets again. The only way to ensure that he didn't was to kill him. They also didn't believe that he would ever give up where Zach was. No matter what, Bar Jonah wasn't going to give them anything.

* * *

The public defender who was charged with defending Bar Jonah was Eric Olsen. He was a relatively new PD and had no experience in defending or managing the kind of media exposure the Bar Jonah case was beginning to garner. The ability to find a neutral jury would be almost impossible, especially with all of the talk about cannibalism now being thrown around. The public defender's office was in a state of chaos. Never had it dealt with a case of this magnitude. It seemed that their phone rang constantly from reporters wanting information from all over the United States and Canada. There were even calls beginning to come in from Europe, Japan, and China. The case involving the three boys was massive enough alone, but they had received word that Bar Jonah was also going to be charged with the murder of Zach Ramsay sometime in the near future. They would have to prepare for this case too. But the resources simply weren't there. The other problem was that in their conversations with Bar Jonah he had been completely uncooperative. He had never done anything to anyone. It was their job to prove it. He shouldn't have to help them, that's what he paid taxes for. Moreover, he had other things he needed to take care of. They had spoken briefly with the boys but had not seen much of the evidence that the cops had taken from Bar Jonah's apartment. Olsen and his assistant Larry LaFountain didn't particularly like Bar Jonah either. But he had rights and they would do their job to the best of their ability. Bar Jonah was not going to make it any easier to defend him against a stacked deck. The initial trial date had been set for January 16th, 2001 on the sexual assault and kidnapping charges. Olsen and LaFountain were working around the clock trying to get prepared. Things were going to become more problematic because LaFountain was quitting the PD office on January 12th. An extension had to be filed.

* * *

Cameron, Theisen, and Wilson were now focusing much of their efforts on going through Bar Jonah's three ring binders. The binders contained the photographs that Bar Jonah had meticulously trimmed and slipped into plastic baseball card sleeves. There were more than 22,000 photographs in all. Most had a name scribbled underneath the picture. It may be the correct first name of the child with a bogus last name or the opposite. It may also be a fictitious name altogether. The investigators spent hundreds of hours between them trying to identify the children in the pictures. In addition to the photographs, there were also cutout pictures of children and families from magazines and catalogs. Most were head shots. None of the images were nude. In fact, the only completely nude image was of Bar Jonah himself. "Putting this damn binder together was a full-time job," Wilson commented.

About a third of the way through the first binder, Cameron flipped a page back and as a matter of routine, began to run his index finger over the photographs. Theisen was standing behind Cameron and Wilson, looking down at the pictures. Cameron turned around surprised when he heard Theisen say in a shocked and angry tone, "Son of a bitch." "That's my brother's kid," Theisen said, pointing to the photograph of a boy taken outside of Lincoln Elementary school. Theisen's voice constricted as he spurted out "Fuck," turned around, and walked out of the room. In most cases there are surprises. Rarely do things line up perfectly. But in the Bar Jonah case, the investigators were discovering that nothing could be taken for granted. You never knew what awaited you. For men who didn't like to admit fear, it was clear they were working the case with trepidation.

Theisen went home and began drinking. It was barely past noon. He was beginning to drink more. He was also always asking Laurie where the boys were. They had two wonderful kids and Theisen wanted to know where they were all the time. He had never been like that before. Great Falls, like most Montana cities, is a great place to raise a family. There is always something to do. Parents seldom have any worries about their kids, unless it's watching out for bears if they venture into the woods. Theisen doubted if any parent in Montana had, before Bar Jonah, ever warned their kids to watch out for cannibals.

* * *

Eric Olsen initially thought Cameron had something up his sleeve when he got the call, asking him to come over to his office at the PD. Cameron would only say that there was something he needed to see. Olsen and Cameron had mutual respect for each other. But they were still on opposite sides. When Olsen arrived, he found Cameron sitting behind his desk holding one of Bar Jonah's photo binders in his lap. After shaking hands, Olsen asked what Cameron wanted. Cameron told Olsen that he had been going back through Bar Jonah's binder and saw a picture that he should see. Cameron flipped opened the binder to a plastic sleeve that he had marked with a pencil, turned the binder around, and laid it in front of Olsen. Olsen looked down. Cameron saw Olsen's knuckles turn white with rage as he clenched his fist. Olsen slipped the fingers of his left hand under the cover of the binder, slammed it closed and walked heavy-footed out of Cameron's office. He went back to his office and drafted a statement to the judge asking to be dismissed from the case for personal reasons. Olsen walked the request over to the judge's office. The judge asked Olsen what his "personal reason" was for wanting to be discharged, as he had only been on the case a few months. Olsen tightened his jaws and said, "The bastard has a picture of *my* daughter in one of his binders." Cameron called Theisen and told him that Olsen's kid's picture was in Bar Jonah's binder too. It wasn't just his nephew. Cameron heard the phone click, as Theisen hung up without saying anything.

CHAPTER THREE

Where are the Jews?

The next day, Judge Neill appointed attorneys Don Vernay and Greg Jackson to represent Bar Jonah. The PD's office was going to have to transfer the case out anyway: best to go ahead and do it now. Vernay and Jackson were the only two attorneys certified by the state of Montana to litigate death penalty cases for defendants who couldn't afford to pay for their own attorney. Jackson was well known throughout Montana as a congenial, handsome, and smart attorney. It was not uncommon to hear Jackson referred to as "a gentleman" by other lawyers and judges. He was also deeply religious and like Bar Jonah, was a member of the Assembly of God church.

Vernay, on the other hand, was known to be as arrogant and abrasive as Jackson was humble and cordial. After law school, Vernay had come to Montana from New York City to teach sailing. He had raced sailboats in the Hudson and saw himself more as a philosopher and artist. Vernay ventured around northwest Montana and Canada collecting scrap pieces of steel. He then sculpted them into abstract configurations, often filling them with holes from his .45. Judges bristled when he entered their courtroom, dreading Vernay's nasally Brooklyn voice decrying, *"Yer Onher"* when the court disagreed with one of his many objections. When Vernay and Jackson took over the case, the first thing they did was to request that the trial be continued, again. They needed time to prepare. Bar Jonah liked both Vernay and Jackson, particularly when Vernay said that the initial stop on the street was illegal and without probable cause. He would get it overturned, even if it was on appeal and then the whole case would fall apart because none of the evidence would be admissible. Bar Jonah was convinced that changing his legal team was another step on the way to the fulfillment of the final miracle, his release.

* * *

Bar Jonah was beginning to collect junk in his cell. Papers were beginning to accumulate. Back in Bridgewater, when he had attended Jewish services on Saturday mornings, he had heard that Jews are buried with their possessions. Jews like to be crowded. That was another reason that he wanted to be a Jew, because they were like him, he said. Jews like to encroach on one another's space. To get up in each other's faces and go at it elbow to elbow and toe to toe. In Bridgewater, at least there were other Jews. There were hardly any Jews in Montana, especially not in jail. He began complaining that he missed his own kind. He wanted to connect with Jewish singles, especially Jewish women who had children and were looking for a Jewish man who could help raise them in the Jewish tradition.

Bar Jonah wrote letters and sent poetry, much of it articulating the eternal struggles of the psalmist David, to the Shiluv organization for the resettlement of immigrants in Tel Aviv, Israel. He wanted to join the Shiluv and was enclosing his application, he said. Bar Jonah said he was planning on immigrating to Israel; he was Jewish and wanted to come to the land of his people. He was a toy collector who specialized in antique steam trains. He also collected pictures of Jewish teens and scouts. He was looking for a lifelong partner with traditional Jewish values. One who would dedicate her life to him, as a woman should in marriage. It was decreed in Genesis 3:16, "Your desire will be for your husband, and he will rule over you."

Even though he was a Jew, he had also dedicated his life to Christ. The mate he was seeking not only had to be a good cook but like him, had to be a Jew for Jesus. Bar Jonah wrote that he was temporarily unable to leave the country due to business matters. But he expected that to change in the near future. The God of Abraham had heard his plight and was working to part the seas of injustice and deliver him to his rightful place among his righteous people. He also added that his parents had never had a Bar Mitzvah for him. Once he got to Israel he would like to arrange for the celebration. Bar Jonah said he would appreciate it if a rabbi affiliated with the Shiluv could contact him and begin to help set up the necessary arrangements.

The guards were bewildered at the number of letters Bar Jonah gave to them to mail daily. But they were even more puzzled at how he managed to get the addresses of so many people from all over the world. Over the entire time that Bar Jonah was in prison, no one ever satisfactorily answered that question.

Andy

Kids go missing all of the time. Usually there is a flurry of initial attempts to find the child and then if unsuccessful, the case grows cold and their picture ends up on the side of a milk carton. This was especially true before communications networks were put into place to try to keep missing children alive in the media. Wilson and Theisen in particular focused much of their attention on where Bar Jonah had lived before and after he got out of prison.

Theisen became focused on a little boy who was reported missing on Saturday, August 21st, 1976 from Lawrence,

Massachusetts. Lawrence was just fifty miles from Worchester, right up highway 290. Angelo "Andy" Gene Puglisi had been running around and playing at the Higgins Memorial Swimming Pool about a hundred yards from the Stadium Housing Project where he lived with his parents and two brothers. Andy was a beautiful boy with medium brown hair. He was also the kind of boy to share his walkie-talkies and give an extra cookie to his girlfriend, Melanie.

On that horrible Saturday, Andy's mother said he called home about 3:30 and talked to one of his brothers. About 5:45 one of the lifeguards supposedly chastised him for running along the wet edge of the pool. He could slip and fall, the lifeguard said. That was the last time anyone remembers ever seeing Andy. There was a big fuss. Everyone was out looking for him. Then as the days went by with nothing turning up, the number of volunteers trickled down to nothing, until finally the last testimonies to Andy's life ended up in a small box, tucked out of the way on a shelf of the Lawrence Police Department. Other than an occasional "missing boy" poster surfacing here and there, he was never heard from again. There was never any direct links between Bar Jonah and Andy's abduction. Theisen tried many times to get the Lawrence authorities interested in the case. But it was long ago and there were other more immediately pressing matters. What could they do anyway? The kid was dead. Theisen couldn't understand their complacency. He had always been a cop who, like Cameron, dogged a case until he had answers.

During interviews that were conducted with Bar Jonah in prison, he would sometimes talk about "Andy." He may have met him once with a friend up in Lawrence. "Who knows," Bar Jonah would say. Lawrence wasn't that far away from Worchester. He got around a lot and met a lot of kids. He couldn't help it, they were drawn to him. He feigned being burdened and weighted down by having to suffer the cursed consequences of being "a kid magnet." There were times that Andy's face would creep into Theisen's mind. He would see him, like he saw his own boys running, playing, jumping into the water. He would even catch himself silently admonishing Andy to be careful. And then, Andy Puglisi would be gone again.

I'll get you, my pretty, and your little cats too

Going through the thousands of photographs of children was arduous. Photo after photo, without any knowledge whatsoever of their relationship to Bar Jonah, made the task seem like a Sisyphus endeavor. Who were these kids? Many of the children they identified as being from the elementary schools in Great Falls. Cameron took the binders around to the schools and met with the principals, getting them to identify as many of the kids as they could. The others would remain nameless. In the back of one of the binders were several loose photographs of Bar Jonah sitting on his loveseat with Stanley sitting on his lap, others of him tickling Stormy. A few of Roland and Stanley spread out on Bar Jonah's bed and one of Bar Jonah holding Stormy, lifting his shirt and tickling his belly. Bar Jonah had his "U.S. Marshal" shirt and hat on in each of the photos. Some of the photos of Stanley had "Allen Tannenbaum" cut out and pasted underneath. Another of Stanley had "Calhoun Abernathie" written below. In some of Bar Jonah's letters to Stanley he addressed the envelope to Stanley Abernathie. He always said he didn't know why. But he liked the name. Stanley thought it was funny, Bar Jonah said.

* * *

It had been a month and neither the inspectors nor Cameron had shown their face back at Doc's. He was feeling better now. The swelling in his leg had gone down and he was able to get around a lot better. He had even been thinking about taking in another boy. There were so many out there wandering around without direction, he wanted to tend to them. Doc was feeling more like his old self. He even joked at the HiHo that he thought he was getting the spring back in his step.

Early one morning in the last week of September, Doc happened to glance out his living room window and see Cameron pull up in front of his house. He quickly sat down in his chair, propped his leg up on his Santa footstool, and pulled the pink cashmere shawl from the back of the chair. As he watched Cameron walk up the sidewalk, Doc pulled the smooth soft cloth around his rolled-in shoulders, and called for Cameron to come in when he heard him on the porch. Cameron opened the door and saw Doc sitting in his cat hair-caked chair looking sallow. "How can I help you, officer," came Doc's small, preoccupied voice, barely audible. Cameron stood in Doc's foyer, gagging back the impulse to vomit, looked at Doc, and said, "I'm going to find out what you know Doc, so you had better be getting ready to talk to me. If you don't, you're going down right beside Bar Jonah. I just came by to tell you that. The health inspector will be by today to see you later too. You're going to be moving I hear." Cameron turned around and walked out the door. Doc sat stunned, shooing away the half dozen cats that were crawling all over him. Just when things were beginning to go better for Doc, some son of a bitch like Cameron comes along and fucks them up. Doc hadn't realized that such a long time had gone by until he heard another knock at his door. He must have fallen asleep, he thought, as he raised his head and wearily told the knocker to come into his home. Doc reached over, picked up his dancing bear cup, and put the rim to his glossed lips. When he took a sip of his coffee, he was surprised to find that it had gone cold. Had he fallen asleep?, he kept silently wondering.

Through his fog, Doc recognized the health inspector now standing next to his chair, his arm extended, handing Doc an official-looking piece of paper. "Mr. Bauman," the health inspector said, "I am serving you notice that this property is now officially, by the authority of the Cascade County

Health Department, condemned. You must vacate the premise immediately. You will have thirty days to clean the place up or it will be demolished." "What, I don't understand, I have lived here for years," Doc stammered in protest. "Mr. Bauman, the conditions here are deplorable. I am surprised someone hasn't questioned your mental capacity, living in this kind of filth. The whole neighborhood is at risk. How in the hell it has been allowed to go on this long is a mystery to me. But you will clean it up or it will be bulldozed into the ground." The health inspector added that animal control was on their way out to collect Doc's cats. The city would house them at the shelter and try to find them homes. If they couldn't, then they would be put to sleep. He was heartless. They were going to take Doc's home and murder his beloved companions. Doc fell back into his chair and felt his insides disintegrating. The morning had been so promising. He had even planned to take a walk around the neighborhood. The school was just a short stroll away and Doc had planned on dropping by, just to say hello to some of the boys that he had spoken with before. He was sure they would remember him. There were a couple that Doc had bought liquor for, but he thought they had moved away. He hadn't seen them for a while.

* * *

Doc's coffee had turned out just right that morning too. He still used a percolator. The bubbling sound of the boiling coffee early in the morning was soothing to him. It had been especially comforting the past few months when he had been suffering so much with his leg. Now in the last few days, when he had been feeling better, Doc would stop and stare at the ebullient droplets of coffee bouncing around in the small glass crown that adorned the top of the dulled aluminum pot. On one occasion, tears welled up in Doc's eyes as he watched the dancing bubbles. He remembered a special time when he was a young boy. He was standing beside his father at the local filling station that had a big green dinosaur on its sign, right at the edge of the small Texas town where they lived. His eyes were riveted to the small red, blue and green bouncing balls, locked under a little glass dome on the front of the gas pump. His father had always been gruff, rarely calling Doc anything other than a damn sissy. But for some reason, on that day, Doc recalled his father being tenderhearted. Even patting the back of Doc's head, to break his fixation on the little balls. Telling him to go ahead and get on in the car.

Doc called his attorney and told him the mess that he believed Cameron had created: it was not just a misfortune. There was nothing wrong before Cameron began snooping around his life, Doc said. His attorney sympathized with Doc. "I understand," he said. However, he had been in Doc's house before and no judge or jury would be sensitive to Doc's predicament. Moreover, the place was a health hazard not only for everyone else but also for Doc; he shouldn't be living in that kind of filth. Doc begged his attorney not to let them do this to him. His attorney thought Doc sounded like a high school girl, pleading with her boyfriend not to break up with her. There was really nothing he could do. Unless Doc could think of some way to clean the place up and place the cats within the next week or so, the city would level the place. With that many cats, the shelter probably wouldn't have much choice but to put most of them down. Nobody would take that many cats.

When Doc fell onto the once beautiful walnut floor, right at the archway to the Easter bedroom, he rolled onto his back. His eyes wet with tears, he looked longingly at his precious toys, stacked as high as his eyes could see. What would happen to them? They were his precious ... They, even more than his cats, had always been there ....

In a panic, Doc's legs kicked and scrambled as he struggled against the thick dusty yellow film that caked the floor. He was finally able to sit up against the wall. Doc then pulled himself up with his cane and began going through the house grabbing the most precious of his dolls and toys. They were not going to rob him of everything! They were not! His breathing became hard and labored. Doc was throwing the dolls and toys he wanted to keep into the Christmas room, listening for the bulldozer to drive up any minute and begin the assault on his home. Several times he thought they were there, only to be relieved when he discovered he was mistaken. Doc sat down on another comfy chair and began collecting himself. He felt crazy. Even if he told Cameron everything he knew about Bar Jonah, it was too late. Everything had been set in motion and there was nothing he could do. He was going to lose it all.

Doc called the number on the notice of condemnation and asked to speak with the inspector. The inspector said that the city would not take any action on demolishing the house for at least a month. But Doc had to be out of the house immediately. If he didn't vacate the premises, the inspector would have the sheriff come and make him leave. If he didn't have a place to go, they would take him to the homeless shelter.

Doc took a deep breath and held back his tears. Could he have another twenty-four hours? It was all he was asking for. This way he could at least get some of his things together that he wanted to salvage. The inspector told him that because of the condition of everything in the house being covered in cat feces and urine, anything he took out of the house would have to be declared free of filth. But the inspector said he wasn't unsympathetic and would allow Doc another day to get his affairs in order. Once he was out though, the place would be padlocked shut and he would not be allowed back in. If Doc wanted it, he had to get it out now. Doc courteously thanked the inspector when he said goodbye. When the receiver touched the cradle, Doc said, "Bastard."

Doc immediately called a friend, a young woman, with many tattoos and silver rings punched through her fat, pored nose, to come and please help him. Never in his life had he needed someone so. Without question she would come, she said. Doc had been her friend. Sometimes in the bad times, he had helped her out too. A bottle here and there or a bag of dope. Doc even shared his pain pills with her when she was in real need. She also knew that Doc kept a supply of pain pills in his medicine cabinet. Maybe while she was helping Doc pack up, she might be able to slip a few bottles in the pockets of her smock.

Doc and his friend worked long into the night. They had moved the stuffed Santas and scary plastic goblins aside to excavate a space in the middle of the living room. There Doc and his friend put the things that he would take with him. It was odd, Doc said, but he didn't feel quite so sad, now that he had gotten over the initial shock. His attorney said there was really nothing he could do, even though Doc knew there had to be some way to fight what the city was trying to do to him. Doc wasn't sure why, but he now felt at peace with the inevitability of leaving his home. He had been there for a long time, so many memories, so many loves gone by. And then there was Zach. It would be good to get a clean start and to begin again. The cats took so much work. But this way he could take his favorite kitty with him and set the others free to find another home in the neighborhood. Doc had tried to sell some of his dolls and toys to a friend of Bar Jonah's, but the unkind man refused to even walk with Doc through his house for fear of "catching something." Doc just as unkindly told the man that he had hurt his feelings and to get the fuck out of his home. He berated Bar Jonah for introducing him to someone so disagreeable and needless to say, obnoxious. Doc remembered Bar Jonah being almost as snotty as the odious antique dealer when he complained to him. Bar Jonah had even made disparaging remarks, saying that if Doc's toys weren't covered in cat piss, then his friend would have bought them all. There were times when Doc had found Bar Jonah to be insufferable. Even if the city condemned Doc's house and turned it into toothpicks, they still had to pay Doc fair market value for the house, minus the cost of tearing it down, of course. Doc knew he would come out with some ready cash without having to expend much effort of his own.

* * *

Doc's lady friend was in the bathroom, rifling through Doc's pill stash, when she heard Doc calling for Puddin. Puddin was Doc's favorite cat. The lady friend thought Puddin looked a bit like Doc too.

Doc's big, brown, furry slippers, with big-eyed moose heads, could be heard shuffling down the hallway. "Shit," Doc heard his lady friend say above the sound of his scuffing slippers, scraping along on the gritty wood floor. Doc's lady friend heard the bathroom door creaking open as she hurried to pick up the last of the pain killers that had fallen all over the floor. When she had grabbed the bottle out of the white metal medicine cabinet, she quickly discovered that Doc had not put the lid on tight. The pink pills had gone flying through the acrid bathroom air like confetti at a Memorial Day parade. There at the door stood Doc, the ends of his thin lips turning slightly downward, making his nose look broader than it was, stroking Puddin roughly between her ears and over the top of her head. One hand was gripping the loose skin at the nape of her neck, just to make sure she didn't leap from his arms. Doc looked at his lady friend and told her he was going to put Puddin in a box. She was absolutely the one special friend that he was going to take with him and he didn't want to have to go hunting for her at the last minute. Doc put his fingers under Puddin's front paws, lifted her up to his mouth and kissed her sweet pink lips, telling her that she could be a little scamp. Puddin snapped her head back and tried to nip Doc on the nose.

* * *

Well into the night, Doc and his lady friend worked. The pile in the middle of the living room was now a hodgepodge of toys, knick-knacks, and clothes. There was no underwear; Doc never wore underwear. He used to laugh at the HiHo and say that should an occasion for pleasure present itself, he did not want to have to waste any time taking advantage of the situation. Some of the men at the bar used to joke that Doc always seemed to have piss stains on his ever-present chinos. When he came back from the toilet, some of the more pitiless patrons used to yell out for everyone to look see, Doc had pissed on himself again. He just couldn't seem to get it right. Doc would become righteously indignant and yell at the milksops to leave him alone. They were just cowards he would say, never had any of them seen the horrors he had seen in Korea. They knew nothing of suffering. They were but a bunch of provincial fools who would remain so until the day they died, good-for-nothings. Doc imagined that he had the final say, by tossing back the one-finger of whiskey left in his two-finger glass and sashaying out the door. You could always count on Doc for a few good laughs. He helped break up the monotony of the day.

* * *

Bar Jonah was now getting spontaneous marriage proposals from the ads he had placed in the Jewish singles magazines. In early October, a letter came from a twenty-five-year-old Jewish woman who lived in Tel Aviv. She had read his ad in Shiluv. He was a good man; she could tell from his devotion to Christ. She, too, had recently found Christ. There were so few Jews who understood the coming of the Messiah. To find a man, a man who had suffered at the hands of the Pharisees like Jesus, was, she believed, "ordained." How could she help?, she wanted to know. Were his lawyers Jewish?, she wanted to know. Were they working hard enough, working in the right way? Clearly, if such a good man was still imprisoned, then they could not be. She would marry him and together they would become a force to be reckoned with, as they crisscrossed their way through the Holy Land delivering the message of their Lord.

Two guards, sat in the bull pin, watched Bar Jonah cross his fat legs and tear open the letter. He sat and smiled. Someone would marry him once he was released on the trumped-up charges. Then he would go to Israel, marry her or someone else that wanted to marry him, and then get lost. In the Holy Land fat Jews were everywhere. He would grow dreadlocks and dress in Hasidic garb. He would never be found. Tangiers was not that far from Israel; he had always been interested in Allah.

Evidence collection

With all of the evidence that was being collected from Bar Jonah's and the bone fragments from Bob's garage, Cameron decided that it was time to get a DNA sample from Bar Jonah. The state would need to compare Bar Jonah's DNA against any of the evidence collected in the case so far. Wilson wanted to compare it against Zach's notebook that Rachel had given him back in 1996.

Judge Neill signed the order to obtain blood and hair samples from Bar Jonah. The hair sample was to include a pubic hair plucked from Bar Jonah's mons pubis. A few hours after Bar Jonah read the letter from his hopeful in Israel, Cameron and a nurse showed up at the prison to take the samples. Bar Jonah had not been told they were coming. He was furious. Why hadn't his attorney stopped them from this indignity? It was a violation. He was going to have nightmares again from when he was assaulted as a child and raped by the guards at Bridgewater. Vernay told him there was nothing he could do about it, given that he was being investigated for deliberate homicide. The state would prevail. They had to choose their battles and this was one they would lose.

Bar Jonah became stiff as a board, refusing to sit down to have his blood taken. "If you want it, you're going to have to hold my arm up and take it," Bar Jonah said. His arms were fat and his veins thin. As soon as the nurse slipped the needle into his arm, thinking she had a vein, the damn thing would collapse or roll away. Bar Jonah did not flinch when she began to probe deep into the fat of his arms for a working vein. Finally, after a half-dozen sticks, blood began to replace the vacuum inside the glass tube. They really didn't need much but it was always better to have more than less. Cameron stood by as the nurse politely asked Bar Jonah to pull down his orange drawstring pants so she could pluck a few pubic hairs. Bar Jonah reached down and pulled the frayed end of the knot, letting his pants fall down around his ankles. By the time Bar Jonah's pants were half way down his legs, four eyes were drawn to the hideous abyss that was once his right thigh muscle. The nurse then asked Bar Jonah to pull down his tattered, jaundice-looking underwear. He refused. "If you want them down, you take them down," he said. The nurse tensed her arms to hide the shake in her hands as she gripped both sides of the blue and red striped elastic cinched around Bar Jonah's waist. Then she slid his shorts down around his thighs stopping halfway down his legs, letting the dangling cotton cover the scar. Bar Jonah stood naked from the waist down before them. His gut hung so far down that it almost completely obscured the head of his dwarfed penis, which barely poked out from a sparse mound of pubic hair. His "BB nuts" were set so high and tight, that they pushed up against his pubic mound. With his drooping gut pressing down from the top and his tight testicles pushing up from below, his pubic hair was sandwiched in between, preventing the nurse from being able to comb out a sample that she could readily pluck. She hesitantly looked up at Bar Jonah and asked him to pull his testicles down so she could retrieve the sample. Bar Jonah looked down at her and smugly said, "If you want it, you move them." The nurse reached up with a gloved hand and pulled Bar Jonah's testicles down far enough that she could run the wide teeth of the comb through his matted pubic hair. She took the comb, pressed the teeth against his pubic bone and began agitating it back and forth, freeing the hairs from each other. When she came to the end of the follicles, the nurse held the comb in place, took a pair of tweezers, gripped a single strand of hair between the forceps' flat ends and yanked. The nurse could see that she had got a good sample, because the root of the hair was almost translucent when it snapped out of the thick, fat, pubic mound. In steady succession she took three more samples. Bar Jonah had stood silent once she began to collect the samples.

After she was done, the nurse stood up and told Bar Jonah he could pull up his pants. As his underwear hung around his thighs, Cameron thought that Bar Jonah's stomach looked like flabby lumps of misshapen bread dough. When Bar Jonah reached down to pull up his shorts, he slipped his thumbs under the stretchy waistband and shimmied the cotton briefs up over his thick gelatinous thighs, letting the elastic snap as it popped against his overgrown belly. Then Bar Jonah grabbed the orange cotton pants by their waistband and pulled them up in one swift move. As Cameron watched Bar Jonah spit on his fingers, jerk the drawstrings together and tie them into a bow, he realized that he was watching a private moment usually only meant to be seen by an intimate. In prison, all that we typically think of as dignity vanishes. Bar Jonah didn't speak as he walked out the door. When he got back to his cell, he wrote the woman in Israel, telling her of the indignity he had just endured. But there was a reason, he was sure. Jesus, he wrote, never gives you more than you can handle. He was sure she would understand.

* * *

The investigators continued to build the case against Bar Jonah. The boys were a worry. One day they were good to go and the next day everything was falling apart. Lori wasn't any better: she was now calling Cameron wanting money. Roland, Stanley, and Stormy always seemed pathetic. They were slow-witted and their future was going to be difficult. Saddled with the baggage of not only what Bar Jonah had done to them but also testifying in court and dealing with the aftermath was likely to ruin their lives. Nonetheless, it had to be done. Cameron and Theisen in particular drew the task of keeping an eye on Lori and the boys; buttering them up, keeping them in line until the case came to trial. Both Cameron and Theisen despised Lori. The next step now was to re-interview Pam and Sherri.

Wish I may, wish I might

The howling winds, spinning up out of the canyons just outside of Great Falls were sounding the warning that winter was rapidly approaching. The plane seemed to be as cold on the inside as it was on the outside and never seemed to warm up for the entire flight to Virginia Beach on that early morning right before Thanksgiving. When Cameron deplaned in Virginia, the muggy air clung to him like a wet sheet. He had grown up in Minnesota and was used to moist air, but this stuff stuck to you. Even in November, it didn't feel like you would ever be dry again. Cameron rented a car and drove to a cheap motel, which was just a walk across the road from the beach. He was only going to be there long enough to interview Pam and then catch an afternoon flight back to Great Falls. It was going to be a long tomorrow. But no matter, he decided to take a walk along the beach. Cameron wasn't sure how long he walked, but the sound of the waves rushing over the grainy sand seduced him into staying out later than he should have. It was almost three a.m. when he finally turned off the tarnished brass plated lamp that was screwed into the wall above his bed. He was up by seven and had to be at the Virginia Beach police station by eight to meet Pam. The VBPD was going to let him use one of their interview rooms to do the interview.

Cameron met Pam when she walked into the police station. It seemed to Cameron that she had gained some weight. She still looked really crazy. When he reached out to shake Pam's hand, Cameron noticed that her eyes seemed to bob in their sockets, like the canon ball jellyfish that he had seen throbbing in the water the night before. He thought you could drop a marble in her mouth one minute and it would drop out her ass the next. An officer from Virginia Beach PD escorted Cameron and Pam to a humid interview room. When she walked, Pam tottered, reaching out a couple of times to balance herself against the wall. Pam stood and looked around at the nothingness of the room and then sat down heavily in a straight-back chair that looked like someone had swiped it from the army. Cameron set up his video camera, not forgetting to take the plug out of the microphone. Then he began conversing with Pam as a way of lessening her nervousness. Pam seemed to grow more comfortable with Cameron, talking about this and that. Sometimes though, it was more this and that than the issue at hand. A lot of what she was saying or responding to made no sense. She was all over the map. In a sudden moment of clarity, Pam launched into a tirade about Sherri, again accusing her of wanting to come between her and Bar Jonah. She also said that Sherri was a "semi-psychologist" and had told her that Bar Jonah had a multiple personality. Sherri knew how to get things out of people through her training in psychology and she was sure that Bar Jonah had a split personality between a little boy and a man.

Cameron began asking her about the funny tasting meat that Bar Jonah had served her. She said she was sure that it was ground-up human flesh. Cameron thought he was finally getting somewhere. This was where he needed to go. He then asked Pam how she was so sure that the meat was human. Was she going to say that Bar Jonah had told her that he had ground up Zach in a meat grinder? Pam looked at Cameron through sheepish eyes and with her head bobbing, said that she had been part of human sacrifices before and had eaten human flesh at the sacrifices. Then she giggled and told Cameron that the cops had to give her brain a rest. "I mean this can cause a major stroke or something." Cameron said, "Oh fuck," reached over, turned off the video recorder, and walked out the door. Pam *was* insane. The prosecution would look like fools if they put her on the stand to testify against Bar Jonah. On the drive back to the airport, all Cameron could hear reverberating in his head was Pam's giggles.

When Cameron got back, he called Sherri. Did she have a nice holiday?, Cameron asked. He wanted to know if she would be willing to call Pam and let him record the conversation. Cameron wanted Sherri to try and get any information she could out of Pam about Bar Jonah. He wanted to know what she wasn't saying.

* * *

Sherri played it to the hilt, making Pam believe that the cops and the FBI were harassing her, wanting information. Sherri wanted to know if the cops had been after her for information too. They sure had, Pam said. They'd even come down to Virginia Beach to find her. For the most part there was a lot of nothing being said. The attention was fueling Sherri's desperation to feel important. She was the detective and the interrogator. She was also the liar, twisting and maligning, trying to rope Pam into saying something about Bar Jonah. Sherri kept asking Pam about the rope and the bloody gloves. But Pam said she didn't remember nothin'. Pam did say, though, she remembered the board in Bar Jonah's closet. She sure couldn't understand why anyone was interested in it. Sherri and Pam also talked a lot about Bob and how they thought he was stranger than Bar Jonah. Bob was the one they were suspicious of. Sherri said she thought Bob was heavy into witchcraft. She should know because she was a witch too. Pam thought Bob was "snakey." The call never seemed to go much farther. At the end of the call, Pam and Sherri said they loved each other and hoped they could talk again, soon.

Giving thanks

Thanksgiving was going to be more special this year than any other. It was to be Doc's last at 1615 7th Avenue N. The inspectors still hadn't made Doc leave and he was determined to make cherishable memories of the time he had left. Tears welled up in his still sleepy eyes that morning when he wrestled himself from his big bouncy bed. That night he had slept surrounded by dozens of hippity-hoppity happy Easter bunnies. He hadn't actually slept in his bedroom for many years. Even though he had been enveloped by the love of his friends, Doc had tossed and turned that night, peeking up out of his covers, not feeling comforted, but watched. Things were just not as they had been for Doc. He felt that something was changing inside of him. But what he did not know. Doc had a couple of friends bringing a big turkey and all of the trimmings over for Thanksgiving dinner. He didn't have to do anything except clear the table of debris, dust the cat hair off his good china, give the tarnished silverware a quick wipe with a damp cloth, and he was set. Doc also had to corral as many of his cats as he could down to his always disagreeably damp cinderblock walled basement. He had stopped feeding the cats every day; it was costing him too much money. It also gave Doc more control over the felines. Of course only feeding them every couple of days made them more of a nuisance too, whining for food and seemingly always brushing up against Doc's legs, climbing on top of him. Ah, Doc would tell his friends, having a generous heart was burdensome at times. That morning Doc went to a box he kept under the overhang on the back patio and took out several large cans of "turkey and giblets surprise" wet cat food. He put them in a canvas bag, picked up a big spoon and a can opener from the kitchen, and walked toward the basement door. Doc gripped the handrail and descended each step with great care, stepping over cat after cat. When he put each foot down, he twisted it around and around like he was rubbing out a tossed cigarette, to get a good foothold on the slick, cat shit-caked stairs. Doc hated going down to the basement. The thick ammonia-laden air made even his eyes burn. Once Doc stepped onto the concrete floor, he reached up and pulled the beaded chain that was dangling from between two of the rafters. The dark basement was now filled with harsh light, yellowed by soggy trapped air. Year after year, the putrid stench had fortified itself, imbuing each and every corner of the wooden rafters and concrete floor, causing one of his visitors, who had taken a hapless turn down his stairs, to call the wretched fetor in Doc's basement, an "alien life force."

Doc reached into the canvas bag and pulled out each of the cans. Cats were beginning to surround Doc now, with their meowing becoming deafening. The moment that Doc cracked the first can with the round sharp blade of the blue-handled opener, cats came scurrying like rats out of a burning sewer. They seemed to come from everywhere. Down the stairs, dropping from the rafters, knocking each other off of the many hair-encrusted cat towers.

It wasn't just the meowing, but the snarling at each other that Doc now found increasingly irksome. Doc decided then that Cameron was not bringing grief into his life, but was forcing him to uncomplicate his life. He had been generous with his friends and now it was time to set them free and for him to move on. The only kitty that Doc had decided to take with him for sure was Puddin. She was not a whiner or demanding. Her demeanor reminded Doc of Zach.

Doc pushed the spoon deep into each can, turning it around like the hands of a grandfather clock, slopping scoop after scoop of wet food onto the floor. The cats were hungry. The more passive ones began throwing up almost immediately from eating so fast, trying to get enough to fill their bellies before the fat cats at the top of the pecking order shoved them aside. As they ate, they began to quiet down. An "ahhh" escaped Doc's lips as he stood satisfied, watching his precious kitties gorge themselves on their every-other-day rations. Doc tried to delicately step over the menagerie, wrenching each time at the screeches of the few tails he was unable to avoid with his pink powder-puff slippers. When he got to the top of the stairs, Doc pushed the basement door closed. When Doc walked back into his living room, he saw that one of the kitties who had decided to forego dinner, was growling under his breath, standing sentry over a freshly killed mouse, that was now tightly drawing up in the throes of death.

Doc's lady friend arrived first. She hadn't had time to cook a turkey, she said, as she dangled the cold cut turkey lunch meat and boxes of dry dressing in a bag slung over her arm. Doc said he didn't mind, there would be other Thanksgivings and he was glad to have a friend thoughtful enough to bring anything to the celebration. After she sat the bag on the table, Doc's lady friend said she had to rush to the bathroom. Her period was especially heavy and she had to change her pad. As soon as she closed the bathroom door, his friend began rifling again through Doc's medicine cabinet. She was sure she had missed some of Doc's pills. In her scurry, she knocked bottles of pills into the sink. "Shit," she said under her breath, waiting for Doc to knock on the door and ask her what she was doing. The knock didn't come. Like she always did when she came over to Doc's, his friend wore something baggy so Doc wouldn't notice her pockets bulging with the contraband. Today was no exception. She filled her pockets with most of the pills from the dozen or more bottles she found that Doc had replaced from her last foray to his cabinet. Not long ago, when she cleaned out Doc's bathroom, she had gotten most of his hoard. She knew that Doc had more pills stashed away and would dig them out and load up his cabinet again. Doc hadn't been thinking that good anyway, so he wouldn't know how much she had taken. His lady friend wasn't worried that she might be found out. She flushed the toilet a couple of times for effect, tossed a handful of downers into her mouth, cupped her hand under the tap and swigged back the water from her palm. She extended her long neck and could feel the pills' dry cake shedding, as they traveled down her gullet. Doc's lady friend took one last look at herself in the mirror, brushed her straggly hair out of her eyes, rolled her lower lip out, turned, and walked out the door. Doc was standing at the end of the hallway, holding a chipped saucer of crackers and cheese. He was smiling. "When are the others coming?" he asked. She wasn't sure, but said that she wasn't feeling well: "Really bad cramps." She didn't think she was going to be able to stay. Doc could keep the food though. It wouldn't take much for Doc to get things ready. Doc sighed sorrowfully, dropped his head, and pitifully hunched his shoulders. His lady friend, pissed off at Doc's counterfeiting manner, suddenly screamed that he wasn't going to fuck up her Thanksgiving. She didn't feel good: if he was any kind of friend he would fucking understand. Just boil some fucking water, pour it over the fucking dressing, take the butcher's paper off the fucking turkey, and he had fucking Thanksgiving dinner. Doc's lady friend stormed out the door. Doc stood in his kitchen with snot bubbling out of his nose and tears running down his cheeks. A few seconds later, the door opened and his lady friend came into the room and hugged Doc. She was sorry, she said. Her cramps were really bad and she could barely stand up. She was just being moody because of her period. She was careful when she hugged Doc to turn herself sideways, so he wouldn't feel any of his pills bulking up her pockets. As she wrapped her arms around Doc's neck, she looked at her watch like a hooker clocking time and said she had to go. The downers would be hitting in a few minutes and she wanted to be sure and get home before they did. Doc thanked her for bringing Thanksgiving dinner and said that he was sure he could manage and she shouldn't be concerned. His lady friend apologized again, kissed Doc on a ruddy cheek and told him that she loved him. He said he loved her too. She was going to help him get moved into his new place in a few days. Not to worry. Then she turned and walked out the door.

By the time she got home, Doc's lady friend felt like she was drifting off into endless Elysian Fields. In her dazed state, she giggled softly and seemed to almost curtsy as she pushed the door closed with a tip of her butt. Doc's lady friend barely felt the splinter slip into her bubbled ass cheek, when she used the door as a brace to slide down onto the floor. Then she curled up into a tight ball, nestled herself into the gritty green shag carpet, looked up at her floating furniture, and died.

* * *

It was a miserable Thanksgiving that year for Cameron. At one point during the meal, his wife sarcastically suggested that they set a place for Bar Jonah; *maybe* they should even get him out of jail and give him the spare bedroom. He was there all of the time anyway, she would say. Cameron wanted to argue but he knew she was right. Bar Jonah was there, he was everywhere. He couldn't get away from him nor could he let him go.

CHAPTER FOUR

Frog on a stick

They were getting ready to charge Bar Jonah with the murder of Zach. Cameron was talking to Rachel, sometimes almost daily, trying to keep her apprised of how the case was going. She would argue with Cameron that Zach *was* still alive. Rachel said she would do whatever she had to do to protect her hope. Cameron wasn't going to take that away from her.

Great Falls was buzzing with nervousness and curiosity. Had they really had a cannibal in their midst and not known it? What if Bar Jonah hadn't killed Zach? Then the killer was still out there and no one was safe.

* * *

Barry had tipped off Adam Kingsland a few days before Cameron had seen him walking down the street. Cameron had been sniffing around and talking to anyone who had ever known Bar Jonah, Barry said. He was probably going to be showing up at Kingsland's door too. Kingsland didn't know anything, he said. He had only seen Bar Jonah a few times, didn't like him, and stayed away from him.

Cameron pulled up to the curb and honked his horn at Kingsland. Kingsland turned around and looked through the windshield at Cameron. Cameron flashed his badge when he got out of his car. Kingsland figured he was being busted for weed. He thought he might as well confess on the spot. It would be easier than being hassled. As soon as Cameron was within earshot, Kingsland began reeling off a string of apologies laced with excuses. Cameron looked at Kingsland and said he didn't care. He wanted to talk to him about Bar Jonah. Kingsland's stupefied eyes lingered on Cameron, trying to make sense of him saying he didn't care about the marijuana. "I don't know nothin' 'bout Bar Jonah," Kingsland slurred. Cameron told Kingsland that if he wanted him to continue not caring about his weed, it would be a good idea for him to start talking. Kingsland's name had turned up in some of Bar Jonah's papers. But he wasn't a suspect in anything, Cameron just wanted to know if he had seen any kids hanging around, when he was at Bar Jonah's. Pinching a smoldering joint between his fingers behind his back, Kingsland told Cameron about seeing Bar Jonah in his underwear while some younger boys were at his apartment. He also said that Barry had told him that the boys regularly slept with Bar Jonah. But Kingsland said, his eyes momentarily clearing, he always had wanted to know what was hanging behind the sheet that Bar Jonah had nailed up in front of his kitchen table. Cameron told Kingsland that he needed him to come down to the police station and give a statement on the record. Kingsland resisted. Cameron reminded him again that he could keep ignoring what Kingsland was holding behind his back or not. They agreed to meet at the GFPD a couple of days later. He needed to be straight when he gave the statement, Cameron said. No excuses, no exceptions. Kingsland agreed.

* * *

Bar Jonah's days had now become routine. He was sure that he could not be convicted for murder, even if he was charged. "There is no body," he would say. The cops had nothing. Even if Zach's skull washed up somewhere, there was nothing to tie it back to him. The other inmates hated Bar Jonah. He wasn't inside with anyone of the likes of Doc, Boone, or Reno. He was also being held at the Cascade County Detention Center, which was a far cry from the county jail. There were lifers there with nothing to lose. To them, Bar Jonah was nothing more than a baby-fucker. Some of the inmates called him "the freak." There was, however, one inmate that Bar Jonah sniffed out, who intimated that they shared a similar "weakness." He and Bar Jonah would sit and talk for hours. They would sometimes talk right up until lights out.

Like any prison, the detention center is obscenely loud. Heavy steel cell doors clang and big-mouth talkers echo off of cold alloy. Even with the chronic intensity of the noise, Bar Jonah would whisper when he talked in his riddles to his inmate friend about Zach. "There is no body," Bar Jonah would chant over and over again. He had done nothing wrong. Rachel had even become his good friend. She not only believed that he couldn't have hurt Zach, she also believed in him. Bar Jonah said he began writing Rachel the day after she visited him and now they wrote back and forth to each other all of the time. She was the best pen pal that he had ever had. He would snicker when he walked into his inmate friend's cell, waving a letter from Zach's mother.

Bar Jonah heard through one of the guards that Rachel was denying to Cameron that they were writing to each other. He didn't care. Rachel had lost her son and he was determined to be a comfort for her. Bar Jonah also told his new inmate friend that he was sure, when the time came, Rachel was going to be a comfort for him too. She was going to help him, the way he was helping her. He could tell she had a good heart. Nonetheless, he had to figure out how to deal with the little Indian bastards who were lying to the cops about him. His inmate friend agreed. It was probably best not to do anything good for anyone, he said, especially kids. They'll just try to fuck you with their lies. That's what they'd done to him too. Bar Jonah said it was because kids who tell lies don't have good moms. He had been lucky though, his mom had stuck with him throughout all of his trials and tribulations. If it wasn't for Tyra, he didn't know if he would have been able to go on for so long. She had taught him how to stay steadfast and true. Most of all she taught him to believe in God. Bar Jonah's inmate friend sat on his bunk and nodded his head up and down. In between each nod, Bar Jonah caught a quick glimpse of his inmate friend's envious eyes. "When my mom comes to visit, I'll make sure that you get to meet her," Bar Jonah said, as he turned to walk back to his cell. His inmate friend said he'd like that, for sure. When Bar Jonah got back to his cell, one of the guards handed him a letter from Doc. Bar Jonah was surprised. He hadn't heard from Doc since he had been arrested. Sitting down on his cot, Bar Jonah tore open the envelope.

> Dear Nathan, I am being bothered by Detective John Cameron. He seems to think that I know something about dear Zach. As I told you many times before, my heart was broken when you took Zach away from me, and even though I have tried, I have never been able to forgive you. I am in the final sunset of my life and I do not want to continue to be hounded by the likes of Cameron. He is forcing me from my home and taking away all that I love. I just found out today that my dear lady friend was found dead. Supposedly she died from an overdose, but I wouldn't doubt if Cameron had something to do with it, just to put pressure on me. You, Nathan, know what I know about Zach going away. But you also know that I am an old man now, who has many medical problems, none the least of which is my poor memory. It would be inconvenient for you and for me if my memory problems were cured. Anything you can do to direct Cameron's attention away from me would benefit us both. I am

sure that you are faring well in jail. Somehow it always seemed to me that you handled being locked up much better than I. In some ways you seemed to prefer it. I leave it in your hands to resolve our sticky problem.

Doc

Bar Jonah seethed with rage. Doc was trying to blackmail him. It was Doc's word against his. "There is no body." Doc had eaten the deer meat he had given him. He had the letter to prove it. Bar Jonah had even sneaked around and checked Doc's freezer a few months after he gave him the meat. Inside was only some cherry popsicles. It helped Bar Jonah to regain his composure when he recalled handing Doc the butcher paper-wrapped meat and jokingly saying that he had brought him some special "dear meat." In a fit of tears, Doc had screamed that he didn't appreciate Bar Jonah's sense of humor. Bar Jonah knew there was nothing to worry about, it had been years ago. The cops had nothing then and they had nothing now. Bar Jonah stood up and folded the note over and over again into tight little squares. Then as he ripped Doc's note into tiny pieces, Bar Jonah imagined that he was a circus strongman standing in front of an applauding crowd, ripping the head off a chicken.

Bar Jonah walked over to the seat-less, stainless steel toilet and in a locked gaze, scowled at the pieces of featheredged paper falling from his fat, nubby hands, swaying in the foul prison air, like Lilliputian ballerinas in their white lace tutus. After all of the inanimate little dancers rested on the water, Bar Jonah leaned his head close to the bowl and thought they looked confused, unsure what to do next, floating about in the grayish liquid. Then Bar Jonah stood back up, turned around, dropped his pants and sat his flabby ass down on the cold rim of the toilet bowl.

A few minutes later his inmate friend walked by Bar Jonah's cell and saw him sitting on his bunk, smiling a big smile and laughing out loud. In an Appalachian drawl, Bar Jonah's inmate friend wondered what was making him so giddy. "Why you got the chuckles," he asked. His inmate friend was taken aback when Bar Jonah lifted his head and captured his eyes with a reptilian gaze and said, *"Like the Great Fish, the little boy had to be swallowed to make him whole. Like the Lord swallowed me and made me whole. And like Rachel, who had to be punished for her sinful ways, the old man, like Jonah had to be punished for interfering in God's work; the little boy too. He'd been a devilfish who made good men transgress the way of the Righteous. The old man had been a good man too. Then the devil boy came and took the old man's heart. You must love the Lord above all others. The old man lost his way. He had been punished and now had to live with the pain and sorrow like Rachel the mother of Zachary."* Bar Jonah's inmate friend said he felt like a frog stuck on a stick.

"Tiger Pultoric"

On the morning of Tuesday, December 19th Cameron and Wilson arrived at the Cascade County Detention Center. The guards knew they were coming and already had Bar Jonah in a holding cell. Neither Cameron nor Wilson had ever met Bar Jonah in person before. In his right hand, Cameron was carrying the forty-six page deliberate homicide and aggravated kidnapping indictment. When Cameron and Wilson walked into the holding cell, Bar Jonah's counsel wasn't there. Without his attorney present, Cameron couldn't speak to Bar Jonah. Cameron turned and walked out of the room to see if Vernay or Jackson had left a message at the front desk. Wilson and Bar Jonah stood for the first time, face to face. The first thing Wilson noticed was that Bar Jonah smelled. Not unwashed, more like something about him was decayed. Wilson thought it was odd. Maybe he was imagining the smell because of the nature of the case. Behind his unkempt scraggly beard, Wilson could see that the deep lines along the side of Bar Jonah's mouth made his floppy jowls seem more pronounced. His eyes were buried behind thick pads of flesh. Their blankness teased Wilson's curiosity. Even though it was a direct violation for Wilson to speak to Bar Jonah, he, at that point, didn't care. Wilson's discerning eyes sought to capture Bar Jonah's elusive glare, and, when they did, Wilson said to Bar Jonah, "Everyone thinks you're crazy, but I don't." Bar Jonah, with an ugly grin and his voice as quick as thought, said, "I know exactly what I'm doing." For a brief second, Wilson felt his bones chill. After that moment, Wilson and Bar Jonah never spoke again. A few minutes later, Cameron came back into the holding cell. Bar Jonah's attorneys weren't coming. He handed Bar Jonah the murder indictment and said, "Mr. Bar Jonah, you are hereby served." Count 1 read: "Deliberate Homicide, A felony in violation of MCA Section 45-5-102 (1) (a) (1995). The above-named defendant did then and there cause the death of another human being, Zachary Ramsay. A person convicted of this offence shall be punished by death, or by imprisonment in the state prison for life or a term of not less than 10 years to more than 100 years." Count II read: "Aggravated Kidnapping, A felony in violation of MCA Section 45-5-303 (1) (b) (1995). The above-named defendant did then and there knowingly or purposely and without lawful authority restrain another person, Zachary Ramsay, by using physical force for the purpose to facilitate commission of a felony. A person convicted of this offence shall be punished by death, or by imprisonment in the state prison for life, or a term of not less than 10 years to more than 100 years."

Cameron and Wilson turned, walked out into the hallway, and motioned for a guard to begin unlocking the series of doors that would set them free. Bar Jonah's protruding belly left the holding cell before the rest of him. He sashayed down the receiving hallway to the guard station. When he passed one of the other prisoners, Bar Jonah slapped the tightly rolled-up indictment on his forearm and said, "It'll never go to trial."

The next day, with his attorneys by his side, Bar Jonah was formally arraigned on the murder charge. He sat with his arms resting on a table and his hands clasped together, as Justice of the Peace for Cascade County, Sam Harris read the charges into the record and asked how Bar Jonah was pleading. "Not guilty," Bar Jonah said. His bail was set at $500,000. The bail on the sexual assault and kidnapping charges of the boys had been previously set at $1.2 million. Bar Jonah's total bail was now $1.7 million. Bar Jonah had appeared on video from the detention center. It was easier than getting a security detail together to haul his fat ass down to the courthouse, one officer said. Death threats were beginning to come in now too. People were afraid. Great Falls had never seen the likes of a Bar Jonah before. They hadn't even imagined it. A small picture of Bar Jonah, captured from the video screen at his arraignment, was printed beside the headline "Bar Jonah Hears Charges of Kidnapping and Murder" in the Thursday *Great Falls Tribune*. A larger photo of a freshly lipsticked Rachel Howard, with her fists clenched, offering encouragement to the people of Great Falls, was printed right beside Bar Jonah's picture. Cameron thought Rachel was elated to be back in the limelight.

Commotion

The night before the charges were read to Bar Jonah, thirty people met at the Great Falls Community Center. How were they supposed to deal with having a cannibal in the community? Were the cops sure they had got the right man? Rachel was there. She was answering questions and offering comfort to the concerned, saying that each of them had to give the other love. Rachel also said, "We're bitter about all of the talk of Zach being cannibalized having ruined my Christmas." Rachel said, "That breaks my heart. People want to enjoy the holidays and be happy, and they are confronted with cannibalism. You're expecting a sugar cookie and you get a salt rock."

The next day the *Great Falls Tribune* published a full page Uncle Wiggily-looking "Playing It Safe Game Board" about how to keep your children out of harm's way, as they walk to school. It was printed right above the photograph of a real police officer, in dress blues, with a cutout of a *real* police badge. The picture accompanied the article "How Kids Can Tell When A Police Officer Is Real." But the paper also published something else. Bar Jonah was not going to sit idly by while the press covered him without having something to say about it. On the morning before Bar Jonah appeared in court, the *Great Falls Tribune* received three letters from Bar Jonah. One was a copy of his last will and testament. The other two were letters adamantly denying that he had anything to do with Zach's disappearance. In one letter Bar Jonah wrote, "I'm innocent pure and simple, no more no less." He also wrote, "Let's get this perfectly clear—I did not, I repeat, I did not kill Zachary Ramsay or anyone else. I won't say I did something when I did not do it. I am not guilty of those charges and I did not do anything with or to Zachary Ramsay or anyone else. So, please, if you know where he is, please, call the police. Thank you!" Bar Jonah also wrote that he did not do anything to Roland, Stanley, or Stormy. Bar Jonah summed it all up with his take on what had happened: the cops framed him. "They are indeed Great Falls' finest who believe they will always get their man either by hook or by crook. That is they can't prove it legally [so] they will set them up and bully people into making a false statement. These cops remind me of the Borg on *Star Trek*. WE ARE THE LAW. Resistance is futile."

On the same page as Bar Jonah's letters was a short article saying that the other inmates wanted to take care of him with "Jailhouse Justice." The article also revealed that on June 29th, five or six of the other inmates happened to find Bar Jonah without a guard shadowing him. They jumped him, smacked him around a bit and told him that he was going to be killed. Somebody was going to beat him to death in the shower with a sock stuffed with bars of soap. One of the men spit in his face. After that, Bar Jonah was never out of the sight of a corrections officer. He refused to identify the other inmates who jumped him. The only thing that is worse in prison than a baby fucker is a snitch. He knew to keep his mouth shut. Bar Jonah did, however, plan to file a suit against the jail for refusing to serve him kosher meals. After all, he was a Jew, he said. To ululate about what he was not getting that he wanted was his God given right.

* * *

"I can forgive; if I hold anger in my heart, I will suffer," Rachel was quoted as saying at a press conference that she called on December 22nd. Rachel said she was getting so many phone calls from the national media, that she wanted to try to answer their questions all at once. A couple of days before prosecutor Brandt Light filed charges against Bar Jonah, he had met with Rachel and her family to let her know the particulars of the case. At that meeting, Rachel told Light that she *would* testify for the prosecution.

Rachel ran outside to smoke a cigarette, before she ran back inside to take the podium. Once at the mike, an out-of-breath Rachel immediately said that she had something she wanted to announce, but that she was going to wait until the end of the press conference. The reporters and the curious were baited with anticipation. "I can be miserable or I can be happy; I choose to be happy. I have two children to raise and they don't need a momma who's devastated. For me to deal with it, I just have to stay strong. That's just how I am," Rachel tearfully said. She also said that she believed that Zach was still alive. He'd be coming home anytime. As the meeting drew to a close, Rachel made her announcement: she had decided to testify for the prosecution. A reporter asked why, if she didn't believe that her son was dead, would she agree to testify against Bar Jonah. Rachel glassily looked at the reporter, turned, and walked back outside of the auditorium for another smoke. The press conference had come to an end.

The next day, right after the mail came, Bar Jonah's inmate friend asked him if he had heard that Rachel was going to testify against him. Bar Jonah folded the letter that he had just read, smiled, and said, "I heard."

* * *

Cameron, Wilson, and Theisen were about as disliked as they could be by the other cops. Wilson didn't have to worry about any of the political ramifications; he wasn't a city cop and the case didn't have any bearing on his advancement. But he was still hated by the cops. The scuttlebutt was that Wilson kept sticking his nose where it didn't belong. Cameron and Theisen thought that Wilson was pretty straightlaced, but for an FBI agent, he was the best they had ever worked with. They tried to get him to go out drinking with them but he always refused, saying that he needed to get home. Cameron thought he was a closet evangelist. The only addictions he seemed to have were soda pop and salt. When Wilson went home at night, he didn't stop working. He obsessed about Bar Jonah's nine words. He dreamed about Bar Jonah's nine words. He worked them over in his head. He imagined what they might mean. He didn't need to write them down, they were indelibly etched in his memory.

Cameron's wife told him that she was through. She'd had enough. Cameron wanted more time. They were just about to bring Bar Jonah to trial. She said she didn't care. It didn't matter. Cameron would never be done with Bar Jonah. Laurie Theisen on the other hand didn't give a shit. No matter what, Bar Jonah was not going to wreck her marriage or her family. She was encouraging her husband to retire as soon as he could. The almost daily fights with his lieutenant were not worth what it was doing to him. He agreed. The only ally he had left was Cameron. They now relied on each other and didn't trust anyone, besides Brandt Light and Wilson. Behind the scenes, Bellusci was still quietly fueling the belief that Rachel had killed Zach. To Bellusci's way of thinking, Rachel still couldn't explain those "missing four hours," on the night Zach disappeared.

* * *

Just before four on Christmas Eve, the report came back from the crime lab on the meat grinder. When the technician had separated the blades of the grinder from the aluminum housing, she found a hair. Assaying the hair, the technician discovered that it was a Negroid hair. However, the DNA was not a match for Zach. The other debris caked around the blades of the grinder could not be identified. Cameron read the report right before he left the office to pick up a couple of last minute Christmas presents.

Receptions

Bar Jonah received visitors on Christmas day. It wasn't too bad. They brought him homemade cookies. He loved cookies. Even if the Lord chose, for reasons that only He understood, to make Bar Jonah go to trial on the murder charges, any conviction would be overturned on appeal. The original police stop by Officer Burton was illegal anyway, his attorneys had assured him of that. Burton didn't have any probable cause. It wouldn't stick and without that, the cops didn't have anything. Everything else fell from that tree, Bar Jonah would often tell his inmate friend. His inmate friend wasn't so convinced though and told him that he shouldn't be so cocksure of himself. If he wasn't careful, he could end up spending the rest of his life behind bars. Bar Jonah said it wasn't likely.

* * *

This was Doc's last Christmas in his house. He had packed all that was important to him. The cats lying everywhere were like little furry Christmas bows, adorning each box of Doc's treasures. Now that his lady friend was dead, there would be no celebration, at least none with any adult. There were, however, a couple of brothers that Doc had celebrated extra special occasions with over the past few years. They were now just going into their mid-teens, one just a year or so older than the other. Usually by that age, Doc was ready to turn kids away. But these were boys that Doc had known for many years. He had enjoyed their favors since they were sprouting striplings. And, they sure did like the different kinds of beer that Doc had introduced them to over the years. They also appreciated the toys that Doc gave them every time they came to see him. On that final Christmas, they were going to come and visit Doc one last time. Doc had wrapped a few special presents for them and put them under his shiny silver Christmas tree. Doc had not been going to put up a tree that year, but at the last minute decided to since he was going to have company and he wanted to make it memorable for the lads. He had even set up the rotating color wheel that reflected a kaleidoscope of colors off of the old aluminum tree onto Doc's smoke- stained walls.

When the boys arrived, they found that Doc had already cut and fanned out slices of cold canned ham. One of the boys even commented that Doc had spread the thick brownish packing jelly on the pink meat. That was the best part, the other boy added. Doc gently rubbed the youth's back and told him to eat up. They could have the whole ham all to themselves if they wanted. He had even bought an extra one because he knew how much they loved ham. The one boy kept stuffing rolled up cuts of pork into his mouth, like he sure was hungry. Their family hadn't made it to the church to pick up a frozen turkey, so they hadn't known what they were going to eat for Christmas dinner until Doc called and invited them over. Doc had lots of their favorite beer to quench their thirst after the salty meat. He hadn't fixed any vegetables, just meat and beer. The boys had been through the routine many times before.

After they ate and got drunk enough, Doc let them open one of their presents. Even if it wasn't Christmas, Doc always gave them presents. After they opened their gift, each boy in turn sucked Doc's penis. The first boy got it going, which at Doc's age took a long time. But once it got hard, the other boy finished him off. Doc would then wipe himself with his stained terry cloth robe, lob his head around until he found just the right spot on the always present thick, feather bolster that he kept taped to the back of his easy chair, and tell the boys in a barely audible whisper that they could now open another present. Then Doc would reach out and take a sip of his holiday hot toddy and fall sound asleep while the boys robbed him blind.

When the boys tore open their other presents, they each found a dried cat piss-caked army man doll, still wrapped in cellophane. They would add them to the pile that they already had gotten from Doc. What they were able to steal from Doc was always better than the presents that Doc would give them. This time though, just about everything was packed up. As Doc was rolling his head around on the pillow, moaning like he might wake up, they helped themselves to one of the smaller boxes sitting by the door when they left to go home. Walking into the alley behind Doc's house, with their army man dolls tucked under their arms, they sat the box that they had lifted from Doc's on top of a galvanized trashcan and ripped it open. Inside was a picture of Doc in an army uniform, with his arm wrapped around a couple of dark-skinned slant-eyed little boys, standing on a dirt road with some scrawny chickens. There were also a couple of purple-heart shaped medals in a black flip-top case. An old webbed army belt, with a dry canteen clipped to it, was lying beside a couple of magazines from a .45. A few rounds were still stacked in the clips. One of the boys pushed out one of the shells and saw that the casing was dark green. He guessed it had probably been from a war somewhere. There was a bunch of letters that looked like they were real old too. One of the boys remembered that one of the letters he looked at was addressed to "Mom" somewhere in Texas. The ink was blue, blotty, and pretty smeared. They also found a bayonet with a ring on the top end and a groove cut into the bottom of the handle, so it could slide over the barrel of a rifle, they guessed anyway. One of the boys wondered if Doc had ever killed anyone with it. The boys split the canteen and the knife between them and each one slipped a .45 clip into a pocket. They each agreed that if they wanted to switch the canteen for the knife sometime, they could. The heavy metal magazines made their pants ride down on one side off their thin hips. If they hadn't had coats on, they would have looked like a lopsided drunk with a full bottle when they walked. They pinned a medal to each of their coats and tossed the cases along with the cardboard box into the trashcan, before they started walking home. With their bellies full of ham and beer, they staggered through the door of their cramped apartment to discover that the church had dropped off a full Christmas dinner with all of the trimmings. The smell of turkey and sage dressing baking in the oven made them hungry all over again. After all, they were growing boys. Their mother didn't ask them about the medals dangling from their threadbare coats, why they were tottering around on their feet like a wobbling top, or the smell of beer on their breaths.

* * *

Doc had woken up when he heard the boys pull the door closed and winded himself as he struggled to get to his feet. He was lightheaded and thought his hands looked blue, probably from the toddy, he thought. There were just a few more things to pack and he hoped to get that done before Christmas Day was over. Nothing too taxing, just a few things to finish up. Most everything was going into storage and the rest he was going to take with him. Doc had decided to temporarily move into one of the local motels on 2nd Avenue North, close to downtown and right next to a 24-hour restaurant. This way he could eat whenever he wanted. He was just getting too old to fuss with too much. There was even a nice warm lobby at the motel, with a gas fireplace, where Doc could sit on cold, windy winter days and watch people blow by, while he stayed toasty, drinking hot chocolate from a machine. Doc wanted to be out of his house before the first.

* * *

Somewhere in the first week of the New Year, the Ladies contacted Cameron and told him that they believed that Zach was indeed still alive. It wasn't just Rachel that believed, they did too. They had evidence, but they knew that he wouldn't listen to them. He should be focusing his investigation on finding Zach to bring him home, not putting all of his efforts into persecuting an innocent man like Bar Jonah. How could Bar Jonah be guilty if Zach was still alive; they didn't understand. Cameron decided it was pointless to argue with them. He had to argue with seemingly every cop on the force, except for Theisen and Wilson, anyway. He didn't want to waste his time verbally scrapping with the Ladies.

* * *

Bar Jonah was constantly complaining to his jailers that the tightness in his chest was getting worse. He was chronically having chest pain and shooting pains down his left arm. The prison should have him transported to the hospital to be checked out. One guard joked that he was in the emergency room more than he was in his cell. But with Bar Jonah's history of having had at least two prior heart attacks, they weren't about to let him die on them before his trial, if they could prevent it. The doctors diagnosed him with chronic angina, gave him nitroglycerin to manage his discomfort and sent him on his way. Every time Bar Jonah showed up in the ER, there was a sense of dread. Like when he was twelve, the physicians and nurses argued, not only about who was going to see him, but also who had to touch him. One nurse said that he made her skin crawl.

* * *

Cameron said that this was a case where nothing would surprise him. But when random people in the community started showing up at the police station with letters from Bar Jonah, Cameron was surprised. Bar Jonah's inmate friend tried to talk him out of writing to the community to tell his side of the story, but Bar Jonah would have no part of it. He was going to write anyone and everyone he could to proclaim his innocence and attempt to taint any jury pool. There was no point in letting his persecutors have an easy time of it. They had already destroyed his good name as an honest businessman. It was going to be really hard to rebuild his reputation when he finally got out. Bar Jonah was hoping that somehow his letters would influence the prosecutors to drop all of the charges against him. It was futile, Bar Jonah told his inmate friend, for the prosecution to continue to pursue him. "No one has ever made me face a jury," Bar Jonah said, and Great Falls wasn't likely to be the first. With somber eyes, his inmate friend told Bar Jonah that he was going to trial and he'd better get used to it. He'd had dealings with Cameron before and he was a dog.

They just keep turning up

A series of letters turned up in Bar Jonah's mounds of paper from a woman named Teresa Sizemore-Bourisaw. She said if she couldn't marry Bar Jonah, she would come to Montana to live with him, once she got out of prison herself. Bar Jonah had met Sizemore through another inmate while he was incarcerated at Bridgewater. They had many things in common, especially their love for children. From her writings, Cameron thought that Sizemore wasn't just crazy, she was also dangerous. In one of her letters, she told Bar Jonah that she had been charged with forcible sodomy of her boys, who were unfairly taken away from her. Her husband, Lonnie, was already doing time for raping his kids and now she was being charged too. In thinking about it she didn't want to divorce Lonnie while he was in prison, even though she had fallen in love with Bar Jonah. But even if the charges of rape stuck, she wanted Bar Jonah to stick by her. He was her true love. They had never met each other in person, but that didn't matter one bit. They were kindred spirits.

Cameron managed to talk to Sizemore on the phone, before she was sentenced on the sodomy charge of her two sons. She told Cameron that after "the kid" in Great Falls disappeared, Bar Jonah would tell her about "little Zach" being his friend and taking "little Zach" to Billings to flea markets with him. Sizemore said she asked Bar Jonah if Zach's mother knew that he was taking her kid on trips. Bar Jonah said that Zach's mother never knew where he was anyway, so it didn't matter. The train conductors used to run Zach out of the rail yard down by the river, Bar Jonah told Sizemore. The kid was all over the place. It didn't sound to Sizemore like the kid's mother gave one fuck about him. She didn't understand how a mother could be that way with her kids.

* * *

Bar Jonah learned from his inmate friend that Cameron had been talking to Pam. He figured that he would eventually. His inmate friend nodded when Bar Jonah slipped a couple of packs of cigarettes into his outstretched palm for helping him out with information. He'd been a snitch on the outside and was a good source of information on the inside. He was pretty cheap too. A couple of packs of cigarettes here and there was all it took. Funny thing was, his inmate friend didn't even smoke. But he had him a little cigarette business that he ran out of his cell. Some of the guards were his best customers, he would say. "Cheap cigarettes for a little bit of snitch juice," and he had all of their favorite brands. Cigarettes were better than running drugs in prison too. Everyone wanted them and most of the men "wouldn't kill you for 'em."

In the middle of February, Bar Jonah thought it would be a good idea to write a letter to Pam and let her know how much he still loved her. Later on that day he wrote a few other letters too.

Correspondence

My Dearest Pam,

I first of all want to say I'm sorry. I put a stop to the wedding because I was afraid. Afraid of a lot of things but one main one was of Sherrie Dietrich's threat. She threatened to kill you if I married you and I believed her. She is one crazy woman. She's one of the ones who brought this on. I spent 14 years in prison for crimes that I did although it didn't happen the way the papers are saying it did but I refuse to go to prison for crimes I did not commit. I'm looking at a minimum of 3 life sentences. In 1999 I had 3 heart attacks and I just can't do time anymore. These cops want me bad and even if I get all these charges dropped I am sure they'll create new ones. I'm tired of fighting. If you receive this letter then you know that I'm dead, either someone has killed me or I did it myself. I just wanted to write and tell you I'm sorry and I love you. I also wanted you to know that I never killed anyone and I didn't do what I'm accused.

Bar Jonah also decided to write a letter to the assistant pastor at the Central Assembly of God.

Dear Pastor Warneke,

I just wanted to thank you for always feeling welcomed by you and your wife. Also, by a few people at the church like the prices, Winklers, Teihs, the Dickoffs, and quite a few more that I can't remember there names off hand but I've never felt that Central Assembly was my home. I have yet to find a church that fits the bill. I've also been like an outsider. Twice I felt like I belonged. The first was when I was working with Royal Rangers but when that was taken away I came close to killing myself. The second time was when I worked the firework stand but that too vanished. Then when Dallas moved I was devastated because I had a family I really felt I belonged. Since Dallas left, I hated being here in Great Falls and Montana, but I never had the means to move even though I tried. Well, now Great Falls is eating me alive and I'm innocent of the charges. These rogue cops are screwing me and my family over and I need to put a stop to it. I love my family too much to allow this to continue so with that I give a fond adue and thanks again.

Sincerely,
Bar Jonah

After he wrote the letter to Pastor Werneke, Bar Jonah wrote two letters back-to-back to his family.

To my family,

This is a letter to tell you that I love you so very much and after talking with my lawyer I can't bear with the Great Falls police to mess with my family. My lawyers feel they are going to arrest Bob and Mom and put them on trial too to squeeze me. I cannot allow that. These cops are evil and rogue. My mom and brother did nothing to deserve this. I've done stuff in my past I'm very ashamed of and God has forgiven me. But I am not, I repeat, I am not guilty of the charges they have me on and I fear that even if I prove I had nothing to do with it, the cops will not stop. Bellucci, Burton, and Cameron are out to nail me even if they have to scare, threaten, and abuse little boys to lie. I believe that they will do everything in there power to put me away legally or illegally even at others expenses like my family. So, I'm putting a stop to this right here and right now. I love you all and I'm at peace with my decision. I haven't been at peace for such a long time but I am now. I love you all.

Love, Nathan

In his second letter, Bar Jonah also enclosed a letter for Bob to send to Roland, Stanley, and Stormy.

I am writing this first of all to say I love you very much and to let you know I tired of this place. I'm here for crimes I didn't commit and as I look at the possible time I could receive—3 life sentences is more than I can take. I don't want to have to kill someone in defense of my life. I've been there and done that and I still live with the nightmares of it. I also know if by some miracle god works as he did before that Bellucci, Burton, and Cameron will try something else and I just can't take going back to prison for crimes I didn't commit. I did my time—14 years although God was there for me, I see no future for me as it's going and I'm tired of the struggle of everybody's prejudice toward me because of my past. All I want is to have friends and a normal life but I don't see that anymore. I knew I should of left great falls when I had planned to instead of listening to bob because of the year 2,000 scare. I'm also tired of the pain and agony I feel in my innermost being. It's time to go home, yes, it is, it's supper time. I love you all very much, be happy for me.

Love ya, Nathan P. S. check with the police before you mail Roland's letter. I don't want you to get in trouble. It's a letter asking them to tell the truth and clear my name.

* * *

Dallas Kallberg and his family had met Bar Jonah through Bob while he was still in Bridgewater. They were a good Christian family who attended the Central Assembly of God Church. They had been planning on testifying as character witnesses for Bar Jonah during the Shawn Watkins debacle. Kallberg was prepared to swear in court that Julie Watkins was a slut, and that Bar Jonah had babysat their kids many times and there had never been a problem. Though they had abandoned Bar Jonah and moved to Knoxville, Tennessee, nonetheless, he forgave them. He thought it would be a good idea to write them too.

Dear Dallas,

This is just a short note to say I miss you and I love you brother. This is also a note to say my last goodbyes. These past months have been really rough on me and it just keeps getting worst. I have been beaten up, received tons of death threats and I've had enough. My life is ruined even if I'm free from these charges I'll never be the same. My name has been slandered by zealot cops. I did not kill anyone and I did not sexually assault anyone. But I'm tired and if you receive this letter in the mail then you'll know that I'm dead, my friend. This is more than I can bear, it really is. I have written to my family, friends, lawyer, and my final words to the newspaper. I doubt they'll print it exactly as I wrote it, but it sure felt good writing it. Who knows, maybe they will print it as I wrote it. I love you, Bro and take care. Goodbye for now. Your brother in Christ.

There was just one last short letter Bar Jonah had to write before the slop came around that they called dinner.

Dear Barry,

This is a letter to say goodbye and to let you know I forgive you for your lies about what happened at the house. You know I'd never do that and if someone was in trouble, you wouldn't slither off to your room and hide. You need to be a man and clear my name. I'm dead so I can't force you to do anything. You have to live with what you've done. Take care my friend. Bar Jonah.

After dinner, Bar Jonah was feeling exhausted. He had worked his mind a lot that day. Still, he had a poem brewing inside of him. This poem was for the people of Great Falls. He wanted them to understand what was happening to their city. Bar Jonah sat down on his bunk and penned *The Night The Lights Went Out In Great Falls*.

> *Oh that's when the lights went out in Great Falls*
> *That's the day they killed an innocent man*
> *Thanks to the deceit of hook or by crook cops*
> *Burton, Bellucci, and Cameron*
> *The man was charged with a simple crime*
> *That they just blew & blew for time*
> *They ran his life out through the news*
> *Distorted as it was, they used*
> *They made him look 100 times worse*
> *And one who should be cursed*
> *A god-fearing man who tried to change his life*
> *But all people gave him was strife*
> *There were people who really cared*
> *And he thanked them for the love they shared*
> *But the evil of this town really abounds*
> *That if the truth be known it would astound*
> *Now it's time for me to die*
> *Built mainly on all these cops lies*
> *For the fight is just knocked out of me*
> *And now I can go to Heaven happy and free.*

The next morning Bar Jonah folded his poem along with a letter he had written several weeks earlier and slid them into an envelope. He told the guard to see that it went out in that day's mail. It was addressed to the Trib.

Asst. District Attorney presenting opening arguments.

Bar Jonah at a court hearing.

Bar Jonah at his video arraignment.

Bar Jonah looking back at the author in court.

Bar Jonah with attorney's Don Vernay and Greg Jackson.

Bar Jonah's mug shot after sentencing.

Zach Ramsay.

CHAPTER FIVE

Chapman and Pierce

Everywhere Cameron, Theisen, and Wilson went, someone wanted to talk about *the* case. At times, the three investigators felt like they were being held hostage by Bar Jonah. Bar Jonah, in his onslaught of letters to the newspaper, declaring his innocence and his dedication to unceasingly praying for those who were lying about him, was in essence Bar Jonah *preying* on the community. He was continuing to troll for victims from his prison cell by invading those susceptible in the community.

* * *

A major snowstorm was pounding Great Falls in late February. Everyone had gotten to the police station late. Cameron, Wilson, and Theisen all seemed to be edgy and pissed. None of them had slept well the night before and the coffee wasn't working to jar them awake. Wilson was sitting on a metal foldup chair and glancing down at a stack of letters that he was balancing on one knee. When he caught the name "Wayne W. Chapman" as the return address on one of the envelopes, he immediately woke up. Chapman had been implicated in the Puglisi case. It was now clear that Chapman and Bar Jonah knew each other. Wilson just didn't know how well.

12/15/1995
Merry Christmas Nathan:

Thanks Nathan for answering my letter. I pray 1996 brings a top position at Hardee's with top pay. My hometown, Jamestown, New York, had two Hardee's in the 70's. I am waiting on a judge to respond to rule 29. It's rumored that the 300 men high jacked to Dallas county jail have offered the governor the opportunity to give all sex offenders statutory good time credits rather than to sue. I heard you are getting married, what married life is like. I think I am going to get divorced myself. More later.

Your friend,
Wayne

As Wilson began to sift through the pile he found another letter dated a few months earlier from Chapman to Bar Jonah.

Chapman had an upcoming parole meeting on April 20th, he wrote. He had spent eighteen years at Bridgewater and he wanted out. Enough was enough. He wanted advice from Bar Jonah about how he would suggest that he approach the parole board. Bar Jonah had been so successful at getting out that Chapman wanted his help. There were a couple of group leaders inside of Bridgewater that were recommending Chapman be released to a lower level of monitoring. His lawyer, Greta Junusz, was working with his doctors, Ober and Sweitzer on a revise & revoke motion to submit to a judge. In Massachusetts, Criminal Procedure Rule 29 says that a judge can revise or revoke a sentence if it appears that justice may not have been done. Chapman said he was hopeful that the judge would see the wrong that had been done to him for all of those years.

* * *

In August 1975 Wayne Chapman had lured two Lawrence, Massachusetts boys into the woods with a puppy he had stolen from a house not far from the woods. After he got the boys into the woods, he broke the neck of the puppy and then raped the two boys. In late September of that same year, newly graduated Bar Jonah said he met Chapman while sitting on a picnic bench watching children playing at an elementary school in Lawrence. Bar Jonah and Chapman hit it off right away when they discovered they both had a liking for police badges, toy pistols, and handcuffs. They also liked rope and tape too. Some of the kids ran past the two men as they sat and smiled at the kiddies. Chapman looked at Bar Jonah and not so under his breath said, "Ummm ummm!" A few of the little ones even stopped to ask the men what they were doing just sitting there on the picnic bench. Bar Jonah said that Chapman was really impressed when he unzipped his light blue police jacket and showed the boys the badge pinned to his shirt. The boys were impressed too. Bar Jonah told them they were working undercover to keep kids safe. As the boys were walking away, a cop turned onto the street. Chapman thought they should leave, "The cop may know me," he said. The two men got up and began walking the other way. Before they came to where the sidewalk split, Chapman told Bar Jonah that he wanted to introduce him around to some other men that he knew. Bar Jonah thought that was a great idea.

Bar Jonah and Chapman agreed that they would not call each other. They both liked to write letters and that seemed like the best way to stay in touch. It didn't take very long before there were lots of letters back and forth and they became real good friends. Chapman thought Bar Jonah had promise, like Doc had thought much later on. Chapman told Bar Jonah that he was going to have to "slick-up" or he was going to end up going to jail. Bar Jonah replied that he had a big hunger and it sometimes got the best of him.

They also had the Lord in common and would spend time when they were together studying their Bibles. Chapman showed Bar Jonah how to keep pictures of boys in his Bible and label them like they were his nephews. No one ever asked questions about your own kin, Chapman said. Chapman and Bar Jonah liked to drive around together. Between the two of them, they could cover a pretty good area in a short amount of time; one slept while the other drove. They would go in bursts, spending time together and then not seeing each other for a while. On one of their trips, Chapman told Bar Jonah a story about the first time he tied a boy to a tree and set him on fire. Chapman said he laughed so hard that he thought he was going to shit himself when Bar Jonah would keep interrupting him, making crackling sounds. At the end of the story, Chapman told Bar Jonah, "I didn't want to kill the kid, I just wanted to leave my mark on him." Chapman didn't like to be forgotten. That story is likely where Bar Jonah first culled the seeds for his fabrication of Kevin being strung between two trees and set on fire while he courageously fought and ultimately saved Kevin's life.

Chapman also worked as a morgue attendant at Miriam Hospital in Providence. He was charged with incinerating amputated body parts. "It came in real handy sometimes," Chapman said to Bar Jonah. Bar Jonah enviously agreed that he could see how it could. On one of their trips together, Bar Jonah said that he and Chapman prayed that the Lord keep them safe. They knew they did things that could sometimes make the Lord angry. However, they were devout in their beliefs and believed that Jesus knew that. No matter what happened, He would keep them out of harm's way. Chapman cautioned Bar Jonah about being too hungry and needing to be careful. Even the Lord couldn't protect someone from themselves. He would then recite one of his guiding Bible passages to Bar Jonah: "For the law having a shadow of good things to come, and not the very image of the things, can never with those sacrifices which they offered year by year continually make the comers thereunto perfect. For then would they not have ceased to be offered. Because that the worshippers once purged should have had no more conscience of sins. But in those sacrifices there is a remembrance again made of sins every year. Wherefore when he cometh into the world, he saith, Sacrifice and offering thou wouldst not, but a body hast thou prepared me. In burnt offerings and sacrifices for sin thou hast had no pleasure." Bar Jonah added, "Then said he, 'Lo, I come to do thy will, O God'." During one of those trips, they agreed that if one was in need, the other would always be there to help. They also made a pact to keep souvenirs for each other. That way, if the nosey cops ever came looking for anything, they couldn't trace it back to either Chapman or Bar Jonah. Chapman told Bar Jonah that he thought he was a genius for coming up with the idea. Bar Jonah later said that he and Chapman were passing through the Lawrence area on one of their drives when the "Puglisi kid" disappeared but that they didn't know anything about it. They had just got off the road to get something to eat and then got right back on. There were just so many kids. No matter where Bar Jonah ended up kids just flocked to him. He wished that wasn't the case because they had always gotten him into a lot of trouble over the years.

On September 5th, 1976, a patrol sergeant stopped Chapman's van on the NYS Thruway, in Brockton, MA. On the dash were dozens of Polaroid photographs of boys naked and in sexually explicit poses. The officer found 8mm child pornographic movies, a blank gun, fake police badges, and an audiotape of Chapman talking to himself while he was following a school bus. The tape was what would ultimately convict Chapman and serve to keep him in prison for the rest of his life.

"There comes two boys now—they look pretty good there—one of them is about eight years old, wearing a light blue snowmobile suit—another school bus just passed loaded with small children. Boy, would I love to get into some of the stuff that's in them buses. Wowee! And sock it to'em but good! Some of them scream, 'It hurts, it hurts'; some of them say 'It feels alright.' You know what that means when they say it feels alright—it means it feels all right man!" (Excerpt from audio tape played at the 1976 sexual assault trial of Wayne Chapman).

In August 1975, the year before Andy Puglisi went missing in Lawrence, two other boys from the projects had been kidnapped and raped up in the woods behind the same pool. The man had said his puppy was lost, could they help him find it. The cops didn't think it would be important to put the tenants in the projects on notice that someone had kidnapped and raped two young boys. When the cops began to investigate Chapman, they realized that he fit the description of the man who had raped the two boys back in 1975. When they took Chapman's mug shots to show the boys, they identified him without hesitation. On August 16th of that same year, Chapman was charged with the sexual assault of the two boys.

In September 1977, Chapman was found guilty of raping the boys from the Lawrence pool. He was sentenced in the Essex County Superior Court to two concurrent fifteen to thirty year sentences. Massachusetts Correctional Institute at Cedar Junction was supposed to be his home for the next thirty years. Chapman didn't think much of the accommodations at Cedar Junction. The other inmates hated his guts. They thought he was a sissy and a baby fucker. Word was out that someone was going to kill him; there was no doubt. He immediately began his quest to be transferred to BWSH. Because he was sentenced as a violent sexual offender, he qualified for treatment as part of his incarceration. In March 1978, Chapman was civilly committed to Bridgewater for a term of "one day to life." Almost as soon as he arrived at Bridgewater, he began writing Bar Jonah, who was now serving his time for attempted murder and kidnapping at Wapole. Chapman extolled the virtues of Bridgewater compared to doing "ordinary time." A short time later, he got a letter back from Bar Jonah saying that he had just killed an inmate by throwing him over the top of the railing, off the third tier of the metal catwalk that ran right outside of the cells. Bar Jonah said that a nigger had come up and grabbed him from behind. He had taken enough. Bar Jonah told Chapman that he elbowed the nigger in the belly, turned around, and threw him over the railing. The jig stopped screaming when he slammed three stories down onto the concrete floor, dead. Bar Jonah wanted to know how Chapman had gotten sent to Bridgewater. He also said that the blacks in the prison had a contract out on him so he was living on borrowed time. Chapman instructed Bar Jonah how to go about getting transferred to Bridgewater. Bar Jonah began his plea.

Tyra helped too by starting a letter-writing campaign to anyone in the Massachusetts Department of Corrections whom she thought would listen. She also went to see Chapman on a couple of occasions to get his guidance. Tyra said she thought he was a very nice man; he was also very helpful. Tyra was overjoyed when Bar Jonah called her and said that his prayers to get help at Bridgewater had finally been heard. The Lord had come through again for him, Bar Jonah said. "The Lord protects his own," Bar Jonah said right before he hung up. Tyra softly whispered, "Amen," as she sat the receiver down onto the cradle.

* * *

Charles Pierce was a lazy-eyed itinerant carnival worker, horrific serial murderer, cannibal, necrophile, and close friend of Bar Jonah and Chapman on the outside. There was some speculation that Pierce may have initiated Chapman into the world of pedophilia at a young age. Bar Jonah always said that Pierce was part of his and Chapman's coven. They kept things for each other, in order to make it hard for the cops to trace anything back to any one of them. Without any doubt, the most important thing Bar Jonah learned from Pierce was that absolute denial, regardless of the kind of evidence that the cops were shoving in your face, was the only way to handle an interrogation.

"You fucked up, fat boy, when you wrote that confession for the cops back in '77. They didn't even have to go looking for anything, you stupid fuck, you gave it to them. You keep your cock sucking mouth shut, fat boy. No matter what they've got, you didn't have nothin' to do with it. You remember too, that if they ain't got no body, they ain't gonna put you in the hot seat. They may be able to put your ass in prison for life, but they can't put your fat ass in Old Sparky. Death row is real hard time. But you ain't gonna get the hot seat without no body." Bar Jonah took Pierce's many years of tutelage to heart. After he was released from Bridgewater, Bar Jonah never admitted to anything again. From that day forward he was completely innocent of everything.

Investigators wondered if Bar Jonah, Chapman, and Pierce were moving bodies around for each other, to prevent the other from being caught. In November 1979, Pierce was charged with the murder of Michelle Wilson. He pled innocent and was committed to BWSH for observation. Bar Jonah and Chapman could hardly wait for his arrival. Pierce was eventually transferred back to Massachusetts Correctional Institute and would spend the remainder of his life there. He died on February 18th, 1999 of prostate cancer. Right before he died, he made a deathbed confession to having killed children around the Lawrence area. Investigators brought out cadaver dogs to search the area but found nothing. Ultimately, they thought that Pierce confessed to murders that Bar Jonah and Chapman committed to throw the cops off their scent. Pierce's confession was his last act in fulfillment of their covenant.

* * *

Bar Jonah and Chapman spent the next twelve years together in Bridgewater. They were the best of friends and spent hours praying and "Bibleing" together. In Bridgewater it wasn't difficult to have just about anything smuggled in. Bar Jonah had many of the letters from his pen pals in Eastern Europe sent to Tyra's. "They were personal," he would tell her, issuing strict instructions not to open anything that came to her house for him. He expected her to bring them to him as soon as they arrived, even if it meant an extra trip that week. The letters were important. They were his only contact with the outside world. Chapman admired Bar Jonah's resourcefulness.

* * *

In early March 2001, Cameron and Theisen flew back to Massachusetts to interview Chapman. They spent almost two hours listening to Chapman's singsong, syncopated voice sound like it was swaying from an incense censer. His words were like smoke. He even denied that he knew Bar Jonah. In between the mountain turbulence on the flight back, Cameron and Theisen talked about Chapman's eyes. It wasn't that they were just ice cold, it was also that there was absolutely nothing behind them. The vacancy in Chapman's eyes was reptilian. They had spent two hours in the presence of a man who would in fact eat his young. The two men also knew he was a pathological liar.

Ober and Sweitzer

On November 28th, 1990, Dr. Liza Brooks evaluated Chapman for Essex County Superior Court. The court wanted to know if he was still a sexually dangerous person. In her interview with Chapman, he told her that he had been working in group therapy focusing on his anger. Chapman said that he had been seeing Dr. Eric Sweitzer for individual therapy at his own expense. Chapman also said he had seen Dr. Richard Ober three months earlier to help him figure out how to go about getting declared a nonsexually dangerous person. Ober was a good man, he said. The documentation that Dr. Brooks reviewed showed that regardless what Chapman said, he had terminated most of his therapy or just refused to go to sessions. He was eventually terminated from therapy for lack of participation. Chapman also spoke of his deep religious beliefs and how these were the cornerstone of his healing and recovery. He said that when he "was a preteen, I found my father's pornographic literature and it stuck in my mind as pleasurable. When I was driving at age sixteen or seventeen, I found porno shops where there was material of nude children and I found that pleasurable and it fed my thoughts." Chapman went on to say that, "There is no more attraction to males, young or young-looking. In the past few months there has been a dramatic breakthrough and I have finally experienced a sense of freedom."

Chapman told Dr. Brooks that if he were released, he would find solace in the church and that he had a job offer to work in graphic arts or as a nurse's aid with the elderly. He also confessed in the interview to sodomizing more than fifty children. Regardless of Chapman's assertions, Dr. Brooks concluded that he was still a sexually dangerous person. Chapman was furious when he was told that Dr. Brooks refused to declare him a non-sexually dangerous person. He decided to have Ober conduct a complete psychological evaluation to see if his conclusions would be different. Chapman was sure they would be. Ober was a Christian like him. They were of like mind, Chapman would tell Bar Jonah when they talked. Bar Jonah recommended that Chapman get a letter from a minister. That went a long ways when the court was looking at you for release, Bar Jonah said. Chapman wrote his former pastor, Kenneth Harman. Harman was pleased to write a letter for Chapman.

The First Christian Church of Hixville
March 9, 1990
Character reference for Wayne Chapman

> During my twelve year tenure as a volunteer Bible teacher at the Bridgewater Treatment Center I have had the privilege of knowing Wayne Chapman. From the outset of my weekly ministry at that institution, Wayne has been a faithful attendant at those Bible studies. From my personal perspective there have been numerous positive changes that have occurred in Wayne's life during that

interval. I believe that the consequence of having been intimately exposed to the Word of God has produced some of the following area of growth and maturity in his life:

1. a revulsion for inordinate sexual practices
2. a sincere repentance from those lustful patterns that originally lead to his incarceration
3. a tender-hearted concern for his previous victims
4. a healthy and genuine love for other people
5. the ability to openly express his feelings and intimate thoughts
6. the social grace to receive suggestions, criticisms, and good-natured kidding.

The above observations are based on a consistent and progressive pattern of behavior and conversations. Should Mr. Chapman be considered for the privilege of additional programs or an early release, I would give my hearty approval.

Kenneth Harman, former pastor of
First Christian Church

* * *

On June 19th, 1990, Ober performed a psychological assessment of Wayne Chapman. In the introductory paragraph to Ober's evaluation he said that the reason for the evaluation was to "render a professional opinion regarding whether Mr. Chapman was currently a sexually dangerous person." Ober states that, "Chapman's sexual activity began when he was about ten, when he forced a young boy to remove his clothes. Then he set the young boy on fire. His modus operandi was usually the same—to get boys to help him in some manner (often to look for a lost dog), isolate them and then ask them to have sex with him. He was usually vaguely threatening like taking their names and telling them he knew where they lived and that people would not like them if they knew what they did. He said that he tied up one victim and left him in the woods. He purchased handcuffs, a can of mace and a starter's pistol. He was placed on probation and briefly incarcerated several times due to sexual offenses with children before the arrests which lead to the convictions for which he was currently in the treatment center. He had homosexual experiences at age 17 and 19 and was sexually active with his wife, 19 years his senior with whom he lived only nine months."

Ober said that one of the reasons that Chapman married was "to be around the stepchildren and not touch them—that is, to test himself and perhaps become stronger." Chapman received "sexual and emotional pleasure from being around children." Ober went on to say that Chapman no longer had sexual thoughts about children. He saw them as children not as objects. He was no longer preoccupied with sexual thoughts. He infrequently masturbated and when he did so he thought of women." Chapman told Ober that the "critical issue" was related to his spiritual stand. He felt being a Christian meant that he should not become involved in a "secular" type of therapy which placed heavy emphasis on introspection, emotions, and understanding of the past. Ober said that Chapman was in individual therapy with Eric Sweitzer, Ph.D., a licensed psychologist in private practice. "Mr. Chapman felt that the similarity of spiritual beliefs between him and Dr. Sweitzer would facilitate the therapy process."

Chapman told Ober that being in therapy with Sweitzer allowed him to see his past behaviors as "sin" and not "disease." He did admit that sometimes he had "flashbacks" of having sex with boys, but that his last sexual fantasy involving a boy was in 1987. In his summary, Ober wrote, "Mr. Chapman was a 42 year old man who was convicted of pedophilic activities and had been determined a sexually dangerous person. A revocation of this status is warranted given his growth over the past several years." Ober was impressed with Mr. Chapman.

In a July 22nd, 1991 follow-up to his evaluation, Ober wrote that his opinion was unchanged from his findings in his original evaluation. During the subsequent meeting, Chapman told Ober that during the interim he had seen an actor on television that he found attractive but he changed the channel. Ober closed his "psychological assessment update" by saying that Chapman's "hope is to leave the institution and become involved in a church and receive therapy from someone who would permit him to express his Christian values. He has hopes of reestablishing a relationship of some type with his wife, although a true reconciliation with her is unlikely and probably not in *his* best interests, in the opinion of this evaluator. Accordingly, it is the conclusion of this evaluator that Mr. Chapman is no longer a sexually dangerous person." Just like Bar Jonah, Chapman now had proof from Ober that he wasn't a sexually dangerous person. Ober was Chapman's corner man.

Chapman was fighting, not for his release from Bridgewater but to be transferred to the Southeastern Correctional Center. There he could serve out the rest of his time in solitary, not have to be pestered by therapists, and when his time came for release in 2004, he could simply walk out the door. No one would have any hold over him. No parole officer, no nothing, he would tell Bar Jonah. Ober, however, encouraged him to continue to petition the parole board for early release. He and Sweitzer would continue to help him, while he was still behind bars and when he got out.

When the transfer hearing came around at the end of June, the hearing judge didn't think that Dr. Brook's arguments were as compelling as Ober's. He ruled that the Commonwealth failed to prove beyond a reasonable doubt that Chapman was a sexually dangerous person. He ordered Chapman discharged from Bridgewater Treatment Center and back to prison, where he would serve the remainder of his time and then be released back into the community. Chapman was rapturous. A miracle had been delivered to him, just like a miracle had been delivered to Bar Jonah. He could, after so many years behind bars, finally see an end date to his incarceration. It would be easy time.

Chapman didn't want the rest of his time in prison to go to waste. There was no reason not to continue to push for an early release. Chapman came up for parole just two years after he was transferred from Bridgewater to Southeastern Correctional Center. On April 13th, 1993, Ober wrote a short letter to the parole board, highlighting Chapman's sincerity and redemption. He fully supported his release.

> I am writing this letter in support of Wayne W. Chapman. I became acquainted with Mr. Chapman when I evaluated him for his Section 9 hearing at the Treatment Center in 1991. Mr. Chapman has impressed me as a man who was truly contrite for his offenses. He has made excellent use of psychotherapy over the years and has an excellent record in the several institutions in which he has been incarcerated. He has improved himself through classes and other groups. He has an excellent work history. His release from the Treatment Center is evidence of how hard he has worked to improve himself. In my opinion he is an appropriate [candidate] for release at this time. He has realistic plans and goals for the future. His application for parole warrants your careful consideration.
>
> *Richard W. Ober, Ph.D.*

To the frustration of Ober the parole board rejected Chapman's request.

By October, Chapman was getting increasingly more agitated. He wanted out. Bar Jonah and Chapman were continuing to write back and forth. "Continue to trust your doctors," Bar Jonah wrote. "With the Lord's guidance they are the ones who can set you free." It was now time to have Sweitzer begin petitioning for his release. On October 3rd, 1994 Sweitzer drafted a letter to the parole board. In the letter Sweitzer asserts that "Wayne has consistently maintained relationships with his fellow inmates and staff who share his Christian faith. He has also corresponded regularly with a network of pastors and other Christians outside of the prison walls. I have no doubt that Wayne will maintain such contacts and will continue to build a supportive network within his religious community once he is paroled and finally released."

Sweitzer then begins to cite Chapman's "arousal pattern" when he was offending against young boys. "Wayne and I have on numerous occasions discussed his arousal pattern when he was offending against boys. During his years of incarceration, Wayne has disciplined himself to avoid 'trigger' stimuli. For example, he will change channels when young boys are featured on television and he senses his temptation to fantasize. However, he has also reported a significant decrease in his degree of attraction towards such stimuli. The use of the plethysmograph to determine Wayne's current arousal pattern has been avoided by him in the past. He believes that exposure to any form of sexual stimuli, with the intent of reconditioning his arousal 'targets', would violate his conscience as a Christian. This certainly could be construed as a form of psychological defense against still deviant arousal patterns. Yet, I believe that Wayne's entire value system has been 'reconditioned' through his religious perspective on life in general. Having known him for nearly 5 years, I have observed Wayne to be rather consistent in applying his belief system to all life situations and relationships. Wayne's Christian values and beliefs have been internalized to the degree that they are part of his very identity and worth as a person. They are not simply external maxims to follow when and if they seem convenient. Therefore, his refusal to undergo a plethysmograph evaluation is not a singular appeal to a religious belief system used in a defensive manner, but is consistent with Wayne's entire lifestyle."

In the October 3rd letter, Sweitzer closed by saying that "Wayne has formed close relationships, particularly with those who share his faith, both inside and outside of the institution. Such ties will provide a network which will facilitate his transition towards probation and release." Chapman sent Bar Jonah a copy of Sweitzer's letter. Bar Jonah thought it was a good letter and praised Sweitzer for seeing Chapman's devotion to God. The parole board again rejected Chapman's plea for early release. Bar Jonah was disappointed that Chapman's request for parole had been rejected. He couldn't devote much time to making suggestions though because he was having his own troubles. Some little bastard that he had tried to help was telling lies about him. He was back in jail. But like Chapman, Bar Jonah was putting his faith in God as his ultimate counsel. He would be found innocent, he was sure.

Sweitzer was undaunted. On June 6th, 1996 he wrote yet another letter to the parole board. This time he was more adamant and formal in his correspondence.

"Mr. Chapman is an inmate at the Southeastern Correctional Center in Bridgewater, Mass., with whom I have had a professional relationship since 1989. I have written numerous letters on his behalf, stating my clinical opinion that he has achieved a degree of rehabilitation that has made him ready for probation, parole and eventually release. As a recovering sexual offender, Mr. Chapman has now had many years of group and individual psychotherapy and continues to serve what has been a lengthy criminal sentence for his sexual offences which occurred in the late 1970's.

"In more recent years I have maintained regular telephone contact, at least once a month, with Mr. Chapman, since we both felt that psychotherapy could not be conducted in the environment of the visiting room at the SECC. As I have stated consistently for the past 4 years, I believe that as time continues to pass, Mr. Chapman has only progressed further in his rehabilitation process. The reasons upon which I have based my opinion that he is ready for release can be summarized as follows:

1. Mr. Chapman has gained significant insight into the reason and motives behind his pedophilia, including his own forms of emotional and sexual victimization in his own childhood. Having such self-awareness, he is able to more fully empathize with his victims, a trait which is crucial in preventing future offenses.
2. Mr. Chapman assumes full responsibility for his actions, and while being aware of having been victimized himself, he does not in any way excuse or justify his offenses against other young boys.
3. He has used his religious faith during his incarceration in a very adaptive manner, rather than as a 'flight into health' to avoid responsibility for his actions and to manipulate others into thinking he has indeed changed. Within the context of his Christian faith, Mr. Chapman has also developed an appropriate support network, both within the walls of the institution, but also with pastors and fellow believers on the outside. This has enabled him to pursue and maintain appropriate relationships in a manner that would be not present for an active sexual offender who would instead tend to socially isolate himself. Additionally, Mr. Chapman's belief system is a restraining force against further offenses, since he clearly understands sexual offenses to be a violation of the basic tenets of his faith.
4. Mr. Chapman has developed a practical and reasonable plan for reintegration into society that incorporates relapse prevention. He eventually desires to return to Jamestown, NY area to be near his family and has already researched issues such as housing, jobs and support systems such as ongoing psychotherapy and a church community."

Sweitzer closed his letter with what sounded like a plea for Chapman not to have to register as a sexual offender if he were released.

I am aware of recent legislation that requires sexual offenders to register with authorities in local communities. Mr. Chapman has some concerns about the risk to his personal safety that might arise if any particular community members make him a target of their wrath. It would be important to be sure that Mr. Chapman's criminal history be kept confidential with only specific law enforcement officials. I trust that this information is helpful and will contribute to a determination in favor of Mr. Chapman's release from many years of incarceration.

Sincerely,
Eric K. Sweitzer, Ph.D., Licensed Psychologist

The parole board continued to be unimpressed with Sweitzer's tenacity. They concluded that Chapman should remain in prison until he had served his full sentence.

* * *

Ober and Sweitzer continued to write letters to the board of pardons, the district courts, and the state supreme court, petitioning for Chapman's release. Chapman sat in his cell watching the hand on his watch tick down the seconds until 2004 brightened the darkness of his prison cell. It would be just a few short months until he would be a free man.

The Essex County district attorney was demanding that Chapman be reevaluated again, to determine if in fact he was still a sexually dangerous person, even though Chapman had proof from Ober and Sweitzer that he wasn't. The court retained forensic psychologist Robert Joss, Ph.D. Dr. Joss had many years of education and experience evaluating psychopaths. He was also a professor at Gordon College and taught in the forensic psychology program. Dr. Joss reviewed dozens of court documents, psychiatric records, and Chapman's institutional history. He wrote in his findings that Wayne Chapman had a particular form of pedophilia that was highly resistant to treatment. Chapman had been disciplined for attending religious services for the sole purpose of transporting contraband in his Bible and for assaulting another inmate. It was the opinion of Dr. Joss that Chapman, regardless of what Ober and Sweitzer were petitioning, should "remain confined to a secured facility." It was also noted that Chapman had refused to participate in any form of treatment that may have in some way been of benefit to him. Dr. Joss cited Ober's comment that Chapman still "had inclinations and temptations" as part of his opinion. He was still a sexually dangerous person. The court agreed with Dr. Joss. The legal bantering about Chapman's rights went on for another three years. In 2007, a judge ruled that based upon all of the evidence presented to the court, Wayne Chapman remained a sexually dangerous person. He was committed back to Bridgewater State Hospital for "one day to life." His status is reviewed annually. Chapman continues to try every year to gain his freedom. And every year an array of witnesses come before the court protesting his release. And now, each year, the court routinely sends him back to Bridgewater. His lawyers now claim that he should be released on humanitarian grounds. Chapman is suffering from dementia and incontinence. Andy Puglisi's mother says who gives a shit.

The dog is out of his cage

Doc decided to dress in real nice clean clothes, right before he had his picture taken in the lobby of the downtown motel where he was now living. He even decided to rewrap his cane in bright red velour. After all, Easter was coming and Doc said he was feeling festive. Doc had taken Puddin with him. He kept her close by at all times. Sometimes he could be seen walking down the street with Puddin meowing in a small cat carrier. He hadn't taken much else with him besides some of his clothes. He had been going to put his things into storage but hadn't gotten around to it before he moved. The city was putting a lot of pressure on him to get out. Now they had to decide what to do about his place and personal property. Even though they said they were going to, they hadn't locked him out. What Doc did refuse to leave behind was the dusty photographs of his favorite boys, which now sat fanned out on top of the pressed wood chest of drawers that sat kitty-corner to the right of his bed. Doc told his friends that he would have been happier than he had been in years were it not for Cameron.

Cameron showed up at Doc's motel on Friday, March 16th. Cameron was pissed. Doc was a wormy little prick bastard. He had it all and he was bullshitting Cameron. Cameron wanted answers. Doc had to know where Zach's body was and he wasn't talking. Doc was expecting one of his friends when he opened the door and found Cameron. For a brief second, Doc was afraid that Cameron was going to hit him. Cameron, gritting his teeth, asked Doc if he could come in. Doc reluctantly agreed, walked over, and sat down on one of two, pale green, vinyl armchairs, sitting in front of a small black and white television, precariously balanced on a chromed wire stand. Doc ceremoniously waved for Cameron to take a seat on the rumpled bed. Cameron looked at Doc and said, "I think not." He then stated, "You have one week to decide what you are going to do, Doc. If you don't tell me what you know about Bar Jonah and Zach, then I am going to arrest you for conspiracy in the murder of Zach Ramsay." Cameron turned and quickly walked out the door. His hands were shaking when he got on the creaky elevator from wanting to grab Doc around his neck.

Doc sat and pondered his dilemma. If he told Cameron about his love for Zach and his anger at Bar Jonah for taking Zach away, then he thought Cameron would leave him alone. That would have to be the understanding between him and Cameron. If Cameron wouldn't agree, then all bets were off and he would catch a bus out of town in the middle of the night and disappear. He had friends who would hide him out until things blew over. Doc thought again about going back to jail. In a few months he would be seventy-two. Doc told one of his friends that the thought of being locked up made him almost wet his pants.

On Monday morning, the 19th, Cameron's phone rang right as he sat down at his desk. It was Doc. He wanted to come and talk to Cameron about what he knew about Zach and Bar Jonah. Doc said he loved Zach and it had been weighing heavily on his mind for a long time and he wanted his conscience to be freed. Cameron scheduled to meet Doc at his office on Wednesday at 1:30.

The appointment

That morning Doc woke up chipper. He went down to the restaurant that was attached to the motel and had the Stomach Buster Breakfast with an extra side order of bacon. Doc usually didn't indulge in such a big breakfast, but that morning Doc told his friend that he wanted to have a full belly when he met with Cameron. After he ate Doc went back up to his room and puttered around a bit, moving this and that, playing with Puddin, and preening what little hair he had left. As Doc preened he also practiced looking pathetic in the mirror. Whenever he had a meeting, with anything riding on it, he always practiced looking pathetic. It gave him an edge, he would say. Doc sat down on the edge of the bed and found his eyes heavy, probably from the delicious breakfast he had just enjoyed. He lay back, took a short nap and then went out for a walk. It was about eleven and the still cool air stung Doc's freshly shaven cheeks.

Doc strolled for about an hour and then headed back to the restaurant to have a nice lunch before he met with Cameron. The waitress greeted Doc with a smile and brought Doc his favorite club sandwich on extra dark toast, with extra bacon and extra mayonnaise. She thought Doc was a sweet man, so she had the cook pile on some extra French fries too. Doc ate slowly, trying to control the nervous quivering that he was feeling inside of his chest. There was nothing to worry about, Doc kept telling himself. Cameron was not going to arrest him; he just wanted to know what Doc knew about Zach and Bar Jonah. Doc was ready to tell him. It was time to stand up to Bar Jonah and set things straight. Right as Doc was about to take the last bite of his sandwich, the waitress noticed Doc's face grow ashen. She walked over and asked him if he was okay. Doc looked up and said he was. He had just realized that he may have to testify against Bar Jonah in court. For whatever reason, it hadn't dawned on him before. But Doc was going to have none of that. Cameron was going to have to guarantee Doc that he wouldn't call him to testify, otherwise he wasn't going to say anything. Doc left the restaurant and walked over to the bus station, which was right downtown too. There was a bus leaving at 4:00 for Seattle. If Cameron wouldn't agree to Doc's conditions, he planned to invoke his rights, ask for an attorney, get up, and walk out. He then would take the long way around to the bus station, hop the four o'clock bus, and leave the state. He had already talked to a friend in Seattle who would meet him at the stop in the small mountain town of Snoqualmie, long before the bus ever rolled into Seattle. Then Doc, like Zach, would vanish.

On the walk down to the police station, Doc encountered one of his old friends. He told his long lost friend that he may be going back to Texas. Doc said he hadn't seen any of his family in so many years that he was thinking of just picking up and heading back down to the land of smoked barbecue and oil wells. Doc's long lost friend was surprised and said that he didn't think Doc would ever leave Montana. "I'm lonely," Doc confessed. He was an old man now and he would like to be near his brothers and sisters. It wasn't going to be long before he would need someone to take care of him. He wasn't getting around like he used to and he was still having problems with his leg swelling. Doc slipped the tip of his index finger behind the bridge of his sunglasses and pulled them down onto his nose, so that his friend could see his lonely, worn-out eyes. His sympathetic, long lost friend said he understood. He wasn't much younger than Doc and things had started going wrong with him too. Before his friend walked away, he told Doc to be sure to let him know if he decided to leave. He might want to come down to Texas to see him one day. Doc nodded and said if he heard he was gone, that's where he'd be. Then Doc threw his arm high in the air and wiggled his fingers as he turned and walked away. Doc knew that his friend was a snitch for the cops. He was probably out looking for a pay phone right now, Doc thought. It didn't hurt to plant the thought in his lost friend's mind that he might be going back down to Texas. It might be a nice insurance policy.

Goddamnit again

The Great Falls police station sits right on the bank of the Missouri River. A large nest of trees separates the parking lot, where the cops park their cars from the embankment that drops down into the muddy river. As Doc approached the police station, he could see the far bank of the great river, to the right of the main doors of the station.

The moment that Doc set his foot on the rectangular cement step that takes you into the lobby of the police station, he felt a claw-like grip take hold of his chest. His eyes began pulsing in their sockets and his clear vision of the Missouri began to dim. Doc's reedy panicked fingers stabbed at the constricting pain running amok in his chest. He couldn't breathe. His hands flew away from his tortured heart and started fluttering like frenzied moths encircling a bright light. In that brief instant, Doc knew that hell had finally arrived. All he could do in his last seconds was to lament his vanishing past. Then Doc took one shallow, final breath and fell over dead. The old woman who had been standing beside Doc, watching him die, thought he looked like a falling bird, whose wings had suddenly given out as he collapsed onto the monolithic slab.

Police dispatcher Helen Berlien saw Doc drop to the stoop. She ran outside, bent down, put her mouth over Doc's dry blue lips and blew. Doc's chest swelled, full of Berlien's warm breath. A police officer, who was now assisting Berlien, was pumping Doc's chest. Berlien would blow her air into Doc's collapsed lungs and the officer would push it back out Doc's broad nose. Over and over again, for ten minutes, she blew and the officer pressed. It was pointless; Doc was going to stay dead.

* * *

Cameron had been on another call and had been running late for the meeting with Doc. When the call from dispatch came over his radio, telling him that Doc was dead, Cameron thought he was being fucked with. He arrived back at the station just as the squad was loading Doc into the back of the ambulance. One of the medics who was working on Doc thought his long-lobed leathery ears stuck out like they had been dried and smoked. His nicotine-yellowed eyes were still open and protuberantly metering like a metronome, to each compression of Doc's lifeless chest. The ancient Greeks didn't have a word for dark blue; Homer called it "wine dark." Doc's face never changed from wine dark, as the medic continued to perfunctorily pump on his chest all the way to the hospital. When they arrived at the ER, a physician said Doc was done. He was officially pronounced dead shortly after two p.m. When Cameron got to his office, he slammed the side of his fist onto the top of his desk. He knew that whatever Doc had been going to tell him, was now dead right along with him.

Trouble gives us the power of waiting

A short time later, Bar Jonah's jailhouse friend took him aside and told him he had heard that Doc had croaked on his way to be a stoolie to the cops. Bar Jonah stood silent, reverentially looked up, and said, "See." Then he turned and went back to his cell. Bar Jonah sat down on his bunk, took out his Bible and began reciting Acts, 8:6, over and over again: *"And the people with one accord gave heed unto those things which Philip spake, hearing and seeing the miracle which he did."*

* * *

Cameron's depression lasted almost a week. So did his drinking. Not a sloshing hard core drunk but never really all the way sober either. Doc, that son of a bitch, had died on him. He had been going to give it up, everything, and now he was dead. The following week after Doc died, Cameron drove over to his house. Cameron parked in front and didn't bother getting out of his car or talk to the demolition crew that was there to level the place.

The Hansel and Gretel fence went flying through the air, like rice paper caught in a storm squall, as the big dozers ran up over the lawn and slammed into the side of Doc's house. Great plumes of dust and debris filled the air on 7th Avenue N, as the house moaned and groaned one last time, before it collapsed into itself. An excavator scooped up the last vestiges of Doc's life, and dropped it into a top loader that hauled it away to the city dump. Cameron sat for a few minutes watching the spectacle unfold, shook his head, and then drove away. The neighbors complained that the stench from the years and years of cat piss and shit hung over the neighborhood for days on end. When he got back to his office, Cameron found a hand scribbled note that said Doc's final resting place was "Section A, Row 6, #43" at the Veterans Cemetery, in Helena, Montana. He wadded the note into a ball and threw it into the trash.

Later, one of the few mourners at the visitation commented that Doc looked his usual whey-faced self, laying stone still in his government-paid-for coffin, with a folded flag placed respectfully beside his head. The little cosmetic smirch at the corner of Doc's misshapen nose, however, made one of the sorrowful indignantly comment that Doc would *never* have gone out of the house with his make-up smudged.

* * *

Bar Jonah's jailhouse friend again took him by the arm and whispered in his ear that Doc's house had been leveled. The pillage had been taken away in dump trucks. Another blessing had been bestowed upon him. Oh Holy Day ... The Lord did not abandon the devout. Bar Jonah slipped his friend an extra pack of smokes and began walking through the corridor, singing at the top of his lungs.

> *This old house once knew his children*
> *This old house once knew his wife*
> *This ole house was home and comfort*
> *As they fought the storms of life ...*
> *This old house once rang with laughter*
> *This old house heard many shouts*
> *Now she trembles in the darkness*
> *When the lightnin' walks about*
> *Ain't a-gonna need this house no longer*
> *Ain't a-gonna need this house no more*
> *Ain't got time to fix the shingles*
> *Ain't got time to fix the floor*
> *Ain't got time to oil the hinges*
> *Nor to mend the windowpane*
> *Ain't a-gonna need this house no longer*
> *I'm a-gettin' ready to meet the saints*

(Hamblen, 1954)

Then Bar Jonah sat and wrote, rejoicing the whole day, feeling the presence of the Lord.

CHAPTER SIX

Pissing match

The sexual assault trial was approaching fast. The cops were preparing for the onslaught of media from around thecountry. It was rumored there was even going to be press coverage from China. Reporters would be screaming, "Talk to me, talk to me," and then sound so dejected, like beggars on a street corner panhandling for change, when the investigators couldn't give them the answers they wanted.

Theisen was continuing to have bad dreams. They always involved being trapped in some way by Bar Jonah, usually somewhere dark, cold, and wet. Cameron's marriage was all but over and Wilson wrapped himself in what seemed to Cameron and Theisen as a marble mantle of privacy. Though they had their differences, Cameron and Theisen also trusted Wilson. They knew he was dealing with the same thing they were. He was consumed too.

With Doc dead, Bar Jonah now began talking about the "old man" who had lived down the alleyway that Zach used to visit. He wasn't sure who the old man was but there was every reason to believe that he had something to do with Zach's disappearance. Bar Jonah was wondering out loud to anyone whose ear he could capture. Even though he was locked up, Bar Jonah believed he should still do his civic duty and help the cops find Zach's killer. He was sure the boy was dead. It was hard for Bar Jonah to imagine that, after all of this time, the kid was still alive. You couldn't even live in a cave that long, he would say. He even sent Cameron another note, shorter this time, offering his assistance to find Zach's killer. Bar Jonah also said that another prisoner, Frank Rohdar had confessed to killing Zach one night when they were all drunk on pruno. Pruno for the uninitiated is a prison liquor, made from fruit, sugar, and ketchup. It is so vile in its putrid taste that even the most hardened prisoners hold their noses when they imbibe. Bar Jonah was known to drink it by the glassful, whenever he had the chance, downing it in one long gulp. Licking his lips at the last drop, always asking for more.

* * *

The three boys were regularly talking among themselves. They were also in psychotherapy trying to come to terms with what Bar Jonah had done to them. Roland especially felt enormous conflict about testifying against Bar Jonah. He still loved him. But Bar Jonah had called him a liar and said that Roland was going to be the one who sent him back to prison, this time for life. Roland also believed that he was going to be responsible for Bar Jonah being killed in prison. There were already rumors going around among the Indians, about which one of the Big Leggins, who was on the inside, was going to gut Bar Jonah after he got convicted. Roland didn't know what he was going to do if Bar Jonah got killed. Yeah, Bar Jonah had hurt him, but he sure didn't want him dead. Roland was also scared of Bob. Bob was real cold, Roland would say. If someone killed Bar Jonah in prison, Roland was afraid that Bob would turn around and kill him. Roland was having trouble controlling his diabetes. Fry bread was his favorite food and it wasn't good for the sugar. Sometimes after a big meal with a lot of fry bread, Roland got so lightheaded that he thought he was going to pass out.

Stanley still didn't talk much about what had happened, although some of his friends would see him at times sitting around rubbing his hands around his neck. They figured that he was thinking about the upcoming trial and what he was going to have to say about what Bar Jonah did to him. The hanging and all. Stanley was still pretty mad that Roland had left him in Bar Jonah's apartment all by himself that day. Roland wasn't just a big kid; he was a big pussy too.

Stormy spent most of his days in dirty clothes with food smeared around his mouth. No matter what Lori seemed to do, Stormy was always dirty. Everyone thought that Stormy had so much energy that he could climb up a straight wall if he put his mind to it. It was real hard to understand much of what he said. Mostly when he talked, his words came out on the tail end of a loud yell.

* * *

On July 20th, 2001, the final report came back from Mytotyping Technologies. There was no possibility of a DNA match from the bones with Zach. They held out some hope that something may turn up in the future as DNA analysis grew as a science. But for now, the results were conclusive. Dr. Melton recommended against trying to get any usable DNA from the smallest bone fragments. The investigators had racked up more than $50,000 in charges to the lab and had nothing to show for it. They still had no body and no DNA. Now with Doc dead, they also had no direct link of Bar Jonah to Zach.

Rachel was sitting at her kitchen table, having a late breakfast of French toast and sausage. It had been a late night at the VFW where she was bartending. She was expecting Cameron. He had called ahead and told her that he wanted to see her. It was already hot in Choteau. Storm clouds could be seen swelling up over the high line just south of Alberta. When Cameron rapped on Rachel's screen door, he heard a low smoker's voice telling him to come in. Rachel offered Cameron coffee. He accepted. It had been a long night between him and his wife and certainly not a romantic one. The coffee looked anemic. Cameron told Rachel that the DNA lab's final report came back and the bones found in Bar Jonah's garage were not Zach's. Rachel looked at Cameron and said, "I know. I told you they weren't my son. My boy is alive." Cameron looked at Rachel and wanted to tell her that no, Zach was dead and was never coming home, but that day he didn't have it in him. He knew it wouldn't make a damn bit of difference anyway. Even if he were able to produce incontrovertible evidence that Bar Jonah had killed Zach, Rachel would never believe it. Rachel would disintegrate, if she even began to entertain the idea that her son was dead, much less cooked and cannibalized by a madman. They then spent a pleasant hour or so just talking about this and that, nothing in particular. Cameron liked looking at Rachel. Even when she looked disheveled, as she often did when she wasn't posing for cameras, she was still a beautiful woman. Too bad she was crazy, Cameron thought. It was a lonely drive back to Great Falls from Choteau.

* * *

In early August the guards abruptly came into Bar Jonah's cell and began tossing it. They didn't say what they were looking for and didn't give him a reason. He told his jailhouse friend they were disrespectful. The guards just told him to stand outside of the cell while they tore everything apart. Bar Jonah thought the guards seemed especially interested in his letters. Picking each one up and looking at it. He figured they were too stupid to know what was important and what wasn't. Bar Jonah was enraged and stood with his short arms hanging down by his side, watching the pile of papers and books getting higher and higher, as the guards threw everything on his bunk. He could say nothing. He could not make a face. He had to wait. The toss took about fifteen minutes. Bar Jonah nodded to the two guards as they were leaving his cell. They took nothing with them. He went back into his cell, took the many letters from his pen pals that he had put in envelopes with Tyra's return address, sat down on the toilet, and with sneering eyes began tearing them into little pieces, dropping them between his legs. He flushed the toilet before he stood back up. Most of his letters from Wayne Chapman and other special pen pals swirled away through the twisting and turning pipes of the prison sewage system. Then he wrote a short poem. *"Demons for sale and monkeys from hell, come in different sizes and will last you all night. Murderer of life, leave me alone. Cut him with a razor and I don't crave it anymore. Now I have peace of mind."*

Tension building

Vernay and Jackson were firing off motion after motion to the court. Judge Neill figured Vernay was trying to set up appealable issues before the trials ever started. They were aggressively trying to have the court declare the original stop unlawful. The cops had clearly and unconstitutionally been targeting Bar Jonah. He had done nothing wrong. Then the cops went so far as to use the unlawful stop as an excuse to search Bar Jonah's home. Nothing they took from Bar Jonah's apartment should be allowed to come into evidence. Cameron knew the impersonating a cop charge wouldn't hold. He could walk around the streets dressed however he wanted. But the other charges would. Bar Jonah was a known pedophile parading around the local schools. The cops had every right to see what he was up too. Vernay and Jackson could go to hell. At the motions hearing, Judge Neill disagreed with Bar Jonah's counsel. The evidence could come in and there was probable cause for stopping Bar Jonah in the first place. That was okay. Now Vernay and Jackson believed they had their first appealable issue. Bar Jonah said that his attorneys told him that they would be really surprised if the Montana Supreme Court didn't see it their way on appeal and overturn Judge Neill's decision. But it was a good thing that Bar Jonah was a patient man. He could be sitting in jail a long time before the Supreme Court agreed to hear his appeal.

* * *

Vernay and Jackson were talking with Rachel too. She was "different", they would say. But she could be useful. Vernay thought it was good that she and Bar Jonah had been writing. He also said that Bar Jonah couldn't have killed Zach. The time line was all wrong. When he watched the interviews that the cops did with the boys, it was clear that Cameron and Theisen had manipulated the boys, especially Theisen. The cops were clearly zealots, trying to destroy a man who had done his best to turn his life around. Cameron was probably planting evidence. He was most certainly lying. Bellusci had a pretty tainted past too, especially being busted from a gold shield detective back to tin star cop. Vernay, especially, appeared outraged.

Vernay and Jackson requested that the September trial date be continued. They just hadn't had enough time to prepare for a trial of this magnitude. Judge Neill agreed. They were new to the case. He granted a continuance. The sexual assault case would come to trial in February 2002. The murder trial would be held in May of the same year. The other thing they began fighting about was that the case had gained too much notoriety for Bar Jonah to be able to get a fair trial in Great Falls. There was much wrangling back and forth. Finally the judge agreed with the defense. They would not be able to find an unbiased jury in Great Falls. The case had to be moved out of Cascade County. The judge reassigned the sexual assault case to Butte. The murder trial would take place in Missoula.

The courts in Butte and Missoula were not happy with Judge Neill's decision. They understood it but they didn't like it. Bar Jonah was hated throughout Montana. Given that Montana had a reputation for vigilante justice, enormous security precautions would have to be taken. Extra cops, metal detectors, figuring out how they would transport not only the jury but also Bar Jonah himself, were concerns immediately high on the list. Jury selection was going to be arduous.

* * *

Cameron, Wilson, and Theisen were continuing their investigation. They had to make sure that their case was as bulletproof as possible. Cameron contacted the woman who now lived in Bar Jonah's old apartment, where he was accused of hanging Stanley.

Jessica Gange met the three investigators at the door of Bar Jonah's old place. It no longer had the reek that it had when Bar Jonah lived there. Cameron walked into the kitchen area, looked up and saw a large area that had been poorly spackled over. The ceilings were short, so he could stretch a bit and press his index finger into the plastered indentation. The area was right below a ceiling joist. That would explain how Bar Jonah was able to anchor the pulley, in order to raise Stanley off the floor. Wilson took photos of the area. Theisen talked with Gange, who wanted to be right in the fray of things.

Liars

On August 15th, Barry was interviewed by Vernay and Jackson. Barry said that Wilson and Theisen came and got him from work and said they wanted to interview him about the Bar Jonah case. He wanted Cameron to be at the interview too. Barry trusted Cameron. The interview went on for a couple of hours, Barry said. He told Vernay and Jackson that Wilson and Theisen put pressure on him and that he said things that he shouldn't have. Barry "didn't know nothing about no rope game" and he got scared and "didn't know what else to do." Vernay asked Barry if he ever saw Bar Jonah "touch any of these children in any kind of an improper manner." Barry said, "No. I did not." He went on to ask Barry if he ever saw Bar Jonah hurt any of the kids or threaten them with a knife. Barry said, "No." "So the statements that you made to the police were really more to please them than to tell the truth, is that fair to say?" Vernay asked. "Yes, I tried to tell the truth and they wouldn't believe me." "Sure, you just wanted to get out of there," Vernay quipped with indignation. Barry agreed with Vernay. What the cops had done to force him to lie about Bar Jonah was wrong. After Barry said that the cops had forced him to lie, Jackson jumped in and took over the interview. Barry said he was interviewed by Wilson and Theisen for about three or four hours. That was way too long and he got real tired. The cops had worn him down, they all agreed. Jackson said to Barry, "So during the time that you talked to them, did you ever tell them things that were not true?" Barry again said, "Yes." Jackson went on, "Can you tell us today why it is that you got to the point that you told them things that were not true?" Barry replied, "Being pressured and I couldn't handle the pressure. I was in real bad tears and I told them to stop. It's been tearing me apart inside." Jackson asked Barry why. Barry said, "Cause I could be putting an innocent man in prison for the rest of his life."

As the interview was winding down, Jackson asked Barry if there was anything else that he thought was important for them to know. Barry spontaneously said, "Well, where the cops said we were both sitting around in our underwear. I never said that." Barry also denied that he had ever been in Bar Jonah's bedroom. The only time he saw it was when he was walking down the hallway and looked in, but he had never been in there himself. Bar Jonah had, of course, said just the opposite.

Close to the end of the interview, Barry again said that Wilson and Theisen had pressed him. "They pressured me to lie about things that didn't happen." Jackson asked Barry about the letters that he had gotten from Bar Jonah. Barry became anxious and said, "He asked me how I was doing and I don't blame him for being mad, but he said, 'Why did you lie to the police?,' and then he said, 'My blood is on your hands.'" Barry added that he didn't feel threatened by Bar Jonah's letters.

* * *

When Bar Jonah got a transcript of Barry's interview, he hand-copied it and sent it along to the *Great Falls Tribune* with a note, "This an awesome recanted statement." Bar Jonah also wrote that, "The 16 year-old was interrogated too for about an hour when he finally broke down and cried and told the cops everything they wanted to hear. I believe the cops forced these kids to lie because we have letters from them saying nothing happened and I received them long before the cops talked to them."

A few days later, Bar Jonah jotted a note thanking Barry for making things right. But at the last minute he decided not to mail it. Barry had put him through enough with his lies. He would just have to keep wondering if Bar Jonah was still pissed at him and if they would ever be able to be friends again. Barry mentioned to one of his friends that he didn't think he'd be able to stay around town if Bar Jonah got set free.

Bar Jonah was elated with Barry taking back what he had told the two-faced cops. The Lord in all of His mercy had brought blessings again. Bar Jonah could barely believe how God continued to shine His light on him during these dark times.

* * *

Cameron sat at his desk looking down into his coffee cup. He had known Barry since he had been a teenager. He had picked him up when he was an adolescent for getting into minor shit, nothing too bad. Barry was always a desperate kid who never seemed to have his oars paddling in the same direction. But getting mixed up with Bar Jonah had been just plain stupid.

Now, as Cameron read the transcript of the interview Barry had done with Vernay and Jackson, he wasn't surprised to see that he had recanted everything he had told Wilson and Theisen. Cameron figured Bar Jonah had gotten to Barry one way or another and scared the hell out of him. It sounded like Vernay and Jackson were going to mount a defense that was going to question the way the investigation was conducted. They had already tried to say that the original stop was unlawful. It was likely that they were going to try other legal antics as well. But, Cameron had to admit, what else could they do? They probably had the most hated and despicable client they would ever have. Cameron thought that the jury would see through any desperation defense that Vernay and Jackson came up with. Kingsland was going to be a far better witness on the stand than Barry anyway. He had been an outsider with nothing to win or lose by telling the truth.

Back in Massachusetts Dr. Patterson was quietly keeping an eye on the newspaper reports coming out of Great Falls.

Agendas

Vernay and Jackson were convinced the boys were lying. They had been coerced by the cops, particularly Cameron and Theisen. They had put words in their mouths. Bar Jonah hadn't done anything wrong. He was being railroaded for crimes he didn't commit. Yes, he had had some problems in the past but he had turned his life around and was a productive citizen who had his own business. Moreover, the prosecution couldn't bring up any of his past crimes in court anyway. One of the first things the defense had to do was to find an expert who would testify that the kids had been duped into saying that Bar Jonah had abused them.

It was Vernay who found Phillip Esplin, Ph.D., a forensic psychologist out of Phoenix. When he interviewed Esplin, Vernay discovered that he had mainly been a National Institute of Health researcher and had limited clinical experience. More importantly, he got hired eighty percent of the time by the defense. Vernay liked what he heard from Esplin. Vernay saw Esplin as a "hired gun." Esplin's fee was $10,000 up front, plus expenses. He also insisted that a bottle of sixteen-year-old Scotch be in his room when he arrived for the trial. Several years earlier, Esplin had written an article for a scientific journal detailing how children could be influenced by police interrogators to say what the cops wanted them to say. In the article he also detailed how defense attorneys could question children to bring out the bias in court. It didn't take Esplin long to say that both Cameron and Theisen had manipulated the boys into accusing Bar Jonah of molesting them. He wanted to see the interview tapes for himself, but from what Vernay had told Esplin he was pretty darn sure that he would be able to say that the cops had forced the kids into making unfounded accusations against Bar Jonah.

Vernay and Jackson were now beginning to put together their witness list for the court. Yes, Barry had recanted his statements to the cops, however, Bar Jonah's lawyers didn't believe that he would be a viable witness for them. Vernay thought the case was seamy enough. Barry's demeanor was only likely to cast more of a cloud over the case. If the prosecution wanted to add sleaze, okay, but that was the last thing that the defense wanted to do. Bar Jonah, though, was pushing for Barry to testify. Since the boys were going to get up on the witness stand and lie, Barry was the one who could set him free. He was the one who had the obligation to set the record straight in court. He was the one that Bar Jonah was counting on to say that the boys were lying.

* * *

The investigators had just about sifted through all of the evidence that had been taken from Bar Jonah's. One snowy afternoon, just before Thanksgiving, Wilson found a discipline report from Bridgewater where Bar Jonah had been written up for hiding needles in his socks and putting them back in his drawer. This way when the guards searched his cell, they would stick themselves. The report said that when he was confronted about the needles he said sarcastically, "I didn't know they were there." Wilson also found the article Doc had given Bar Jonah on autoerotic asphyxiation. He thought it would be good to show it to the jury at trial.

* * *

Lori always tried to get money out of Cameron or Theisen the same way. Whenever they would call, Lori answered the phone breathless. Before Cameron or Theisen could say what they wanted, Lori would launch into a singsong diatribe about "Not having enough money, init." Cameron and Theisen would argue about who had talked with her last. They always tried to pawn it off on the other.

Roland's problems seemed to be getting worse to Cameron. He knew this was going to be hard on him. Roland had to testify. No one else was a key to the case like Roland was. A big Indian kid getting up on the witness stand and saying in public that he had been sexually assaulted by Bar Jonah was going to be devastating to the defense. No matter who the defense presented as witnesses they couldn't possibly overcome Roland's testimony. Still, the boy was fragile. They were going to have to take it real easy with him on the stand.

* * *

Regardless of Vernay's boisterous indignation, he knew that it was unlikely that the defense was going to prevail. Bar Jonah was difficult on good days and impossible on bad. Vernay and Jackson also had to spend a lot of time with Bob. Vernay in particular didn't like him. He thought Bob whined constantly. Bob called all the time wanting to know how the case was going. Vernay, it seemed, got stuck with most of the calls. He had to be sure to always add a slightly exasperated edge to every answer to every question that Bob posed. If you were too congenial with Bob he would talk your head off.

Tyra had gone back to Massachusetts to live with Lois and Lee. Lee was an aeronautical engineer who was designing and manufacturing components for spy satellites. They had a lovely white, New England style home with a wrap-around slat rail porch, adorned with the stylish accoutrements one would expect of a well-educated, successful family. Adjacent to their house was Lee's R & D firm.

Lois and Lee had converted a section on the side of the business into an apartment for Tyra. It was crowded but quaint, with pictures of Bar Jonah, Bob, and Lois neatly sitting atop a polished mahogany chest of drawers with well-worn brass handles. Vernay also talked regularly to Tyra by phone. She was getting weary of the turmoil, she would say. It had gone on for so long and she didn't have the energy that she used to. At this point in her life, she just wanted some peace. Vernay and Jackson could see, even with Tyra's quiet pronouncements of exhaustion that she wasn't about to abandon Bar Jonah. He still called her, collect, at least once a month and they wrote back and forth continually. Whenever Vernay and Jackson met with Bar Jonah, he wanted to know if they had talked with "Mom." She was a good woman, he would say. Vernay figured that Bar Jonah would never say anything about killing Zach as long as the old woman was still alive.

* * *

Cameron didn't trust Rachel. He thought she was beautiful and sexy but he didn't trust her. She was a wild card and reveled in the attention. The rumbling around the jail was that Rachel and Bar Jonah were writing to each other. On one occasion, Cameron asked Rachel if she was communicating with Bar Jonah. She said no. Bar Jonah said different. He was telling his jailhouse friend that they had become the best of pals.

She was willing to help him in any way she could. Rachel and the Ladies were hard at work, continuing to follow up on new leads in Zach's case. There was always something new, but unfortunately the trail would go from hot to cold. Like all of the other times, Franz and Joan Cook always seemed to be one step ahead of them. They all continued to be followed just about everywhere they went. It was frustrating not being able to turn to law enforcement with the leads that they came up with.

Rachel thought Cameron's heart was in the right place, but his pursuit of Bar Jonah was misguided. Cameron didn't have a body, but Rachel did. She had dozens of "Zach sighting" reports from all over the world. It would be expensive to keep Zach hustling from one place to the next. The money was probably coming from Franz's family. She guessed that that was what Franz was doing with Zach's child support because he sure wasn't paying her. Fortunately, the Ladies were still offering their help when things got tight.

Pam had thought and thought and thought about the phone call from Sherri a while back. It always had bothered her. Sherri had just called her up, right out of the blue. It wasn't sitting right with her. Cameron had called Pam too, just a bit of a while before Christmas. He wanted to know how she had been doing since the last time that they had talked. She said she'd been doing just fine. Her sciatica had come back but that didn't last none too long and she was doing real good now. The letter she had gotten from Bar Jonah, not all that long ago, was real sweet with him saying that he still loved her and all. But she wasn't even thinking about going back with him. It sure had been good there for a while, but she had a new life now. She had just met the man of her dreams and she didn't want Bar Jonah interfering with her happiness. Cameron told her that she would probably be subpoenaed for the murder trial. Pam wanted to know if they could make her come back, since she lived out of state and all.

After Cameron hung up with Pam, he called Sherri. She was still having serious financial woes. It would really ease her burden if Cameron could get her some work with the police helping them find bodies. She wanted to know if Cameron had put together a search team to look for the place she had seen in her vision. He said he hadn't had time to do that just yet. Cameron told Sherri that she would have to testify at the murder trial too. Like Lori, Sherri wanted to know if the cops could pay her a little something for her testimony.

CHAPTER SEVEN

Sizing them all up

Christmas that year was depressing for Bar Jonah. He had hoped to be out long before now. Usually the Lord didn't keep him waiting. This Christmas was particularly bad though because on the 20th, Detention Officer Grubb noticed that Bar Jonah had made a few hack marks on his upper thigh. When he was confronted, Bar Jonah admitted that he found a razor that had been left in the shower. It so happened that the holiday care packages were going to be delivered that day. Grubb refused Bar Jonah his. Bar Jonah was outraged. He had rights and he demanded his presents. Grubb was adamant. Bar Jonah would not be eligible for a care package that Christmas because of his behavior.

* * *

When Eric Olson was still Bar Jonah's defense counsel, he had retained Montana psychologist, Michael Scolotti, Ph.D., to conduct a sexual offender evaluation as part of his initial defense strategy. Scolotti had a stellar reputation as being an astute evaluator. He didn't like bullshit and he was known to see through the facades of psychopaths. With Scolotti, the chips fell where they may.

* * *

In early September, Vernay and Jackson thought it would be a good idea to see if Bar Jonah was appropriate for placement at Warm Springs State Hospital, instead of going to Montana State Prison, if he were found guilty. After all he was crazy. It seemed that the court might entertain placement at a state hospital at mitigation; if it came to that. They already had Scolotti, who had come over with the case from the public defender. But Vernay thought they needed more, especially if Scolotti's final report didn't paint Bar Jonah in a good light. Vernay got a recommendation for Phoenix neuropsychologist Paul Beljan, Psy.D., to evaluate Bar Jonah. Beljan was a man of impeccable credentials and unimpeachable integrity. Beljan only agreed to come on the case if Vernay understood that he was *not* a "hired gun." If he found clinical indications that Bar Jonah might benefit from placement at the state hospital, he would say so. If he didn't, he would say that too. Vernay agreed. Beljan also wanted to interview Bob, to get some basic family information.

* * *

Bob still lived in the duplex that he had shared with Bar Jonah when he first got out of Bridgewater in 1991. It was a well-maintained white stucco building with a well-manicured, though somewhat dried-out lawn.

Bob had told Beljan to come to the back door. He had just moved out of the upper apartment and was remodeling the basement to serve as his place. Bob arrived a few minutes late, carrying a couple of bags of groceries down a slightly curvy walkway, leading from the garage where Mr. Popcorn Head used to live. No one seemed to know what had happened to Mr. Popcorn Head. He just seemed to disappear. Beljan noticed that Bob walked upright, very upright. He looked stiff as a board. The grocery bags were perfectly balanced on arms turned at 45° angles. His hair was slightly windblown. Beljan caught Bob's cautious eyes when he opened the back door and invited Beljan in. The back entrance hadn't been fully framed up, so they walked in between the skeletal 2 × 4's and sheetrock leaning against a cinderblock wall. There was a separate entrance a little ways into the basement that opened directly into the back of Bob's kitchen. As soon as Beljan walked into the apartment he noticed how austere it was. Everything seemed to have an exact place. It wasn't just a sense of being neat and orderly. It was more that each object could only live in the position that Bob had placed it. Knickknacks were ostensibly set as perfect, matching cusps; one intersecting with the another. Bob pointed to an early American couch with a quilted throw laid precisely over the back and told Beljan to please sit.

Bob went back to the kitchen, opened a box of cookies, placed them in a neat circle on a plate, and carried them back into the living room. "Here, have a cookie," Bob said to Beljan. Beljan politely said that he was fine and thanked Bob for the gesture. With barren eyes Bob looked at Beljan and insisted, "Have a cookie!" Beljan picked up a cookie and bit off a small corner. Bob smiled and seemed pleased. As they were beginning to talk about Bar Jonah, the phone rang. Bob excused himself, walked over to the return off the side of the kitchen counter and picked up the receiver of the yellow princess phone that was fastened to the wall.

To the left of the couch, against the wall, was a large bookcase, with a few books, a television, and several elegant dancing glass figurines. Like everything else, the little obedient dancers were right where they were supposed to be. Beljan got up from the couch and walked over to the shelf. Bob's gunnersight eyes locked onto Beljan as soon as he stood up. Beljan stood with his hands clasped behind his back, admiring the figurines. Bob's voice was now beginning to slightly stammer as he was becoming increasingly distracted by Beljan. Then Bob saw Beljan reach out and pick up one of the figurines, gently turning it around in his hand and comment, "This is very nice." Bob screamed in a panic, "I have to go." Try as he might, Bob in his state of disarray over Beljan's insolence couldn't quite get the receiver to stay in the cradle. Each attempt culled more frustration until finally, Bob simply let the receiver drop onto the counter top right as Beljan sat the figurine back down on the shelf, being sure to turn it in the opposite direction.

Bob slid around the return like a crouched down speed skater rounding a bend. In a flash, Bob was standing exasperated beside Beljan. Bob reached in front of Beljan, took the coryphée by her ceramic neck and twirled her back into perfect position. Then he exhaled. Things were better now. Beljan turned and walked back over to the couch and sat back down. Bob stood for a moment and then said to Beljan, "Finish your cookie!"

A few minutes later, Bob, now having collected himself, told Beljan that the cops had torn up his yard looking for evidence against Bar Jonah. "It wasn't right," Bob said. Bob asked Beljan if he would like to see where he had replaced all of the sewer line from his house to the alleyway. Beljan said he would. They got up and walked over to a doorway, off a short hallway. The door opened into another section of unfinished basement. Bob pointed toward a small shop area where the mortar was clearly roughed up differently than other parts of the floor. Bob stood in between two peg-board walls, carefully hung with tools of every size and description. He pointed down to the cement scar on the otherwise smooth concrete. "This is what the cops wanted to dig up again, tear this whole area up, completely disrupt my life even more than they already had when they ripped up my backyard. And for what, some animal bones. Well, there were some ancient bones that were human. They had probably been there for more than a hundred years," Bob said. As they turned to go back into the apartment, Beljan caught a glimpse of the washer and dryer, which were tucked into a small alcove, under a frosted block window. Beljan's startled eyes saw thick dribbles like fingers of a copper-red liquid that had been spilled onto the washer and dryer. For a moment, Beljan thought it was blood and in that moment, he had the disquieting thought that Bob was going to kill him with an axe. Bob softly spoke and broke Beljan's trance, "I spilled some paint a few weeks ago. Looks like blood. Ha ha." Beljan was so glad to get back into the apartment, he voluntarily ate another cookie.

During the interview, Bob told Beljan that Bar Jonah had got a lot of money from the state of Massachusetts after he got out of Bridgewater but he spent it on "junk" within a couple of days. It had infuriated Bob, especially when Bar Jonah kept asking him for money. Beljan thought Bob wanted to appear that he cared more about Bar Jonah than he really did.

The defense had had some blood drawn to have Bar Jonah tested for Prader-Willi syndrome, a genetic condition that results in an insatiable appetite, obesity, and other anomalies, all of which Bar Jonah demonstrated. Bob said that he and his family had been wondering if some of the blood could be tested against their DNA, just to make sure that Bar Jonah was really their "blood brother." The family had been speculating that maybe their "real brother" had gotten switched at birth and been given to another family. They would never abandon Bar Jonah, Bob said, regardless of the results of the test, but they sure would like to know. Beljan suggested that Bob talk to Vernay.

* * *

From Bob's place, Beljan went over to the detention center to begin his evaluation of Bar Jonah. The detention center looked like every other prison. As Beljan stood looking at the green tile walls and cold colorless concrete floor, it seemed to him that all jails must have been designed by the same person. An enigmatic creator who travels the world, birthing prisons in his own likeness; he must be a god. Beljan pressed the button on the wall. An anonymous voice came resounding back through the scratchy, metallic speaker asking Beljan to identify himself. A camera rotated above his head. Beljan told the androgynous voice that he was there to evaluate Bar Jonah. The speaker clicked off.

A few minutes later, a guard came through a tawny steel door and halfheartedly looked through Beljan's testing material. He scoffed at some of Beljan's supplies but finally acquiesced when Beljan protested that he couldn't do the evaluation without them. The guard made sure to count Beljan's pencils and told him to make sure that he left with the same number that he was going in with. He was going to count them when Beljan left.

The guard motioned for Beljan to follow him through the heavy, cumbersome door, pulling it closed behind them. They were now in a long, sealed, narrow corridor, at the end of which was another door. When they got to the other door, the guard rapped on the door's cross-hatched wire window with his callused knuckles. Shortly, a set of anonymous eyes peered through the shatterproof glass pane. A few seconds later, the anonymous hand that belonged to the anonymous eyes slipped a gold ankh shaped key into the keyhole and turned one way, then the other. The bulkhead cracked open with the peal of a muted cymbal.

The moment Beljan stepped out of the free world, his eyes were drawn to the fortified glass-encased holding cell door. There, standing pressed up against the thick crystal was Bar Jonah. Naked. Beljan stopped and stared. He was surprised how Bar Jonah's fish-belly white fat seemed to wobble against the glass even when he was standing still. When Bar Jonah stepped back from the glass door, his copious belly swayed and his dwarfish genitals momentarily came into view.

The guard whispered to Beljan that Bar Jonah had been put in the holding cell the night before because he said he was suicidal. The guard didn't believe it. Bar Jonah's orange prison garb was lying in a pile in front of the door. The guard looked at Bar Jonah, looked at Beljan, and then shook his head. He unlocked the cell and kicked the orange pants and sleeveless shirt through the door. "Put your clothes on," the guard said brusquely.

The guard turned and unlocked a wooden door on the other side of the hallway to the room that was normally reserved for attorneys to meet with the prisoners. "Go on in and have a seat and I'll bring him over," the guard said to Beljan.

* * *

The room felt like more of a closet really. The stark echo made it seem colder than it was. Inside were a small wooden desk and three short wooden chairs, all showing deep blemishes from years of wear. When the door opened, Bar Jonah caught Beljan's eyes. He had to make a good impression. Bar Jonah didn't care so much what the tests showed. What was more important was that Beljan became his friend and among other things, saw how the gang-rape when he was such a young boy had changed the course of his life. He would have to hang his head low, as he told Beljan how those eight boys had made him have to suffer. It wasn't fair. But most importantly, he had forgiven them.

Beljan extended his hand. That was a good sign. Vernay had said good things about Beljan. When Beljan felt Bar Jonah slip his hand into his, he was struck by how powdery soft and feminine it seemed. Harmless? Then Beljan imagined Bar Jonah's hand was like a colloidal gelatin, molding to the form of his hand; seeping into the crevices of his *Jeevan Rekha*, the palmist's life line. When Beljan pulled his hand away, he felt Bar Jonah's overtly limp, damp fingertips linger along his palm. Bar Jonah's beseeching eyes peered into Beljan's. Beljan leaned in slightly toward Bar Jonah and tightly held his gaze. Then, Beljan undid their ocular knot by turning away.

Bar Jonah turned around on one foot and sighed deeply as he sat down heavily behind the desk. Beljan told Bar Jonah that he was there to evaluate him, to see if he had any mental defects that the defense could use as mitigating circumstances, if he were to be convicted. He was going to give him a series of tests. It would be helpful if Bar Jonah would cooperate by giving his best effort. It would make things go a lot easier. Bar Jonah said he would do his best. He had been evaluated a lot, he said. But most of the psychologists and psychiatrists had misunderstood him. There were only two, Ober and Sweitzer, who had ever truly understood him. They were devout Christians, men of God themselves, he said. Bar Jonah told Beljan that while he was in Bridgewater, he "trained fifteen psychiatrists to think like me. I don't know how I did it, but after a while they all began thinking exactly like I did. That sure helped me a lot when I talked to them. It was just like talking to myself."

Beljan casually asked Bar Jonah about Zach Ramsay. Did he have any idea what happened to the boy? Well, there was one guy who had confessed to Bar Jonah there in prison and then there was the old man, who lived down the alleyway that Zach used to visit all the time. Bar Jonah said he had done his own research. He had even written a book about Zach's disappearance and given a copy to his attorneys to help in his defense. Bar Jonah said Zach's grandmother was in the hospital dying the day the boy disappeared. Zach had been seen walking toward the hospital. Somebody could have probably just snatched him then. Bar Jonah told Beljan that he and Zach's mother were friends. They wrote each other all the time, back and forth, he said. Then with popped-out eyes Bar Jonah looked icily at Beljan. Deep-cut lines framed Bar Jonah's faint thin lips as he told Beljan that the murder case would never go to trial. "There is no body," Bar Jonah said. "I've got a surprise for them right at the last minute. I'm not worried about the murder charges. I just need for the jury to see that these kids are lying. They really turned out to be brats."

* * *

As the interview was beginning to unfold, Bar Jonah's scanning eyes saw a two-foot piece of wood, sitting to his left, leaning against the concrete wall. He guessed another prisoner had ripped it off of the desk. Beljan was sitting directly across from Bar Jonah. He noticed the piece of wood and saw Bar Jonah catch sight of it out of the corner of his eye. As the two men continued to mark their territory, Beljan noticed that Bar Jonah would periodically cast his eyes over to the wood. Beljan thought it looked like a walnut billy club. He also wondered why it was sitting out in a room where a prisoner could get his hands on it.

Bar Jonah leaned backwards and forwards, adjusting his butt on the seat, sighing, and glancing to his left. Finally, after a few minutes of choreography, Beljan quickly shifted his eyes like he saw the wood for the first time. Then he stood up and shaking his head in staged disbelief said, "What the fuck is that leaning against the wall? Why in the hell would someone leave something like that sitting around?" Beljan looked into Bar Jonah's eyes and told him to hand him the piece of wood. Bar Jonah looked passively back at Beljan, reached over, picked up the wood and gently laid it in Beljan's outstretched palm. "Thanks, I'll just take this down to the guards' station." Beljan opened the door and began walking down the hallway. One of the guards snapped to when he saw Beljan in the monitor carrying the piece of wood down the corridor. He took his feet off of the desk, pushed himself up out of the chair and darted around the corner. "What in the hell are you doing with that," the guard demanded. Beljan didn't answer, he just passed the baton off to the guard, turned, and walked back to continue interviewing Bar Jonah. When Beljan got back into the room, Bar Jonah looked up and said, "Whew, that was a close one." Beljan sat back down, indifferently looked at Bar Jonah and said, "Actually, it wasn't."

Beljan began asking Bar Jonah questions about his family background. He was struck how reverentially Bar Jonah spoke of Tyra. He resented his father for the many beatings, loved his sister, and never got along with his brother. Bob was the oddball of the family. Even Tyra thought so. It didn't take long before Bar Jonah told Beljan about the assault by the neighborhood boys. He hung his head in mock shame when he spoke of the rape and torture. From there, he launched into his tale of suffering of having been sexually assaulted by the guards. Beljan listened and feigned empathy to Bar Jonah's melodramas. He had worked with psychopaths before. Bar Jonah was pretty transparent. Beljan's task was to administer a battery of neuropsychological tests to look for any deficits that might help the defense, if Bar Jonah was found guilty. At one point during the testing, Bar Jonah told Beljan that he figured his IQ was at least 150. Beljan doubted that. He had a subspecialty in evaluating giftedness. Bar Jonah didn't come close to fitting the profile.

It didn't take long for Beljan to see how impulsively Bar Jonah responded to the test questions. There were times that he responded even before Beljan instructed him to begin or had finished giving him instructions. At one point, Beljan chastised Bar Jonah about beginning a task before he was told "go." Bar Jonah looked at Beljan and said, "Sometimes you just have to break the rules. I make up my own rules."

* * *

About noon on the second day of the evaluation, a guard opened the door and sat a plastic tray in front of Bar Jonah. A soggy looking hamburger, French fries, a few leaves of wilted pale lettuce with a dab of gray dressing, and yellow pudding were each neatly arranged on the tray.

In what seemed like a blur, Bar Jonah's fat fingers seemed to fly around the food. One hand grabbed the sandwich and pushed it past his thin lips into his mouth while the other hand gripped a clump of French fries, mashing them into a starchy ball, dropping it onto his now protruding tongue, chasing right behind the hamburger which was followed by

Bar Jonah's hand, now freed by the devoured beef, taking the plastic fork, stabbing the lettuce with one jab, rolling it around on the tray in the smidgen of ashen dressing, feeding it to his hungry mouth still chewing the remnants of the sandwich and French fries, then anxiously pausing for but a brief second for the tan pudding.

Beljan sat and stared, his eyes fixed wide in disbelief. He had planned on going out and getting a bite to eat before he continued with the evaluation but lost his appetite after witnessing the spectacle of Bar Jonah devouring his food.

As Beljan continued to administer the psychological instruments, he thought that Bar Jonah was showing signs of being brain-damaged. Later Beljan would write in his report, "Bar Jonah's problems lie at the front of his head, at the region of the prefrontal cortex and the subcortical circuitry connections with the limbic system and the basal ganglia region." Beljan also noted that Bar Jonah was highly resistant to treatment because of his cognitive rigidity. Part of Bar Jonah's way of relating to the world was to believe that he was right, when in fact he was almost always wrong. Then he would argue his position, finally concluding that everyone else was the problem, not him. Bar Jonah, in explaining himself, pointed to his orange jumpsuit and said, "If I say this is orange, then it is orange and don't try to tell me something different or that something is something else, when I know different."

Beljan was also curious about Bar Jonah's claims that he blacked out when he had attacked his victims in his past. Bar Jonah said, "I just couldn't help myself, something just took me over. I don't remember any of it though, I'm just going on what I have been told that I did." If Bar Jonah had blacked out then he would have likely dissociated, like he was standing outside of himself, watching what was going on without being a participant. In fact, Interconnections Counseling Group, in their 1994 evaluation in the Shawn Watkins case, said that Bar Jonah likely suffered from "dissociative episodes," because of his history of "being molested." However, Beljan found nothing to support Bar Jonah's assertion that he had ever "blacked out."

During one of the breaks Bar Jonah told Beljan that Vernay's legal assistant had become his close friend. Bar Jonah would send her cards, when he could afford it, and she would send him some too. She really understood his plight and his loneliness. Beljan was astounded when Bar Jonah told him that he was also serving as her son's editor. "He is thirteen and likes to write short stories. His mom knows that I have a degree in journalism and asked me if I would help him out. So she sends me his stories and I write suggestions, correct his grammar, and then send them back to her. He sends me thank you cards, all of the time. He is a sharp kid."

About 4:30 on the second day, Beljan finished testing Bar Jonah. As he stood up to walk out the door, Bar Jonah reached out to shake Beljan's hand. Beljan couldn't bring himself to touch him again; he kept his hand down by his side. The guard who escorted Beljan back to the lobby didn't bother to count his pencils.

A cold wind clipped Beljan's face when he walked out of the prison. He would only have to see Bar Jonah again if Vernay and Jackson lost the case and he had to testify at mitigation. Beljan couldn't imagine Bar Jonah winning. It had been a rare experience for Beljan to be in the presence of someone so immensely dislikable. As he was pulling out of the parking lot, he thought about how Bar Jonah's overt emotions were almost imperceptible. His personality was like the movie set façade of an old Western. Bar Jonah worked hard to create the illusion that he was an itinerant white-collared reverend, who wandered into dirt-floored beer parlors, carrying the Good Book under his arm, ready to save any wanton soul. But when the saloon doors were swung wide, all one could see was an empty lot.

* * *

Beljan felt like someone had thrown a bucket of raw sewage all over him. Before dinner, he went back to his hotel and took a long, very hot shower. Beljan said he was trying to steam Bar Jonah out of his pores, maybe his soul. That night for dinner, he was sure not to get anything that remotely resembled what had been on Bar Jonah's lunch tray.

When Beljan calculated Bar Jonah's full scale IQ, it came out to 95. There was some question though that Bar Jonah was malingering. Beljan thought he was cagey. Given the fact that he did have a diagnosable neuropsychiatric disorder, it seemed reasonable to recommend sending him to the forensic unit of Montana State Hospital if he were convicted. The prosecution wanted him to go to Montana State Prison. Beljan would testify that he had a mental disease, diagnosable through neuropsychological testing, but unlike Ober, he wasn't going to be Bar Jonah's corner man.

Cameron and Theisen were upping their contact with Lori and the boys. They didn't want them backing out at the last minute. But Lori and now the boys too wanted money. "You guys make a lot of money, can't you help us out some? That Fed guy, I bet he makes more money than both of you put together, think he'd have any money he could spare, init."

Cameron and Theisen's nervousness was not going to go away until everyone had testified. The last thing they wanted was for Lori or the kids to get up on the stand, face to face with Bar Jonah in the courtroom, and recant everything they said during the interviews. The cops were also getting nervous about testifying themselves. Both had been in court hundreds of times over the past twenty years but a lot was riding on this case. They especially didn't want to get tripped up by Vernay. Not because he was so good at cross-examination but because they both hated him so much. They were concerned their hostility may come through on the stand. Cameron had been told that Vernay liked to take on high profile cases because he enjoyed the media attention. He had also heard that Vernay didn't win many of his cases either. Cameron figured that Bar Jonah's presence alone in the courtroom would be enough to convict him.

* * *

Vernay and Jackson met with the prosecution in late January 2002 to see the physical evidence. Prosecutor Brandt Light had all of the evidentiary exhibits ready for their inspection when they arrived. Light watched when Vernay and Jackson seemed to perfunctorily glance through the three ring binders filled with 14,000 pictures of kids, the stun gun, a piece of yellow rope. But Light was elated when he saw Bar Jonah's defense team completely miss the article that Doc had given Bar Jonah on autoerotic asphyxiation. They didn't even seem to notice it. The entire process took less than an hour. They didn't ask any questions and only seemed to nod to each other a couple of times. Jackson thanked Light when they left the room. Vernay just walked out.

Bar Jonah's lawyers didn't believe that the state had a solid case. It was the boys' word against Bar Jonah and they weren't going to let him take the stand. They had thought about calling Barry but were concerned that he wouldn't be a credible witness or that he might flip his testimony again. Barry also looked greasy. They knew that the prosecution planned on calling Adam Kingsland to testify about Bar Jonah walking around the apartment in his underwear and the sheet covering the area by the table. Light was also going to parade Lori and the three kids in front of the jury as well as the boys' psychotherapist. Vernay was sure she was going to get up on the stand and say the boys were suffering from the aftereffects of being sexually assaulted by Bar Jonah. Of course, Bellusci, Theisen, and Cameron, the liars, would all be called to testify too. Vernay wanted to figure out how to bring up Bellusci getting busted down from a gold shield detective to driving around in a patrol car handing out speeding tickets. Jackson said there was no way. It couldn't be done.

After everything was considered, Vernay and Jackson decided to call only one witness in Bar Jonah's defense, Phillip Esplin. They knew their case depended upon their cross of each of the state's witnesses, most especially the boys. Under no circumstances could they come right out and call the kids liars. Even though they believed they were. If they did, they would lose the jury. They had to save the rough stuff for the cops and let Esplin cast a negative light on the boys' story. The boys had been coached, Esplin asserted. Cameron was the one Vernay most wanted to expose as a liar. He was sure that he had fabricated evidence.

CHAPTER EIGHT

What eyes could have seen the good in such horror

Bar Jonah was continuing to write letters. Many of them were back and forth to Wayne Chapman. Chapman cautioned that Bar Jonah should make sure that he flushed all of his letters. He would do the same, just in case the Feds ever decided to search his cell. Chapman cautioned Bar Jonah to be a "good boy" when he was in court. That would go a long way with the jury. He had to look like the innocent man that he was. Let his innocent countenance make the brats look like the liars they were. He and Bar Jonah had been through it with little bastards who lie on them. That's the biggest cross to bear when you dedicate your life to loving boys.

Chapman wrote that he was still trying to get out. Ober and Sweitzer were helping all they could. They were good Christian men like he and Bar Jonah. They had dedicated much of their professional lives to bringing the Word to men who were many times wrongly convicted of loving boys too much. In those rare cases where a man had made a mistake and taken their love too far, Ober and Sweitzer were able to see their repentance and many times champion their release from the Pharisees who refused to follow the Law of Moses and forever became misguided, the punishers. Chapman and Bar Jonah were true believers and like the Israelites, they too would be released from bondage. It was good that they had each other and many others like them, who believed the same way, to strengthen them in those moments of weakness, guiding them back to the Redeemer. Each time Bar Jonah got a letter from Chapman, he read it over and over again and then folded it up, tore it into little pieces and flushed it down the stainless toilet in the middle of the night.

* * *

New poems were flooding Bar Jonah. He said they helped him purge his past, doing for him what the years of treatment at Bridgewater couldn't. For many of them he was merely acting as a scribe. Bar Jonah was sure they were divinely inspired; offered to him by the Lord. Healing poems. On January 20th, Vernay's legal assistant received a large envelope in the mail. Inside were a letter and a collection of poems.

> *I have enclosed some of the new poems I've written. I hope you like them. They are yours to keep. Also I've enclosed a book for your son. I hope he doesn't have it in his collection. It's a first edition of Star Wars (1980). It is just a little something to thank him for the stories he wrote and sent to me. They did more than he'll ever realize. Well, not much else except I'm enclosing a poem called "Zeus." It's a poem I wrote from Kevin's point of view from what he told me as we sat and I rested to get my strength back. This poem and the other I'm listing. I cried as I wrote them. The other poems are, "Ode To Nathan," "Kevin," "I've Reached My Gethsemane," "Healing The Shame, Healing The Pain," "Pater," and "Lake Chargoggagogga what?" I'm also enclosing the poem God gave me called "All is Well" and a few others.*
>
> *Your Friend,*
> *Nathan*

The poems amounted to a small chapbook of writings. Bar Jonah said he wanted to make sure that his attorneys would know how terribly he had suffered. It would help them in their quest to save his life. They would be able to see his torment through his poems and make right all of the wrongs that had been done to him. Vernay's assistant diligently read each poem. She was touched by all that Bar Jonah had endured in his life. She didn't know if she would have been able to go on, if she had to bear the scars of such torture and torment. In closing Bar Jonah requested that Vernay's legal aide send him some recipes. He was planning on writing a cookbook.

Hi There!

I'm looking for some recipes. Can you help me? I'm looking for the following:

1. Blackberry Cobbler cooked in a sugar-water bath & butter
2. Banana Foster
3. New York-Style Hot Pastrami Sandwich
4. Chicago-Style Pizza
5. Peanut Butter Chiffon Pie with a pretzel crust (It's really delicious)
6. A good Native American Fry Bread Recipe
7. A recipe for Swedish Rye Bread

Thanks!
Bar Jonah

* * *

Preparations begin

There was and still is a strong sense of independence that bores deeper into Butte's heritage than the copper mine. Voir dire would take about a week. The defense and the prosecution would try to stack the deck against each other by choosing the right mix of jurors. Each claimed they wanted an impartial jury, when of course what they really wanted was a jury that would agree with either respective side. The prosecution wanted a jury who believed in vigilante justice and the defense wanted a jury who would see Bar Jonah as the victim of many years of circumstance. The defense especially wanted the jury to see that the cops coached the boys into saying that Bar Jonah had sexually assaulted them. Yes, Bar Jonah had a tainted past but he had been trying to do his best to help out a neighbor in need. It wasn't the kids' fault. They hadn't gone to the cops. Remember ladies and gentlemen, the cops had gone to them. During voir dire, the prosecution put great emphasis on saying to the prospective jurors that Bar Jonah was innocent during the course of the trial. The jurors' job to determine his guilt or innocence did not begin until the trial ended and they had been given their instructions by Judge Neill. Vernay and Jackson focused most of their questions on media attention and getting potential jurors to acknowledge that there are "good cops and bad cops." They also wanted to know if any of the potential jurors would give more credibility to something that a police officer said. The implication was that they were fabricating evidence.

* * *

On the morning of February 20th, Vernay and Jackson were going to meet at the courthouse. It was 27 below in Butte that morning. Vernay had just had a remote starter hooked up to his truck. About fifteen minutes or so before he left for the courthouse, he looked out the window, pointed the dongle on his key ring toward his truck and pushed the button. He heard the soft whine of the engine coming to life on the frigid morning. His new truck, that he bought with some of the fees he had charged the state for the Bar Jonah case, had electric seat warmers too. Vernay arrived at 8:30. The trial was set to convene at nine. Bar Jonah was already there. The cops had been afraid that someone would try to kill Bar Jonah if they kept him in the Butte jail. It was decided to house him about thirty miles away in Boulder. They would take him back and forth each day in a blue, unmarked van with tinted windows. He would be wearing a bulletproof vest. They would keep him in the holding cell that was right next to the judge's chambers. Each person in the gallery was given a special pass and had to be screened before they were allowed a seat. The jury was also bussed in because someone had threatened to kill them. The sheriff's department set up a metal detector that everyone had to pass through. None of Bar Jonah's family planned to attend the trial. At ten minutes until nine, Vernay was getting nervous. Jackson still was not at the courthouse. "Not like Greg," he commented to his legal aide. Right before nine Vernay saw Jackson looking out-of-sorts, coming through the metal detector. That morning, as Jackson was about to go out the door of his motel room, he realized that he needed to use the toilet. It would be better to go ahead, rather than have to rush once he got to the courthouse. After he finished, Jackson leaned over and pushed the handle on the toilet. Nothing happened. Jackson flushed again. One large bubble effervesced, like a lifeform from the brown water. Jackson leaned over the bowl and pressed the chrome handle again. The toilet bowl burped and then exploded raw sewage, covering Jackson.

* * *

The tribunal begins

When the jury arrived, they were escorted to the jury box, which sat directly to the right of the witness stand. The prosecution was seated at the table closest to the jurors. Binders and bagged evidence were stacked in front of the prosecutors. Judge Neill would look to his left when he addressed Bar Jonah's defense team. A few chairs in the gallery had "RESERVED FBI" taped to the seats. A couple of agents from the Behavioral

Analysis Unit had come for the trial. Wilson arrived just before the bailiff called for all to stand. He dashed through the metal arch of the metal detector, flipping his black leather badge case open with his right hand, so the sheriff guarding the entrance would know not to question him. His suit coat briefly snagged on the butt of his recently issued Glock 22. In one move, Wilson slipped his badge holder back into his inside pocket and familiarly brushed his hand back, freeing the trim of his coat from the butt of the Glock.

Wilson picked up one of the "RESERVED FBI" cards and slipped it into his black leather binder. He looked over at the jury. They were ordinary people sitting there waiting to decide the fate of someone whom Wilson considered to be one of the most dangerous men he had ever investigated. Bar Jonah had been slick before and managed to slither away from justice. Wilson hoped this jury would see how menacing Bar Jonah was and slam him into the ground.

You could tell the jurors had all worn their Sunday best for the trial. One juror had his going-to-church white cowboy hat resting on his lap. Many of the female jurors wore print dresses. One had a white fresh flower pinned to her bodice. As they sat, waiting for the call to order and the arrival of Judge Neill, the eyes of the jury were unblinkingly set on Bar Jonah. Each juror had their own vantage point from which to explore him, cataloging his breathing, his deceptive make-believe eyes, his size.

* * *

Bellusci was called to testify for the prosecution first. Light ran him through his contact with Bar Jonah. He knew Bar Jonah's defense team was going to challenge the initial stop, where the cops arrested him for posing as a cop and carrying a concealed weapon. They didn't have any right to stop him in the first place; he was just walking on the sidewalk, not bothering anyone. Bar Jonah's rights had been violated by rogue cops. Light brought up the stop first. He wanted to establish why the cops were interested in Bar Jonah in the first place. It didn't take much. The jury was attentive. Bar Jonah sat at the defense table, his hands crossed in front of him, looking around the courtroom. Every now and then he would sigh loud enough for the jury to hear.

Greg Jackson took the cross of Bellusci. He asked Bellusci about questioning Lori after Bar Jonah was arrested. "She indicated to you that the children had indicated nothing inappropriate had happened?" "Yes," Bellusci responded. Bar Jonah "humpthed" under his breath. Jackson followed up with, "And you were the child abuse specialist?" Bellusci answered "Yes," again. "And you let it drop, didn't do anything further, did you?" Bellusci this time said "No."

Cameron came next. As with Bellusci, Light led Cameron through the development of the case. The prosecution also now began to focus Cameron on his interview with Roland. He described to the jury how Roland initially was okay during the interview. Then Cameron said, "Then at one point, he broke down bawling and had to be given a tissue." The jury's collective eyes now sterned up, as they turned from Cameron to Bar Jonah. Bar Jonah sat and glared at the "liar cop on the stand." Cameron also explained to the jury that once Roland disclosed what Bar Jonah had done to him, he and FBI agent James Wilson drove to Frazier to interview Stanley. Light asked Cameron, "During the interview, did Stanley disclose any abuse?" "Yes, he did," was Cameron's response. Light: "Did he indicate to you who abused him?" Cameron: "Nathaneal Bar Jonah."

On cross, Jackson structured his questions to make it look like Cameron had scared Roland into saying that Bar Jonah assaulted him. As Cameron tried to respond, Jackson would interrupt with, "Would you please just answer my question." Jackson also framed Cameron as a liar. During the interview with Roland, Jackson said that Cameron told Roland, "We won't tell anybody what happened."

"Yes," Cameron responded, "we were trying to make him comfortable to tell us what happened. Yes."

"You said we won't tell anybody, we won't go blab, we won't tell your mother, right?" "That's right," Cameron said unapologetically.

Jackson continued to drive home that Cameron lied to Roland, wanting the jury to believe that Cameron's dishonesty somehow turned Roland into a liar too. "You told him nobody else would know what you tell us?"

"That's correct."

"You told him that the kids at school wouldn't find out?"

"That's right."

"You told him all those things, and every one of those things that you told him occurred?"

"Eventually ended up happening," Cameron acknowledged.

Jackson also hit Cameron with the videotape recorder breaking down. He didn't believe it. The tape looked rehearsed. Cameron said it did look rehearsed but regardless it was the truth. On redirect, Light skillfully went through each point that Jackson had hit Cameron on. Jackson objected to Light leading the witness. Consistently the judge overruled Jackson's objections. The next witness was one that the defense had dreaded getting up on the stand, Roland. They knew they were going to have to tread very carefully when they crossed him.

"The state calls Roland Johnston to the stand." Through the heavy oak door, a dark-complected, obese Indian boy walked into the courtroom. The bailiff pointed Roland toward the witness stand. He seesawed back and forth as he scooted his feet along the polished hardwood floor. His sneakers were swelling at the sides and untied. The moment that Roland spoke, it became obvious that he was slow. His words were carried out of his mouth on shallow, breathy waves. Were it not for the microphone hanging above his head, he could not have been heard. The jurors looked at Roland with sympathetic eyes. As Light gently began to question Roland about the time period that he knew Bar Jonah, the jurors fixed a silently enraged gaze on Bar Jonah. Light walked Roland through the manipulation that Bar Jonah used to lure him into trusting him. Bar Jonah looked unmoved, his eyes darting around the courtroom, crossing and uncrossing his fingers. Then Light began to turn his questions to the night of the assault in Bar Jonah's bedroom. "Roland, was there ever a time that you were in the defendant's residence and he touched you in a manner you didn't like?"

"Yeah," the jury heard Roland softly say.

"And where in the apartment would that have been?"

"In the bedroom."

"And how did you get inside the bedroom?"

"I went in there."

"And when you went in there, what happened?"

"He told me to take my pants down."

"Did you take your pants down?" Light asked.

"Yeah."

"Roland, why did you take your pants down?" Roland didn't answer as the first tear rolled down his cheek. The jury became transfixed. Light continued. "Once you took your pants down, what, if anything happened next? What happened after you pulled your pants down?" Roland began to sob. Several of the jurors were wiping their eyes. The big cowboy in the front row pulled off his oversized glasses and patted his eyes with the corner of his plaid sleeve. "Roland, can you tell me what the defendant did?"

"He touched my butt."

"Did he touch you anywhere else?"

"In the front."

"Roland," Light asked, "Do you mean your penis?" Roland was sobbing uncontrollably. In a pathetically lonely, anguished voice, Roland looked down and said "Yeah." The cowboy juror glared at Bar Jonah like he would take him out back and hang him himself.

"When he did this, did he have his pants up or his pants down?"

"Down."

"He took his pants down?" Roland couldn't speak; he nodded yes. "Roland, when he took his pants down, did he ask you to do anything to him?"

Roland muttered, "Yep, he did."

"What did he ask you to do?" Light asked.

"To touch him."

Roland, a seventeen-year-old Blackfoot Indian kid, pushing two hundred and fifty pounds, was now heaving on the witness stand, rocking back and forth, trying desperately to gain some sense of composure. Desperate not to feel so terribly isolated and alone. Knowing he had just betrayed the man that he once said was like a father to him. Roland rubbed the palms of his hands up his snot-and-tear-coated face and wiped them on his pants.

Bar Jonah was cockily leaning back in his chair listening to Roland's lies. He had his arm draped over the back of Jackson's chair, which was pushed against the wooden rail separating the spectators from the goings-on of the trial. Jackson sometimes struggled with sudden drops in his blood sugar. He always carried small boxes of raisins in his brief bag, which he kept behind his chair for such an occasion. The hollow courtroom echoed Roland's amplified gasping sobs when he told the jury what Bar Jonah had done to him. Bar Jonah continued to look this way and that, when suddenly he glanced behind Jackson's chair and saw the open brief bag with the small red boxes of raisins lying right on top. Like the jury's sorrowful eyes transfixed on Roland, Bar Jonah's hungry eyes transfixed on Jackson's raisins. Jackson, not unfazed by Roland's testimony, listened compassionately. He too was trying to maintain his own decorum as Roland continued to cry. He felt sorry for Roland. No kid should ever have to go through this. And then, Jackson felt Bar Jonah lean over and whisper in his ear, "Greg,

Greg." Jackson subtly raised his right hand slightly off of the table indicating for Bar Jonah to be quiet. Bar Jonah leaned over and louder this time said, "Greg, Greg." The rich acoustics of the old courtroom bounced Roland's sobbing around like a bullet ricocheting off the walls of a canyon. To shut Bar Jonah up, Jackson finally tipped his ear. Then, for a brief stunning moment, what Bar Jonah said to Jackson stole him away from Roland's agonizing testimony. "Greg, I sure could use some of those raisins right now. Can you slip me a box of those raisins? I'm pretty hungry, Greg." In that second, everything became quiet for Jackson, as he leaned away and stared back at Bar Jonah in disbelief. For the first time since taking the case, Jackson cringed in the presence of Bar Jonah's reptilian indifference.

When Roland said that Bar Jonah told him not to say anything to anybody about what had happened, he doubled up again. He said Bar Jonah had scared him. Bar Jonah now sat up and leaned his elbows on the table and looked at Roland with pleading eyes. The heads of the jury turned from Roland and cast a vengeful gaze at Bar Jonah. Light asked Roland if he had ever visited Bar Jonah in jail. He said he had and that was where Bob had told him, "Don't talk to anybody." Light asked Roland if he was afraid of Bob too. When Bar Jonah heard Roland say that he was, he whispered to Jackson, "He's lying." Light closed by asking Roland, "Is the man who sexually assaulted you in the courtroom today?" Roland tearfully said, "Yes." Light asked him to point to him. Roland shakily raised his right arm and pointed at Bar Jonah, "He's right over there."

Jackson stood up to cross Roland. During the questioning Jackson read one of the letters that Roland had dictated to his sister for Bar Jonah. "Nathan you really treated me nice. You never harmed me in any way. I really miss you, big guy, you were like the dad I never had." Then Roland started sobbing again. Jackson sighed and paused. When Jackson continued, he tried to set things up to look like all of the media coverage, especially the cops and most especially Cameron, was the real reason that Roland was saying that Bar Jonah sexually assaulted him. It wasn't his fault. He was a victim just like Bar Jonah. They were both being victimized. When Roland was excused from the stand, he wiped his nose with his sleeve, pushed his heavy body up out of the chair and stumbled out of the witness box. The jurors were relieved when he was excused. But there were two more kids to go. One of the jurors later said she didn't know if she could take another round like that.

Light took a breath and then called Stanley to testify. Stanley, tall and lanky, timidly walked into the courtroom. The questions that Light asked Stanley were almost exactly the same as those he had asked Roland. Stanley said that Bar Jonah took some pictures of him and Roland in his bed. When Stanley told the jury that Bar Jonah had touched his penis when he was sitting on the couch, Bar Jonah murmured, "I did so much for that kid; he's a liar." Like with Roland, the jury listened intently. Then Light began asking Stanley about the rope and the night Bar Jonah strung him up in the kitchen. "It was braided. He put it around my neck." Once Bar Jonah had the rope around his neck, "He began pulling on it," Stanley said, looking right at the jury. In hushed tones, Bar Jonah continued to say how much of a "fibber" Stanley was.

"What happened to you when the defendant pulled you up with the rope?"

"I just started choking and I went up."

"Did you get scared?" Light asked.

"Yes sir," Stanley replied.

Vernay took the cross of Stanley. One of the first questions he asked was if Stanley "had a hard time remembering things." "Yes," Stanley said. Vernay thought this might throw some doubt on Stanley's testimony. He didn't challenge any of Stanley's testimony about the hanging incident or Bar Jonah touching his penis directly. That would be the kiss of death. But he did question Stanley about telling Jackson during a pretrial interview that Bar Jonah had stabbed him with a knife. There was never any mention of a knife before. When Vernay raised the issue with Stanley, Light called for a sidebar conference with the judge. Light and Vernay walked behind the bench. All you could see from the gallery was Judge Neill's glinting bald crown, Light's lightly brushed dome, and Vernay's dark thick curls, periodically popping up and down like ducks in a carnival shooting gallery. The audience could tell the sidebar had ended when they saw Light and Vernay genuflect in unison toward his Honor. Judge Neill ruled that Vernay could ask Stanley about Bar Jonah stabbing him. As Vernay resumed, he saw that Stanley had been crying during the sidebar. "Are you okay?" Vernay gently asked. Stanley said he was. Then for a brief moment, Stanley looked over at Bar Jonah. Bar Jonah caught sight of Stanley's wet wounded eyes and wouldn't let them go. The tears started streaming down Stanley's face as he sat held by Bar Jonah's predatory gaze. One of the female jurors, sitting closest to Stanley, looked back and forth between Stanley and Bar Jonah. Then she began coughing and coughing and coughing. She was having a coughing fit. Another juror leaned over and asked her if she was okay. When she saw Stanley turn his head and look over at her, she said she was. Then Vernay continued with his questions. Vernay subtly tried to portray Stanley as a liar. His questions continuously implied that Stanley wasn't being truthful. He hoped the jury was taking the bait. Light redirected. "Stanley, when the pretrial interview took place with Mr. Jackson and Mr. Vernay, had you ever met them before?"

"No, sir."

"Did you know who they represented?"

"No, sir."

"Did you want to talk to them?"

"No, sir."

"Were you kind of scared and afraid?"
"Yes!"

The state's next witness was Stormy. When Light called Stormy to the stand, he added that it was going to take a few minutes because Stormy was down on the first floor of the courthouse. A few minutes later, Stormy came bounding into the courtroom dressed in a pullover shirt and blue pants. He stopped, flipped out his palms and yelled, "Where do I go?" Judge Neill cocked one brow and subtly looked admonishingly at Light. The bailiff walked over to Stormy and guided him to the witness stand. As the seven-year-old boy climbed onto the chair he looked up and smiled when he saw the microphone hanging above his head. When Light asked Stormy his name, he pushed himself up and screamed into the mike, "Stormy!" There was momentary anxious giggling in the courtroom. Bar Jonah sat up and with pitiful eyes drew Stormy to him. Stormy waved his happy hands at Bar Jonah like windshield wipers. Bar Jonah smiled wryly while trying to continue to cast a pathetic feel-sorry-for-me persona. Stormy pushed himself up closer and closer to the microphone as he answered each of Light's questions. Light asked Stormy if it would be the truth if he told him that he was wearing blue pants. Stormy, this time not satisfied with just pushing himself up, reached up and grabbed the microphone, pulled it down to his mouth and screamed, "The truth." Judge Neill looked sternly at Light. "I'm sorry, Your Honor," Light said. Bar Jonah was snickering now. The bailiff took the mike from Stormy and put it back above his head. Throughout his testimony, Stormy continued to yell and scream his responses to Light's questions. Still Light cajoled and persisted. Most everyone but Bar Jonah was irritated.

When Vernay crossed, he sat down in front of Stormy, thinking it might help to quiet him down. After a few minutes, Stormy did seem to settle down a bit, sit back, and answer Vernay's questions. Everyone in the courtroom breathed a sigh of relief when Vernay said that he had no more questions. Light didn't redirect. Bar Jonah sighed and frowned when Stormy jumped out of the witness box.

* * *

Soft gasps could be heard when Lori walked into the courtroom to testify for the prosecution. She was wearing a velour jumpsuit that clung so tight to her rotund body that it looked like she had blue skin. By the time she got to the stand, Lori was panting and had to take a few minutes before she could be sworn. Light started out asking Lori to describe her relationship with Bar Jonah. How she had met him and what kind of contact he had had with the boys. Lori looked straight ahead or at Light when she answered. She never looked at Bar Jonah. Light also asked Lori if Bob had told her that if she talked social services would take her kids away. Vernay objected. He was overruled. Lori said "Yes, he sure did."

Vernay again took the cross. "Bar Jonah was a good and generous person?" Vernay said in the form of a question. "Yes," Lori said. Then Vernay took Lori through a series of questions portraying Bar Jonah as a nice guy whom Lori trusted with her kids. He had never given her any reason to think otherwise. Vernay also had Lori read excerpts from the letters that she and Bar Jonah had written to each other. He put a special empathic twist on his words when he asked Lori if Roland missed Bar Jonah after he was arrested. Vernay softened his normally abrasive tone and feigned compassion when Lori answered that Roland had missed Bar Jonah.

When Vernay rose to question any witness, the jury collectively bristled and seemed to listen to Vernay's interrogatives with jaundiced ears. The cowboy juror looked at Vernay like he wanted to hang him right alongside Bar Jonah. On Light's redirect of Lori, Vernay objected to the first question.

Light rephrased.

"Objection, Your Honor," Vernay's voice resounded.

Light rephrased.

"Objection. Leading, Your Honor."

"Sustained."

Light asked Lori, "What was the reason Roland was being harassed?"

"Objection, Your Honor, personal knowledge."

"Overruled," said the judge, clearly irritated with Vernay.

Lori answered Light, "Because of what Bar Jonah did and he had thought he was his friend."

Light closed, "Nothing further, Your Honor."

The state called witness after witness to bolster their case against Bar Jonah. But no witnesses aside from Roland and Stanley were more devastating to the defense than Adam Kingsland. Kingsland testified that he saw the sheet covering the opening to the kitchen. During direct, Light asked, "When you were at Bar Jonah's, did you notice anything unusual about his dress?" Jackson fired off an objection this time. "Overruled," the judge growled. Kingsland said that Bar Jonah would walk around the apartment "only in his underwear, tight white ones."

"Were the children in the apartment?" Light queried.

"Yes," Kingsland replied.

Jackson crossed. "Other than your concern about Mr. Bar Jonah's dress, you didn't see anything at all that he did that was inappropriate toward these children, did you?"

"No," Kingsland said. "But I felt uncomfortable around him just wearing his underwear around the children." Jackson tried to soften the impact of Kingsland's testimony but he knew the damage had already been done. It was no longer just the kids' allegations. Now an adult said that he had seen Bar Jonah parading around half-naked in front of the kids. Jackson closed out his cross by asking a couple of other questions that he didn't think would compound the damage. Light was pleased with Kingsland's testimony. There was no reason to redirect.

As the prosecution began to bring witness after witness to the stand to support the boys' allegations, Bar Jonah began to sweat.

When FBI agent and child interview expert, Kim Proyer, MSW, took the stand, Bar Jonah pulled up the sleeve on his secondhand sport coat and wiped his forehead with the cuff of his starched white shirt. Proyer said the boys weren't lying. She had interviewed hundreds of victims of sexual assault crimes and they were telling the truth. The sweat wouldn't stop coming. Now it was beginning to drip from under Bar Jonah's armpits and from the folds of fat around his abdomen. Proyer kept responding to Light's questions, further indicting Bar Jonah. Then, the pains began pulsing up and down Bar Jonah's left arm. His chest began to tighten. Short, quick, shallow breaths were now replacing Bar Jonah's usual chest-expanding breathing. Jackson and Bar Jonah looked simultaneously at each other. Bar Jonah looked ashen. "Greg, I think I'm having a heart attack," Bar Jonah said. Jackson stood up and asked the court's indulgence, while the sheriff's deputy ushered Bar Jonah out of the courtroom and rushed him to St. James Hospital. An hour later, the deputy knocked on the judge's chambers and told him Bar Jonah was back. Judge Neill ordered the trial to resume. Jackson thought Bar Jonah still looked pasty when the deputy brought him back to the defense table. As he sat down, Jackson asked him if he was okay. Bar Jonah curtly responded, "Don't worry about me. I'm fine." However, Bar Jonah was hungry. Going to the emergency room was an ordeal. "I need something to eat," Bar Jonah barely whispered to Jackson. Jackson tried to shush him, but Bar Jonah would have nothing of it. He was hungry and he wanted something to eat. Bar Jonah said he was stuck in the hospital at lunchtime; it wasn't fair. "I need some food in my belly," he said. Jackson again asked for the court's indulgence, explaining that Bar Jonah had missed getting his lunch. The judge took a deep breath and granted a thirty minute recess. Light didn't object.

* * *

When court finally resumed, Light called Phillip Rector, Ph.D., a psychologist from Wyoming. He testified that Native

Americans tend to be more stoic with their feelings, especially males. The idea that three young Native American boys had got together to make up a lie about being sexually abused and then to speak of it publicly simply didn't make any sense. Pushing toward five on the second day of the trial, the prosecution rested. Bar Jonah didn't have any more chest pains.

Panic

A storm was blowing into Butte the night before the defense was to begin presenting its case. Vernay's hotel room was right at the end of the main hallway. It was a large suite set up with case files and a large table where he could work. Jackson was on the second floor. Vernay could also look right out at his new white truck that he joked Bar Jonah had bought for him. The snow was flying and the temperature was plunging. It was expected to be at least twenty-five below before morning. Phillip Esplin was expected to arrive at 7:30. Vernay offered to pick him up at the airport, but he said he would pick up a car and drive over to the hotel himself. He had been booked into a room just down the hall from Vernay. They would have a strategy meeting with Jackson before his testimony the next day. At 8:30, Esplin still had not shown up at the hotel. By 9:00, Vernay was beside himself. "Where the fuck is he," Vernay kept saying as he paced around his hotel room. At 10:00, Esplin still had not arrived. Vernay was frantic. Esplin was the only defense witness. If he didn't show it was unlikely that Judge Neill would grant a continuance. It wasn't the court's problem. Jackson was getting worried too. At 10:35, a bus pulled up and let three passengers off under the hotel canopy. Were it not for the blizzard that was now in full force, they would have stayed dry on their short jaunt to the lobby doors.

Vernay's legal assistant happened to be checking to see if Esplin might have checked in without anyone knowing. A tall, slightly bearded, irritated man with a pocky face came through the door, shook the snow off his shoulders like a dog, and still dripping presented himself to the clerk behind the counter. Vernay's legal assistant quickly introduced herself and asked Esplin why he was late. The plane had been diverted to Bozeman, a couple of hours east of Butte because of the blizzard. Then they had to bus the passengers over to Butte. "It was a fucking long trip," Esplin said. As he signed in, Vernay's legal assistant noticed Esplin's hands shaking. While Esplin finished checking in, she walked over to the house phone and called Vernay. He slammed down the receiver and came stomping down the hallway. Esplin grabbed his bags and started walking toward his room. Vernay, taking long angry strides, saw Esplin walking toward him and yelled, "Where in the fuck have you been?" Esplin stopped for a moment and started to explain, then he looked at Vernay and said, "I need a drink. You got that bottle in my room, right?" Now dragging his bags, which had flipped over in his rush, Esplin found his room number, dropped his luggage and pushed his way through the door. Vernay, his legal assistant, and now Jackson, who had joined them, were right behind. As soon as Esplin walked into the room, he eyeballed the bottle of Scotch, sitting on a round table in the corner. Vernay had even thought to put a glass he had found in the bathroom beside the bottle. Esplin's trembling hands picked up the bottle, twisted out the cork top and poured almost a full glass of scotch, neat. He then tossed back his head, downing the single malt without taking a breath. Esplin sat down on one of the Naugahyde chairs and began deploring about how arduous the trip had been. Then he poured himself another whisky. Vernay looked over at Jackson in astonishment and said, under his breath, "Jesus!"

It was now past 11:00. Vernay and Jackson wanted to get to work. Esplin seemed more interested in drinking the rest of the Scotch. Vernay was pissed but didn't want to alienate their only witness. They began asking Esplin questions about his testimony. Each time Esplin responded with some kind of equivocation. He had been more decisive on the phone after he had reviewed the interview tapes of Cameron and Theisen talking with the boys. Finally, Vernay and Jackson began telling Esplin not only how to respond to their questions but also what they anticipated Light's cross would be. Esplin continued to drink his Scotch and nod his head in agreement with Vernay and Jackson's suggestions. After an hour or so, Esplin said he wanted to get a shower and go to bed; it had been a long day. He wanted to be fresh in the morning. A round of handshakes ended the night. On the way back to his room, Vernay, in his Brooklyn drawl, said that he thought Esplin, "Just wanted to finish off the fucking bottle of Scotch alone."

Hijacking

When court was called to order the next morning, Esplin was to testify first. Vernay stood up and told the judge that their witness was on his way. He had been briefly held up. The court ordered a fifteen minute recess. About ten minutes later Esplin arrived. Vernay hoped he was sober. Esplin was dressed in an expensive, pin-striped gray suit with his hair slicked back, making his acne-scarred cheeks and gin-blossom nose more obvious. Vernay led Esplin through his background. "Graduated with Ph.D. in '78, expert on handicapped kids and a co-researcher in a number of studies involving child witnesses. These would be children that have either been a victim or an alleged victim of a crime. And our work involves looking at methods to obtain information from children that's reliable." Esplin also said he had developed an expertise in the "area of the psychology of interrogations." Jackson asked him to elaborate. "Part of my professional interest, as well as some research interest has to do with why people may make statements against their own self-interests, why children or adults may come to either say things that are not correct or come to believe things that are incorrect. It's important to look to see if you can identify individual traits that would increase the susceptibility of those individuals to make inaccurate statements, and then develop procedures that lessen the degree of that proposal." Even though Vernay saw Esplin as a "hired gun," for the defense, Jackson wanted to impress on the jury that he had also worked for prosecutors too. When Jackson asked "Have you presented or taught to prosecutors or district attorneys," Esplin offered a convoluted answer, "They have been in attendance. I have not been invited by a district attorney's association to give a formal presentation in this country." He had though presented to the Ministry of Justice in *Norway*. Jackson didn't pursue the question any further. After Jackson led Esplin through his qualifications, he moved to have him declared an expert. Light didn't object.

Esplin was good when he responded to Jackson's questions. He looked right at the jury, trying to find any available accessible eyes and talk directly to that juror. He gave a lengthy overview of the importance of understanding that "memory is not like a tape recorder." He also said that children with "special needs" are more easily influenced. Native Americans were even more susceptible to influence, especially by "Caucasians." Then Jackson directed Esplin to the interviews that Cameron and Theisen did of the boys. "Have you rendered an opinion?" Jackson asked. Esplin said he had.

"With Roland, what did you find to be significant?"

"There was a substantial amount of information," Esplin said, "that came to the children's knowledge before the forensic interviews, that cast the defendant in a negative light." Jackson was pleased with Esplin's answer. He also said that with Roland being developmentally delayed, it was especially likely that he had been influenced by the bad press about Bar Jonah.

Light objected, "Hearsay," he said adamantly."

"Overruled." Jackson continued. Esplin pointed out that some of the interview methods employed by Cameron and Jackson violated some of the fundamental rules for interrogative interviewing. He thought they had more of an "interrogative flavor" than an "interview flavor." Jackson liked that too. Esplin had been bothered by Cameron lying to Roland. "They weren't in a position to make a promise, and it was deceptive." Roland's disclosure was not "spontaneous." He was responding to "direct questions" put to him by Cameron. Cameron clearly influenced Roland to say what he wanted him to. Jackson then moved on to the interview with Stanley.

Esplin expressed concern that Cameron had "re-interviewed" Stanley when the videotape recorder supposedly didn't record his first "disclosure." Then Esplin surprised Jackson when he said that he saw Roland's emotional tone "shift when the interviewers went to the subject under investigation, that I think is noteworthy. Roland became more somber." Light lifted his head up from his yellow pad and looked over at the jury." He saw the cowboy juror drop his chin down to the right and shift his ear out to the left, seemingly to want to more carefully hear what Esplin was saying. Jackson, recovering, said, "What significance do you put on that?"

"I don't know how to interpret it, at least scientifically." Jackson didn't like Esplin's response. Then Esplin began a monologue that sounded like he was reciting a paragraph from one of his scientific papers.

"Let's talk about Stormy," Jackson abruptly interrupted. Again Esplin was "concerned." Stormy was not just young in age but even younger emotionally. But Esplin then followed his "concern" with almost nothing specifically about Stormy. Instead he sounded like he was giving well-rehearsed excerpts of one of his lectures. When Esplin began pontificating, the cowboy juror sat back and crossed his legs. Jackson closed his direct by asking Esplin, "Doctor, do you have an opinion as to whether the defects and flaws in the interviews substantially affect validity and reliability of the interviews?"

"Yes," Esplin responded. "I think that the mistakes that were made seriously compromise relying on information obtained during those interviews." Jackson was pleased again.

After a ten minute recess, Light began his cross. Light couched a statement with the inflection of a question about the percentage of time that Esplin had testified for the defense. "It was 80%, correct, Doctor?" Esplin affirmed. "How many times have you testified in total?" Light asked.

"In various forms, several hundred times," Esplin replied.

"Did you look at this case to determine whether or not any of the statements made by the boys had been corroborated by other evidence?" Light wanted to know. Esplin said he had. "Wouldn't you agree, Doctor," Light prefaced, "that when Stanley indicated that he had been choked by the defendant and he described the color and type of rope, that when an officer then recovers a photograph that shows the same color and same type of rope, that could corroborate his statement, couldn't it?" Esplin had to answer "Yes." Light continued, "And if Stanley indicated that one end of the rope was hooked to the ceiling, and after that disclosure they go back and they find a photograph of a patch in the ceiling, that could corroborate Stanley's statement, couldn't it?" Again Esplin had no choice but to answer in the affirmative. "Now, you indicated with Roland that you found his shift in demeanor to be noteworthy, isn't that correct?"

"Yes."

"And actually that shift we're talking about was about a thirty-five minute crying period, wasn't it?"

Esplin's previously assured comportment was now slipping. His words were breathy, his neck flushing. "Yes," he said.

"What you saw, that fear, the somberness you saw could mean he was abused. It could be the effect of finally disclosing it, couldn't it?"

"Yes," Esplin softly said. With Esplin's response, Light had successfully hijacked the defense's only witness.

Vernay and Jackson sat and watched their expert, who had testified "hundreds of times," look like a rank amateur. But Light wasn't done with Esplin.

"I want to talk to you a little bit more about some of your articles. I noticed that you referred in most of these articles when you got down to the references that almost every article referred to Bruck and two authors. Is that correct?"

"They're two authors that we've referred to frequently," Esplin replied.

Light continued, "And, in fact, they have written extensively on child testimony and suggestibility, haven't they, Doctor?"

"Yes they have."

"And would you agree that they were some of the first authors to do some type of research who write extensively on this?"

Esplin answered, "They were among the first that conducted a series of laboratory experiments on suggestibility issues." Vernay and Jackson were wondering where Light was going with this line of questioning. But they didn't object. It seemed benign enough.

"Doctor, have you ever read the Bruck article titled 'Child Witnesses: Translating Research into Policy'?" Esplin said he had. "Okay, and wouldn't you agree with me that this is one of the, I don't know the word, hallmarks or one of the first things that may have come out on suggestibility in child research?"

"It was 1993," Esplin said. "I think the first serious work, well not serious but definitive, was the book from the Cornell Conference, the suggestibility of children's recollections, that was put out by the Office of Scientific Affairs for the American Psychological Association. That is later. But I think that's an authoritative document." Light was pleased at Esplin's elucidating response.

"And certainly if one looks at this, this would give them a general understanding of the research that was being done on suggestibility, would that be correct."

"I would agree with that," Esplin responded.

"And also in here, Doctor, I noted, and I thought it was interesting, they have a section on what expert witnesses on child suggestibility should tell the court. So they talk a little bit about the right and wrong of experts in the field; would you agree?"

"Yes."

"So, if a person didn't know very much about child witness suggestibility, or experts in the field, would this article again give them a general understanding of these topics?" Vernay and Jackson were frustrated with how Esplin seemed to be having a conversation with Light, it was like he wasn't aware that he was a defense witness. Their *only* defense witness. But, there was nothing they could object to. They had allowed Light's questioning to go on too long to object now.

Light was again pleased with Esplin's response, "Yes, I think it would."

"Okay, Doctor, you talked about the resources that you were provided by the defense. Were you made aware that this very article was found in the defendant's residence in December of 1999?"

Then on Esplin's answer, the jury collectively gasped, "No, I was not."

On redirect, Jackson said, "Very brief, Your Honor." Jackson led Esplin through a series of questions about good interviews and bad interviews. He also got Esplin to talk about the difference between "developmental age" and "chronological age." Certainly the jury listened, but they didn't seem to care. Light had effectively eviscerated Bar Jonah's only witness.

When Jackson was finished with his redirect, Light said he had nothing else either. In an unusual move, Esplin looked up at Judge Neill and said, "May I be excused then?" Esplin was on a tight schedule. He had a plane to catch for another court appearance. Esplin stood up, smiled and nodded at the jury, and walked out of the courtroom. With that, the defense rested.

Before the prosecution rested, Light briefly recalled Cameron to the stand. When Cameron took the witness box, Light handed him "State's Exhibit Number 93," and asked Cameron to tell the jury what he had just been handed. "It is a Social Policy Report, by Bruck. It's regarding child witnesses and abuse cases." Someone sitting directly behind Bar Jonah in the gallery heard him say, "The cops planted it, I was framed." Where did the article come from, Light wanted to know? "It was recovered from Nathan Bar Jonah's apartment," Cameron replied. Light then said, "With that, Your Honor, I'd move for the admission of State's Exhibit Number 93 please." Jackson said he had no objection. What was the point? And with the defense's lack of objection, the trial was over.

Wrap-up

At 1:20, Judge Neill gave the instructions to the jury. Then the closing arguments began. Light began his closing with a recitation of Roland and Stanley's words, "He touched me on my penis and my butt." "I was scared." "I thought I was going to die." The jury was restless, fidgety. It had been a long, taxing trial. Certainly this jury had been witness to allegations against one of the most ill-famed defendants in the history of the Montana judicial system. Light then said something that quelled the jury's restlessness. As though they were one body, all of their vertebra seemed to snap into place at once. One set of communal ears attuned to Light heard him emphatically say that throughout the entire trial and throughout all of the rebuttals of the prosecution's witnesses, not once had the defense said or even implied that, "It didn't happen." "Not once. There has been no evidence that has been submitted that says they weren't abused." With that statement, Light had deftly untangled the smoke and mirror defense that Vernay and Jackson had mounted. Even those sitting in the courtroom saw the jury snap to. So did Bar Jonah.

Light continued, saying that the only thing the defense had done was to challenge the way the boys were interviewed, not what they disclosed. Like in a point-counterpoint Bach fugue, Light pressed the testimony of the state's witnesses while at the same time preemptively raising and countering the anticipated arguments likely to be put forth by the defense. When Light said, "The defense's own witness," the jury knew he was talking about Esplin. But Light had to walk a tightrope with Esplin's testimony. He had turned Esplin into his witness. It would not be prudent to discredit him. He had to capitalize on the parts of his testimony that undermined the defense's arguments. So, Light said, "The defense's own expert agrees with us about …" Light would repeat this over and over again.

* * *

Jurors were seen wiping their eyes when Light reminded them about Roland. "He was fifteen years old when this happened. When you saw him two years later, he was a seventeen-year-old young man who was still traumatized by what had happened to him. That emotional flooding is because he was living it again. Think about that moment in the courtroom. Go back there. Do you remember how quiet it was? The only thing that you could hear was that young man trying to hold back his emotions as he described the defendant grabbing his penis. Ask yourself, did you feel something swell in your eyes? Did you feel an emptiness in your stomach, a sad innocence in your heart as he was testifying? I submit, ladies and gentleman, that what you were feeling was the trauma that Roland was suffering at the moment. It was real and it was sincere." Finally, Light closed his lengthy summary with, "Don't allow the defendant to put the officers on trial. Don't allow the defendant to call the boys liars. And don't forget what I think is one of the most important pieces of evidence that you saw in this trial, the testimony of Roland Johnston. Think about that when you are deliberating this case. Think about how you felt when he was talking about the defendant grabbing his penis. I have great confidence that you will come back in this case and find the defendant guilty of all counts." A fifteen minute recess was called before the defense offered its closing.

* * *

When Vernay approached the jury, the first thing he did was offer an apology. "We did not come here to attack anyone. We didn't come here to attack the police. We didn't come here to attack their experts, and clearly we didn't come here to attack these children. We came here because we have very serious concerns about this case, particularly the atmosphere under which this investigation was conducted, and these children." Vernay also offered what one juror called a soliloquy, about the media and how, in essence, the cops had been out to get Bar Jonah. He also subtly hinted that the jury had in fact been influenced too. Not only would this make their job hard but most likely impossible to do fairly. But then, about halfway through his closing, Vernay began to refer to Roland in a way that infuriated several of the jurors. Light had consistently referred to the boys by name. He was respectful and compassionate. But as Vernay continued to talk, he seemed to become more disinhibited with his language and began referring, particularly to Roland as "kid." At one point, he said with a thick drawl, "We don't know what happened to this kid in his background." The cowboy juror literally snarled at Vernay. Referring to the pictures of Stanley that the prosecution had entered into evidence, Vernay said, "You don't see a traumatized kid." Several members of the jury later said they just wanted him to shut up.

Vernay only made a two line reference to Esplin in his entire closing argument. He tried to use one sentence of Esplin's testimony to support his contentions that no one really knew what had happened to the boys in their past, implying not that they weren't abused but questioning by whom. Bar Jonah was an easy and obvious target. There wasn't much more he could do at trying to establish reasonable doubt. Vernay continued to pound on the media exposure the boys had been exposed to. The media had painted Bar Jonah as such a "bad man" that the boys had lost their minds collectively and believed everything the media was portraying about the man that Roland saw as the father he had never had. "Sure, they may have been touchy," Vernay said. But because of the media, "Any touch that he ever gave to these kids had to be bad touch."

Then Vernay began a narration about Roland being teased in school. One minute he was happy and the next one he was sad. When the teasing stopped, Roland was fine. Vernay didn't understand how anyone could say that he was traumatized. The jury found Vernay's shrill voice grating. But, the coup de grâce for the prosecution may have been when Vernay called Roland "this kid" while calling the defendant "Mr. Bar Jonah" in the same breath.

In his final summation, Vernay said, "It is their burden to prove their case beyond a reasonable doubt to a moral certainty. And there's just too much here, the well is too contaminated for you to be able to do that. And so I'd ask that you enter a verdict of not guilty. Thank you."

Light had one last shot with his rebuttal of the defense's closing arguments. Throughout Light's final statements, he continued to quote Esplin. He hammered on the article by Bruck and said again and again that not once had the defense ever said that Bar Jonah did not assault Roland, Stanley, and Stormy. "I submit to you that a person who has groomed and sexually assaulted three young Native American boys, that's the kind of person that reads about child suggestibility before it ever even happens. What's this mean, ladies and gentleman? This means you can take their defense and you can throw it in the trash. That's what it means. Because as long as he's grooming them not to tell, but if they did tell, he was ready. He was prepared. He knew about the topic. I believe the state has shown through the expert witnesses, through the testimony of these three young boys, through the officers that, in fact, the defendant is guilty of all charges. The people of Cascade County, the people of the State of Montana, now safely put this case in your hands. Find him guilty, find him guilty, find him guilty. Thank you."

Deliberation

At 4:30, the bailiff began escorting the jurors to the jury room to begin their deliberation. The cowboy juror took one last look at Bar Jonah. This time, Bar Jonah looked back at the man who had sat through the entire trial with his Stetson in his lap and, on this final day, was dressed in a pressed, checkered flannel shirt and scrimshaw string tie. Then barely perceptibly, Bar Jonah nodded, softly pursed his lips together, slowly closed his blameless eyes as though he were drifting off into sleep, and lowered his thick chin onto the fingertips of his praying hands.

The creaky raised floor of the jury box bent and bowed to the spur-ish rasp of the cowboy juror's snakeskin boots, as he made his way past the empty chairs to join the other jurors in deliberation. Right before he walked through the doorway leading out of the courtroom, he swore that he felt Bar Jonah's eyes.

The courtroom was aflutter with nervousness, as the sheriff's deputy led Bar Jonah back to the holding cell. He walked with his shoulders held back and his chest pushed out. There was no reason to feign contriteness now that the jury was out of view. He hated Brandt Light, whom he saw as the personification of the Devil. Light had pursued him like no one ever had. But, Bar Jonah believed that in his darkest hour, the Lord would come through for him. Jesus had suffered the darkness of men like Light. He was no different. Vernay and Jackson expected the jury to be out for at least a day. There was a lot for them to consider. Clearly, the cops had coerced the kids. The media attention to the case had turned the kids against the man who had been better to them than anyone ever had. However, in more private moments, when Vernay was asked if he believed in Bar Jonah's innocence, he would respond, "Well ..."

Light went back to his hotel room and spent the next several hours pondering the trial. It was odd. In most trials Light had been involved in, there were multiple defense witnesses. Especially in a trial of this magnitude. But Vernay and Jackson had called only one witness and Light had turned his testimony around to support the prosecution. In effect, Bar Jonah didn't have any witnesses. They had not even called one character witness to speak on Bar Jonah's behalf. It galled Light because he and his staff were working eighteen and twenty hour days for civil servants' pay. Vernay and Jackson would stand to clear close to a million dollars by the time the sexual assault trial and the murder trial were over. Not to mention the appeals.

Shortly after 8:30, Light's phone rang. The jury was back. Vernay and Jackson got the call a few minutes later. They had deliberated just four hours. At 9:30 p.m. the court was called back into session by Judge Neill. "Let the record show that a note received from the jury says, "Judge Neill, the jury has unanimously agreed on all counts except count 4." Count 4 was the sexual assault charge against Stanley. The jury said they were deadlocked. After considering, Light agreed that the state would go with the deadlock on count 4. "It's been long enough," Light said exhaustedly.

Verdict

When the jury was brought back into the courtroom, the judge queried them for the record. "Have you reached a verdict?" he asked. "Yes sir," the foreman answered affirmatively. The foreman then leaned over the polished oak rail that had heard the fate of thousands of men, some let go, while others hung. The bailiff reached out, took the folded-up piece of paper and handed the verdict to Judge Neill. Neill unfolded the verdict and handed it to the clerk to read into the record.

"We the jury," the clerk read, "Impaneled and sworn make the following verdicts: Count 1, on the charge of aggravated kidnapping, a felony against Roland Johnston, we the jury find the defendant, Nathaneal Bar Jonah, *not guilty* ..."

Bar Jonah, for an exquisite moment, felt the Love of the Lord wash over him like he was being immersed for the first time in the waters of Holy Redemption. The other sinners in the courtroom would now see him being taken down from the Cross. He would forgive them as he had all of the others. But he knew it was going to take many hours of prayer to forgive Light and Cameron; they were the biggest liars. Cameron and Theisen were sitting together, directly behind Light. Theisen said all of the wind left him. He was breathless, not even enough air to panic. Cameron thought his heart had stopped. Light's propped-up elbows felt the sudden pressure of his wet palms catching his face as his head fell forward. Vernay and Jackson turned in unison toward the jury, stunned in disbelief. Judge Neill sat motionless, while the twelve heads of the jury spun like tops casting twenty-four angry eyes on the clerk. For a split second there was no sound to echo throughout the courtroom. Then the clerk, realizing her mistake, emphatically said, "*GUILTY.*"

Light, Cameron and Theisen sprang tall, jubilation now replacing the emptiness of their momentary despair. Vernay and Jackson, realizing that the clerk had mistakenly said "Not guilty," now hung their heads in somber defeat.

When Bar Jonah heard the clerk change his fate forever, he angrily whipped his now pale as wax face away from the jury, as though he was taking away their privilege of his presence. The clerk continued reading the verdict on each count. "Count 2, on the charge of sexual assault, a felony, against Roland Johnston, we the jury find the defendant Nathaneal Bar Jonah, guilty. Count 3, on the charge of assault with a weapon, a felony against Stanley Jones, we the jury find the defendant, Nathaneal Bar Jonah, guilty. Count 4, on the charge of sexual assault against Stanley Jones, we the jury find the defendant, Nathaneal Bar Jonah, deadlocked. Count 5, on the charge of sexual assault, a felony against Stormy Ackerman, we the jury find the defendant, Nathaneal Bar Jonah, not guilty." Bar Jonah now sat stunned. He was sure the Lord would come through for him. Satan had likely taken over the voice of the clerk, when she mistakenly said "Not guilty," just to torture him. The Evil One was always lurking about. Before Bar Jonah was led away by the sheriff's deputy, he was already praying for Jesus to forgive Roland for his lies and lack of strength in standing up to the crooked cops.

Aftermath

The rotunda of the Butte courthouse was filled with reporters. Floodlights and mikes seemed to be everywhere. Not since a good hanging had the courthouse seen so much activity. Vernay and Jackson made their way down the marble stairs before Light. Bar Jonah had been railroaded. There was no way he could escape the specter of the Ramsay case. "It's a human impossibility to set aside accusations of killing a child and cannibalism," Jackson said. "Obviously we are disappointed. But if not for the publicity, we feel like we would have gotten a full acquittal." When one of the reporters asked how Bar Jonah was handling the news, "I think he's numb right now," Vernay piped in. They waved off any other questions and made their way out the heavy brass-framed doors onto the dark street. It had been a short news conference at the end of a long day. Now they had a murder trial to prepare for.

Light stood in front of the reporters. How did he feel about the verdict? "I had absolute confidence in these three young boys and that the jury would believe them. We were always hoping for all counts but the counts they found him guilty on were the strongest we had. At sentencing, we will bring up everything the judge needs to hear to show this guy needs to be off of the streets for the rest of his life." When Jackson was leaving the courthouse, Light watched the Butte winds work their way under Jackson's long coat, flaring it out behind him. He stopped for a minute, still feeling perplexed why Vernay and Jackson seemed to put up such a paltry fight. They had motioned everything before the trial. "We are going to do this," and, "You can't do that, how dare you do this." In the end, Light thought their defense had been full of hot air.

* * *

The next day Bar Jonah was taken back to the Cascade County Detention Center. He was getting more and more agitated, saying that Vernay and Jackson were "fuck ups." "Vernay was a ladies' man, with his dyed hair and perm. He loved being in front of the camera. He couldn't get enough of himself," Bar Jonah would say. "Jackson," Bar Jonah said, "didn't seem as lazy as Vernay, but he was still a pretty boy." The first letter Bar Jonah wrote was to Chapman. He had been jerked around by the law dogs just like Chapman had been. His lawyers were lazy, he wrote. They were going to prepare for the murder trial. But Bar Jonah hadn't trusted them to take care of that alone. It didn't matter what Vernay and Jackson did. There was no way Bar Jonah was going to face the death penalty. He had insurance. It would never go to trial, he bragged.

Bar Jonah spent the next few days reading his Bible. Like Jesus, he had not only been falsely accused, he had now been wrongfully convicted. He was hung on the cross for all to see and to suffer public condemnation. Bar Jonah wondered to his jailhouse friend if the cops had "cast lots" for his most prized possessions. The ones they had stolen from him right before Christmas in 1999. He said he would proudly wear the crown of thorns that Brandt Light had twisted upon his head. A constant recitation of John 19:23–24 now became Bar Jonah's dirge of suffering. "Then the soldiers, when they had crucified Jesus, took his garments, and made four parts, to each soldier a part; and also his coat: now the coat was without seam, woven from the top throughout. They said therefore among themselves, Let us not rend it, but cast lots for it, whose it shall be ..." Bar Jonah figured Cameron had ended up with his prized cookbook collection.

On the morning of February 28th Bar Jonah decided to write a letter to Vernay and Jackson. It was time they knew how he felt. Bar Jonah took out his personal stationery, sat on his bunk, and prepared to write. In the upper right-hand corner of the page was a drawing that he had sketched of an airplane piloted by a duck. In the middle was his address at the prison, notably leaving off any reference that the letter was from the detention center.

Dear Greg and Don,

I was very disappointed in the way you defended me because you weren't properly prepared for the battle and I suffered. You went to battle with a cap gun while Brandt Light came in with heavy artillery. I guess you did the best you could with the cap gun but you didn't do your homework. I was so shocked when you rested with only one witness for my defense. That was unconscionable. You made promises of a great defense, that we didn't need Barry. You had crap. We NEEDED Barry big time because you didn't do your homework. With what you had I would have even testified. To prepare for this case you should have had the following, at least:

1. 2 doctors backing Esplin.
2. Barry should of got on the stand or at least kept there in Butte in case we needed him because Adam Kingsland's testimony killed us. Barry's testimony would of off set that along with Stanley's testimony on the pulley.

> 3. *To back up Barry you should have had George or Ralph to testify on when they patched that hole. They have to keep records of the repairs.*
> 4. *Further back up—You should of hired a professionally licensed carpenter, building contractor or building inspector to use a stud finder on the patched hole and I bet they could of given you their professional opinion on if it could of held the weight of a child.*
> 5. *You should of entered into evidence Stanley's complete interview with you to create reasonable doubt.*
> 6. *You should of brought up my medical condition at the time of the incident. I had 2 heart attacks—March & June. I was on limited work and couldn't lift a lot of weight nor had the energy. There were medical records to back that up.*
>
> *You guys didn't due your job to the best of your ability or up to your reputation. You should of crossed every T and dotted every I. Also, if I do go to Deer Lodge or possibly any other correctional facility I am a dead man. Deer Lodge is run by the Native American population and there are many Bigleggins and their relatives are there. I've met 8 in here but they didn't know the supposed victims at the time. They do NOW! My only hope is the appeal or to be kept at Warm Springs State Hospital. At Deer Lodge I'll be very lucky to survive till the end of the year. Well, there isn't much else so I'll close for now. I hope you will take this letter as criticism and not a berating. I do appreciate all you have done for me but you need to do your homework.*
>
> *Sincerely,*
> *Nathan Bar Jonah.*

Mitigation

Now that Bar Jonah had been convicted, the new goal of the defense was to have Bar Jonah sent to Montana State Hospital.

Most everyone knew the state hospital as Warm Springs. Like most state hospitals, it is an architecturally beautiful, turn of the century facility, with cathedral ceilings, sprawling grounds, and a working farm.

Like most lunatic asylums, it is still haunted by the ghosts of many abandoned wives, whose husbands pulled their carriages up to the ornate doors, made a declaration of their wife's insanity, pushed her into the hands of the compassionate, and trotted away; never to return again. In those days, involuntary commitment was the equivalent of a psychological death sentence.

Over the years Warm Springs evolved into a relatively modern psychiatric hospital, with a forensic unit for treating the criminally insane. Vernay and Jackson had ultimately retained Dr. Beljan to support their argument that Bar Jonah was mentally ill. Dr. Beljan more or less agreed.

After Bar Jonah was found guilty, the defense claimed that it was stretched too thin. Not only did they have to prepare for sentencing but they also had to prepare for the upcoming murder trial. Moreover, it was a capital case. Bar Jonah was facing the death penalty. There was no way they could adequately represent Bar Jonah in the murder trial without a continuance. When the motion was filed the state and Judge Neill agreed; Bar Jonah got an eight-month reprieve. He wouldn't have to face the murder charges until October.

* * *

"May those who fear you rejoice when they see me, for I have put my hope in Your Word," were the words Bar Jonah read over and over again. He sat in his cell on the morning of May 23rd, waiting for the guard to come and shackle him. It was his day of reckoning. Today Bar Jonah would find out how long he must sit in prison until his appeals would be heard and he would ultimately be freed. He would wear no suit this time. How he was dressed was not going to impress the judge.

Light arrived at the courthouse early to make sure there would be no foul-ups with a video he was going to show to the court. He was sure there would be objections from Vernay and Jackson. Light doubted the judge would side with Bar Jonah's counsel. A few minutes after Light arrived, a slight, distinguished man with intelligent eyes walked tentatively into the courtroom. His hand slightly trembled as he extended it to Light. Light thanked him for coming such a long way. "You're doing the right thing," Light said. The man anxiously cinched his tie and nodded. Light subtly swiped his palm against his suit pants damping away the sweat residue from the slight man's hand. The slight man then sat down on one of the oak bench seats on the left side of the courtroom.

At 8:45, the courtroom was beginning to fill. Vernay and Jackson got there about the same time as Dr. Beljan, who would be testifying about the results of the neuropsychological evaluation he had conducted on Bar Jonah. One of the now many reporters remarked that the courtroom looked like a church sanctuary. Judge Neill's bench served as a pulpit for Themis, the Goddess of Justice, to render her clear-sighted and impartial judgment. The jury box was choir stalls for the voices of the innocent to sing the praises of one side and to crucify the other. A panorama of stained glass windows reflected the wrath of the sword of justice. At 8:55, a door to the right side of the bench opened and revealed Bar Jonah, standing in orange prison coveralls. His hands were shackled to his waist. A thick linked chain connected the heavy bracelets that wrapped around Bar Jonah's ankles. With the exception of the slight man, who sat with his head down, all other eyes watched Bar Jonah shuffle to the defense table. Jackson reached over and pulled out an oak chair for Bar Jonah, patting him on the back as he plopped, more than sat, on the chair. At exactly 9:00, the bailiff called the court to order.

* * *

Light made a brief statement and then called Cameron to the stand. It wasn't so much that Cameron had anything new to say. But Light decided to take a circuitous route to get a piece of evidence introduced. Cameron had prepared a slide presentation of several of Bar Jonah's handwritten confessions from his previous convictions. Light asked Judge Neill if he could present it to the court. The court had no objections. Try as he might, Cameron pushed this button and monkeyed with that switch to no avail. Finally after several attempts, Cameron declared that the slide presentation was not going to work. Recovering, Light began asking questions about the confessions. Light asked Cameron if he had interviewed Bar Jonah's 1975 victim, Richard O'Connor, the little boy Bar Jonah kidnapped and beat in a parking lot. "Did you ask Mr. O'Connor to describe the incident and the effect it had on his life?"

"Yes," Cameron said.

"And did you videotape that statement?"

Then, Light indicated he wanted to show the videotape to the court. Vernay, indignant, stood up and objected, saying that to allow the tape to be viewed went beyond sentencing policy, adding, "I think it is improper." Light countered, citing Montana law to neutralize Vernay's objection. The court agreed and overruled Vernay. Cameron left the witness box and pressed the ON button on the videotape player, causing the television screen to scratchily come to life. A ruddy-faced, wavy-haired man with deep, sad eyes appeared on the screen. Then the ruddy-faced man began to speak. O'Connor told the court what Bar Jonah had done to him twenty-seven years before. He was just walking to school, he said, when the "policeman" pulled up and told him to get into the car. Then he tried to kill him. He had almost beat him to death. O'Connor had never really been able to get his life back on track. It was always "just off." As the tape wound through the squeaky pad rollers, O'Connor looked like a man who wanted to sound decisive, forcefully clear. But his words trailed off, like a train losing steam going up a steep hill. Light then asked Cameron what consequences Bar Jonah suffered for trying to kill O'Connor. "One year probation," Cameron said. When Light directed Cameron to talk about the 1977 attempted murder and kidnapping convictions, he wanted him to focus on the psychiatric evaluations that Bar Jonah had received over the years. All of them, other than Ober and Sweitzer, had said Bar Jonah was dangerous and shouldn't be released from Bridgewater. Ober and Sweitzer had been paid by Bob, Cameron said, to evaluate Bar Jonah. Then Light asked the court for permission to show another videotape where Sweitzer had said during an interview that Bar Jonah had duped him. This time Jackson objected. He was overruled.

Vernay crossed Cameron. "Are you a psychologist?" was Vernay's first question. "No," Cameron replied, thinking that the question didn't make any sense. Did Vernay really think that he was going to influence the judge by pointing out that he wasn't a psychologist? However, Vernay didn't have anywhere else to go. After Cameron was dismissed, Theisen was called forward. Light wanted Theisen to say again for the court that Bar Jonah had used the stun gun on Roland. Jackson objected. "Overruled," came from the bench before Jackson finished his objection.

Lori Kicker had been the probation officer assigned to do the pre-sentence investigation. The question was whether Bar Jonah was a candidate for probation. Vernay and Jackson had already seen the report Kicker had prepared for the court. They thought they may get some headway with the judge if they were able to show how biased she had been toward Bar Jonah. Kicker's report was seventeen pages, outlining Bar Jonah's criminal history. Light couldn't have been more pleased with her findings.

Vernay and Jackson were determined not to let her get away with her obvious prejudice. She wasn't giving Bar Jonah a fair shake. Light had Kicker go over Bar Jonah's entire conviction record on the stand including summarizing Dr. Scolotti's report. Kicker's recommendations were brutal. "This officer would recommend that the court sentence Nathaneal Bar Jonah to the Montana State Prison for the maximum on each offence, for a total of 130 years."

When Jackson stood up to cross, it was clear he didn't like Kicker. His tone was clipped and brash. "He has a mother and a sister and a brother and nieces and nephews," Jackson toiled to make his point to Kicker. Kicker was a "victim's advocate." She was a voice for Roland, Stanley, and Stormy. How could she possibly be unbiased? Kicker didn't budge. Jackson wanted to know if Kicker had done anything to contact anyone that knew Bar Jonah. Kicker said she had not. Her concern was not for Bar Jonah or his family members' well-being. Her concern was helping to ensure that Bar Jonah never be allowed to victimize another child. Jackson, in more of a monologue than an interrogative, accused Kicker of failing to pay enough attention to Bar Jonah's psychiatric history and his lifelong struggle with mental illness. Did Kicker not care that Bar Jonah would be targeted as a "child molester" if he went to the state prison instead of to the state hospital? "Everyone's at risk in a prison setting," Kicker retorted. She made no apology saying, "Yes, other inmates view child molesters as the scum of the prison."

Light kept his redirect short. He pointed Kicker to the last page of Dr. Scolotti's report and asked her to read the final two paragraphs from the evaluation. Kicker did. "Emotionally, he is a vacuum. There's nothing really inside of him. He is only a shell. However, it is a very dangerous shell, having abused at least five boys that are documented. There is virtually no hope for rehabilitation at this time."

During each of the state's witnesses' testimony, Bar Jonah sat with his arms folded across his chest. He had not said a word to Vernay or Jackson. But now, the witness that Vernay, Jackson, and Bar Jonah dreaded most was about to take the stand. Jackson was going to vehemently object but he knew it would fall on deaf ears. The objection was leveled. The prosecution countered. He had come a long way to have his say, Light said to the court.

The slight man

Judge Neill leaned forward and looked directly into the doleful eyes of the slight man sitting back in the pews. Then he looked over at Bar Jonah. "Overruled", the judge said. Light spoke, "The state calls Dr. Robert Patterson to the stand." The slight man stood. He gripped his thin black tie between the thumb and forefinger of his left hand and pinched the slightly off-center Windsor knot with his right. By the time he was on his feet, the knot of his tie was squarely cinched.

Bar Jonah coughed as Dr. Patterson stepped into the witness box. The state asked Dr. Patterson to state his name. He did. He also stated that he was a specialist in nuclear medicine. Dr. Patterson had come to testify at his own expense. The prosecution hadn't asked him to come. Dr. Patterson said he had known Bar Jonah when he was David Brown. He and Brown had lived across the street from each other. Light then asked Dr. Patterson if the "defendant had molested him?" The slight, dignified, Georgetown-trained physician, sniffled back the now flowing snot like a young boy. He pulled his shoulders back and said in the funeral silence of the courtroom, "Yes." Bar Jonah, making sure others would hear, piped up and said, "He's lying. Those eight boys who raped me are the ones who did it, not me. He's lying." Vernay looked admonishingly past Jackson at Bar Jonah. There was nothing to say.

As Dr. Patterson began to describe the abuse that he had suffered at the hands of David Brown, he began to sob. He didn't stop crying until he had described each circumstance when David Brown had sexually assaulted him. The defense offered no objections. Judge Neill listened intently, periodically glancing over at Bar Jonah. Vernay and Jackson sat helpless. After more than thirty years, a psychological apparition was appearing out of Bar Jonah's murky past to haunt him. Light asked Dr. Patterson what impact the "instances of abuse" had had on his life. "That is not actually an easy question," he responded. "In retrospect, when you are looking at your life, analyzing things that may have gone wrong, and ways you could improve yourself, I came to the conclusion that there are certain interrelationships I have very hard problems with, particularly reactions or interactions with children and particularly fat children. That is something I particularly avoid, and in my profession that's somewhat difficult to do. But it's something that I have come to manage."

In closing, Light asked Dr. Patterson, "Do you have any input that you would like to make as to what type of sentence you would like this judge to make?" Vernay, enraged, immediately objected. The prosecution withdrew his question and then rephrased. "Was there anything, Doctor, aside from a recommendation, that you would like to say to the court?" Dr. Patterson in that moment was not only one of Bar Jonah's victims but now was an undeclared expert and a seeker of revenge. His comments were devastating.

"In the forty-six years," Dr. Patterson said, "that he has been in existence, his behavior has progressed from one in the beginning when my first event with him was nonviolent. It is clearly now violent. And it's continuing to progress. Thirty years of behavior is not correctable. There's no medication out there that will do that. There's no degree of therapy that will do that. He needs to be in a place where the rest of these children will not be affected by him. And that's what I ask you." Bar Jonah's defense did not cross.

Beljan

After Dr. Patterson left the witness box, Light said the state rested. The defense immediately called Dr. Beljan to the stand. Beljan went through his ample qualifications that qualified him as an expert. He walked the court through Bar Jonah's neuropsychological evaluation. One aspect that kept emerging was how the testing pinpointed Bar Jonah's rage. The Minnesota Multiphasic Personality Inventory showed that Bar Jonah was consumed with aggression. Another psychological test instrument, the Thematic Apperception Test revealed that when Bar Jonah looked out at the world, he misperceived almost every social cue. Dr. Beljan also testified that Bar Jonah's "story" of being beaten and raped by the eight boys was utter fabrication. So was the "rape" by the prison guards at Bridgewater. He was also not complimentary about the 1994 sexual offender evaluation that diagnosed Bar Jonah as suffering from post-traumatic stress disorder. The diagnosis of PTSD was just as bogus as the alleged assaults. Controversially, Dr. Beljan said that by definition Bar Jonah was not a pedophile. It wasn't sexual gratification from children that he had sought. Rather, they were the objects of his profound rage. Bar Jonah, in the 1977 attacks, made the two boys strip as a way to gain dominance and to humiliate them. It is also harder for a naked child to run away. He also showed obvious signs of brain damage, particularly in the frontal lobes. The frontal lobes are what make us human. They are what differentiate right from wrong. He was wired wrong, Dr. Beljan said, and no matter what anyone did, "He could never function in the outside world, he simply can't."

When Light crossed, he took Dr. Beljan to task for not diagnosing Bar Jonah as a pedophile. Again, Dr. Beljan tried to explain. Bar Jonah was not a man seeking sexual gratification from children. For the most part, he could not care less about sex. He was a man who used his "sexual assaults" as a conduit for his rage. This actually made him *more* dangerous than most pedophiles, Dr. Beljan said. He also reiterated that Bar Jonah should be confined for the remainder of his life. When the defense redirected, Jackson asked for Dr. Beljan to make a recommendation based upon his evaluation. Dr. Beljan recommended that Bar Jonah go to Warm Springs State

Hospital. He had no investment in revenge. Dr. Beljan was speaking as one of the top neuropsychologists in the country. Clinically, Bar Jonah was neuropsychologically impaired. That was an indisputable fact. He should never be permitted to be outside of an institution. Factually, his brain was broken. Hearing Dr. Beljan's recommendation, Jackson returned to his seat and said the defense rested. As Beljan was making his way out of the witness box, Bar Jonah leaned over to Jackson and said, "Gee, I thought he was my friend."

Closings

Not surprisingly, Light said in his closing arguments that Bar Jonah should receive the maximum sentence. "Montana State Prison is where he should spend the rest of his life." Jackson's closing statements were somewhat surprising though. "It is obvious," Jackson said, "that from all of the recommendations that have been made to this court today, by all of the experts, that there is unanimity in terms of recommendations that Mr. Bar Jonah receive, in essence, the maximum term." That was not the issue. The issue before the court was where Bar Jonah should be sentenced to. On that, Bar Jonah looked up and said, this time under his breath, "I guess Greg's not my friend either."

Judge Neill called for a recess while he made his decision about how long and where Bar Jonah would be sentenced to. People sitting in the gallery stood and casually meandered out of the courtroom. Vernay and Jackson thought it would take the judge several hours to review the testimony and come to a decision. The court deputy took Bar Jonah back to the bailiff's room to await his fate. He sat down in a screeching swivel chair and rocked back and forth. Then Bar Jonah said to anyone who was listening, "It doesn't matter what the judge decides. It will be overturned on appeal and the murder case will never go to trial. I'll be out in a year and then I'm sure not going to stay in Great Falls."

Judgment of the court

As Vernay and Jackson stood outside of the courtroom making lunch plans, the bailiff walked up and said, "Judge's back." It had been less than twenty minutes. The word spread quickly. Soon the courtroom had filled again to capacity. A clicking of Judge Neill's leather soles against the marble floor leading from his chambers could be heard by the people in the gallery. All heads turned to the left to see the judge's judicial garb flowing freely out behind him as he made his way back to the bench. He was carrying two pieces of paper. "Is there any legal reason we can't proceed with sentencing?" Both Light and Jackson answered, "No." Then Judge Neill read his decision.

"It is the judgment of this court that Mr. Bar Jonah be sentenced as follows:

> On Count 1, to 10 years to Montana State Prison.
> On Count 2, to 100 years to Montana State Prison.
> On Count 3, to 20 years to Montana State Prison.

Said sentences shall run consecutively for a total of 130 years. The court further orders that the defendant shall not be eligible for parole for the protection of society." When the judge said he would grant 526 days for time served, Bar Jonah shoved a note to Jackson. Jackson corrected the judge and said that Bar Jonah had just informed him that he had served 898 days not 526. Judge Neill nodded in agreement and said that he would amend the sentencing order. According to Vernay and Jackson, Judge Neill had made his inability to remain neutral in his decisions clear from the beginning of the trial. He was clearly for the prosecution and against the defense. Almost all of the court's decisions were littered with his bias against Bar Jonah. Vernay and Jackson assured Bar Jonah that each one of the judge's biases and prejudicial errors would be pointed out on appeal. Bar Jonah said that his attorneys were confident the conviction would be overturned by the Montana Supreme

Court, based upon the judge's misconduct. Nonetheless, Bar Jonah's defense team still had the murder trial coming up. If Bar Jonah got convicted of capital murder, the sexual assault conviction was the least of his worries.

Bar Jonah, in the meantime, continued to fire off letters. Later, the recipient of those letters would flatly deny that they had ever even written back and forth. Bar Jonah would say they were lying. They were the best of friends.

There was no DNA evidence, there were no eyewitnesses, and most importantly there was no body. Even the DNA from the remains found in Bob's garage didn't match Zach. There had been rumors, Bar Jonah said, that Bob's house had been built on an ancient Indian burial ground. The bones were probably the remains of some dead Indian kid. But, it didn't matter anyway. Bar Jonah was dead certain the case would never go to trial.

When the police received the videotape from Italy questioning whether or not "Zack" was "Zach," they took every step to determine if, in fact, it was. Of course he was not. In January of 2001, at the urging of Bar Jonah, Rachel Howard took a copy of the videotape to Greg Jackson. She wanted them to help her find her son. Clearly finding Zach would get the charges dropped against Bar Jonah. Vernay maintained that he told Rachel that they did not have the means to conduct an investigation but that they would do all they could. Bar Jonah's defense team had not known about the existence of the videotape before Rachel brought it to them. There would be no need for them to know. It wasn't a factor in Bar Jonah's defense. Within three months Vernay and Jackson learned that the boy in the videotape was not Zachary Ramsay. The FBI had tested Zach's DNA against the boy's DNA in Italy. Vernay and Jackson, however, didn't bother to tell Rachel. In the meantime, Bar Jonah continued to write letters expressing his incredulity at the incompetence and underhandedness of the bastard cops and the Devil incarnate, Brandt Light.

CHAPTER NINE

There is no body

The venue for the murder trial had been changed to Missoula. Like the sexual assault trial, argued the defense, Bar Jonah could never get a fair trial in Great Falls. Like Butte, the city of Missoula would have to upgrade their security at the courthouse to insure Bar Jonah's safety. It wasn't just a matter of electronic security, but also officers' time and administrative costs. The total outlay of cash for Missoula was more than $300,000. All of the security measures were tested and ready a full week before the murder trial was ready to commence. The Missoula county sheriff's office was going to make sure that nothing happened to Bar Jonah while he was in their custody. Light and his team were working day and night on trial prep. Light was exhausted, irritated. It was going to be an uphill battle, even with Bar Jonah as the defendant. Cameron and Theisen were working with the prosecution, point-counterpoint on the evidence. What-if scenarios were worked out. But, there was no DNA, there was not one shred of physical evidence, their witnesses, Pam and Sherri were crazy and as Bar Jonah would regularly say, "There is no body."

The weekend before the trial was to begin, Light went to a store to pick up a few things he would need for his stay in Missoula. When Light turned a corner in the store, he and Rachel came face-to-face. Rachel threw her arms around Light and began crying, saying how much she appreciated everything he was doing, thanking him for all of his hard work. Light sympathetically patted Rachel on the back and told her that he was sorry for all she had been through. Rachel nodded, turned, and walked away.

Loose ends were being tied up the night before the trial was to begin. Files were organized in succession to establish the foundation of guilt against Bar Jonah. Missoula was three hours from Great Falls. Boxes of exhibits had to be carted to Missoula; nothing could be left behind. It was about seven when Light told his assistant prosecutor to get some dinner. He would stay and work at the office. "Go eat," he said.

The assistant prosecutor pulled on a long, light trench coat, slung her bag over her left shoulder, and walked hungry and exhausted to her car. There was an upscale neighborhood restaurant not far from the prosecutor's office. She went there a lot, knowing the service would be quick. The restaurant is more of a haunt for locals. The lighting is Casablanca-ish, almost romantic. A heavily leaded stained glass "D" sits in the center of the thick mahogany door that opens onto a corridor lined with yesteryears' photographs of Great Falls. The assistant prosecutor made her way to a podium that instructed her to wait to be seated. As she stood waiting for the maître d' to come and seat her, she casually scanned the other restaurant patrons. Then her turning head stopped. In almost a clichéd move, she shook her head back and forth, disbelieving what she was seeing. She shifted the angle of her head. It wasn't a mirage. No more than twenty feet away sat Don Vernay waving his arms, pontificating about something. Greg Jackson was nodding his head, while cutting his steak. And Rachel Howard seemed to be enjoying her thick-cut pork chop at the table for three.

Over dinner, it was worked out that Rachel would testify that she believed Zach was still alive. She would emphatically state that the cops had failed to do their jobs and look for other suspects and that the cops had threatened her. Most importantly, she would look directly at Bar Jonah and say that she, the mother of Zachary Ramsay, believed him to be innocent of murdering her son.

Light's assistant prosecutor was still in shock, as she made her way through the neighborhood back to her office. Rachel had told Light that she would testify for the prosecution. Just days before, she had thanked Light publicly for making Bar Jonah face justice. Now, Rachel sat being wined and dined by the defense. Light's assistant was incredulous. When Light heard the news, he wasn't incredulous. He was enraged.

Clearly Rachel had intended to testify for the defense all along. Light felt betrayed and scammed. He had already put Bar Jonah away for 130 years. The state didn't have to go through the time and expense of trying the murder case. All Vernay and Jackson had had to do was to file a motion for dismissal, based on the fact that the mother of the victim was going to testify for the defense. After a lengthy discussion, Light reluctantly drafted an order, dismissing the murder charges. Bar Jonah had been right; the case would never go to trial. The next morning, Judge Neill even more reluctantly signed the motion vacating the murder trial.

* * *

Cameron came out and publicly said Vernay owed the people of Great Falls an apology. He had misled Rachel Howard about the boy in Italy being her son. Rachel wanted, above all else, to believe that Zach was alive. He wasn't. The defense knew that. Bar Jonah knew that. Yet they let Rachel believe that he was. Vernay said, "The cops took everything and turned it and they lied." He also said that it wasn't the defense's job to inform Rachel. That was the cops' job. They were the ones who had found out the kid was not Zach. Why should it be the responsibility of the defense to tell Rachel it wasn't Zach? When Rachel was asked to make a statement, she said, "I have been lied to too much. I do not believe that our justice system is a game. I'm not playing along. This has not been easy. The focus has always been on Bar Jonah. The defense is trying to clear him and the prosecution is trying to win." When asked how she felt about the defense not telling her they knew the boy in Italy wasn't Zach, Rachel said, "I don't know how to respond. I have been told one thing and found out another. Anymore, I am skeptical of everyone." Rachel did however say that, "Brandt Light's decision to drop the charges against Bar Jonah was an answer to my prayers. It is further proof that God was telling me that Zach is still alive."

Cameron called Wilson right before the decision was announced to the press. "Light dropped the charges," Cameron said. The usually stoic Wilson was enraged. How could Light drop the charges, regardless of whether Rachel testified for the defense. Make her look like the crazy, grieving mother who wants to believe that her son is still alive regardless of the evidence. But don't drop the charges. Publicly, however, Wilson said that he backed Light's decision. Wilson said, "The ultimate goal is to find out who the child is whose bones were buried amongst Bar Jonah's stationery in his former garage."

* * *

Bar Jonah received the news right after Vernay and Jackson had been notified of the dismissal. He was not surprised. Then he sat down and wrote Rachel, praising her for having the courage to stand up to the crooked cops and to say that he hoped, now that all of this was over, that Zach would come home soon. When he won his appeal, Bar Jonah said he planned on dedicating his life to helping Rachel discover the truth. Then Bar Jonah pulled an itchy wool blanket around his shoulders and began reading out loud. *"About midnight Paul and Silas were praying and singing hymns to God, and the prisoners were listening to them, and suddenly there was a great earthquake, so that the foundations of the prison were shaken. And immediately all the doors were opened, and everyone's bonds were unfastened"* (KJV, Acts 16:25–34).

CHAPTER THIRTY-SIX

Pounding the same old nail

After the murder charges were dropped, a young, enterprising reporter named Alia Mahi, who worked for the television station, KECI, in Missoula, sent Bar Jonah a request for an interview. Initially, Bar Jonah refused to grant Mahi an interview but then finally agreed.

Hi Alia Mahi,

I received your letter and I was really glad to hear from you. As to a videotaped interview? No, I don't think I will unless my lawyers, Don Vernay and Greg Jackson, decide on a news conference and then I would but not unless they decide to do one. I do know you want to ask me questions about Zachary Ramsay but I can't give you any answers. The reason is because I don't know what happened to him. All I know is that I didn't do it and that if the cops did there job better Zach might have been home 10 days after he disappeared. I have all of the police reports and I wrote a book to help my lawyers to defend me with. I also hope to one day publish it. I think it might even help find out what happened to him. Zach's mom, Rachel Howard, had a great suspect, yet the cops just blew it off. Rachel

Howard, Darlene Gustovich and Cheryl Whitehawk suspected 2 classmates at the Vo-Tech of taking Zach so they could make her boyfriend look like a hero when he found him. David drove a 1984 (blue) Olds Cutless. Marvin Henry, a 16 year-old boy saw a 1985 Olds Cutlass near Zach before he disappeared. Roger Marshal saw Zach get into a (blue) older type car with a man. Jenna Stevenson saw a vision of a large older type car (blue or green) racing toward Browning with Zach and a male and a female inside. It could have been David and Danette. Rachel Howard's suspects. The cops never talked to him. He was not in school all that day and his girlfriend was nervous all day according to Cheryl Whitehawk in a report. There were several suspects the cops didn't really check out like they should of like Ralph Pate Jr., John McPherson, David Nadeau and Danette Habets, to name a few. No one knows whether Zach was abducted or simply ran away. Many of Zach's friends said that he had a "plan." Kyle Green and Matt White said it too plus that Zach was acting funny all week before he disappeared. On the day he disappeared his teacher saw him in the alley and a 3rd grade student, Kendra, claims she saw him in school going down the stairs. At 8:15 A.M. Evelyn La Boy claims she saw Zach walk past Long Fellow School heading in the direction of Benefis West Hospital which is about 20 blocks from where he was suppost to of disappeared. At around 4 pm he was seen by Levon Ostuka near Zach's church near 25th Street North and 6th Ave. North. This is about 17 blocks from Benefis West Hospital. His grandmother was in a local hospital at the time. I don't think Zach knew which one. He was later seen around 8 p.m. several blocks from Benefis Hospital walking east away from the hospital near Hastings on 10th Ave. South. Two days later he was seen by Zachery Outlen near Yellow Stone Truck Stop. Also during the months of January and February of 1996, there were at least 6 attempted abductions plus one in Harlem, Montana. 3 of the attempts were at or near Whittier School (Zach's school) before and after he disappeared. Yet they really weren't investigated, at least according to the reports that I have. On 2/28/96 there was an attempted abduction in Harlem, Montana. The log # is 815233. Melissa Loucks claims that someone tried to abduct her 5 year old son from Whittier School on 2/12/96. According to her the lead detective just brushed her off. According to Julie Doney on 1/18/96 some tried to abduct her son, Dustin, near Whittier School. Zach supposedly disappeared near Whittier School on 2.6/96. Brenda Dubois reported an attempted abduction after Zach disappeared. Anne Wilson reported on 2/9/96 an attempted abduction of her child around 37th St. and 2nd Ave, South. Jack Olds reported that his son and 2 others were almost abducted around the corner of 13th Ave. S. and 9th Street South (near Holiday Village Mall) on 2/9/96. His son Jeremy Olds and Christopher and Chantelle Gotts (parents—Kim Schele and Jack Workman). On 1/13/96, Jerid Denny, reported that his son, Josh Tonasket, was almost abducted in the same area of Holiday Village Mall as the Gotts kids and Jeremy Olds. On 2/29/96, Matthew Brockte, was almost abducted near Parkdale (6th Ave., S and 15th St., South). His mom's name was Patricia Brockte. None of their descriptions fits me. I still loudly proclaim I am innocent and I'll continue to do that as long as there is breath in my lungs. Zach was also seen by Jerry Ouellett at 7:45 near 7th St. and 4th Ave. North, just a block away from the school on 2/6/96. Zach was still alive at the age of 12 according to the cops who had a photo of him. He disappeared at the age of 10. On 8/12/99 they received the taped photo from a lady in Chinook, Montana. Well, with that I'll close hoping to hear from you soon.

Sincerely,
Nathaneal Bar Jonah

Mahi wrote Bar Jonah back and continued to ask him questions about the Ramsay case. On October 22nd, she received a response to her queries.

Hi Alia,

I received you letter and I was very glad to hear from you. As to the Ramsay case? Everything I told you came directly from the police reports that I have and are all present in the book I wrote for my lawyers to defend me with. I also still hope to get it published. As to what it's been like all these year to be blamed for a crime I did not commit? Pure hell for me and my family. What reputation I had built for myself in my business as being honest and well respected has been shot to hell. My mom was so hounded by the media back in Massachusetts she had to get an unlisted phone number and go under a doctor's care. She'll be 87 in November. My sister has lost business because of the media coverage and brother's life was upturned many times because of the cops and their threats. The cops have even falsified documents and peoples statements to fit their agenda. My lawyers have proof of this and we intend on sueing the GFPD when I am released which will probably be in less than 5 years when I win my appeal on the original stop to which was definitely illegal. I was convicted of crimes that I did not do. What I was guilty of they dropped. *I did carry a stun gun for my own protection because I hate guns. I did tamper with a witness according to the letter of the law. In my mind though, I was simply reminding Barry of all I did for him and simply wanted him to tell the truth. There was no threat at all. Finally, over a year later he came forward and recanted his statement and stated that I never touched those kids and that the police (Det. Theisen, FBI Agent Wilson and another cop) forced him to lie. As to the one on one interview? That is still up to my lawyers. I have no problem doing it as long as they say it's okay. It's their call. I do not trust the media and that's thanks to the G. F. Tribune.*

I also think that on all that I sent you, you should talk to those people I named, especially Rachel Howard who would love to talk to you, Darleen Gustovich, Cheryl Whitehawk, Marvin

Henry and so on. These people are real and not made up. They made official statements. Also, the cops really do have a picture of Zach at the age of 12. He was alive 2 years after he disappeared—Yet I was suppose to of killed him in 1996 and served them to friends. I did not. I am an innocent man doing life without parole. I have received tons of death threats and still do and I was attacked by 5 inmates—2 were golden gloves at the jail. This state and the county of Cascade will pay dearly for all that I have suffered. The best way to make them pay is in the wallet along with the city of Great Falls. I also lost a lot of personal property—some can't be replaced like my old cookbooks from the late 1800's and early 1900's, my old Christmas decorations and family decorations, my antique dish set from 1887 and other items that were dear to me. Well there isn't much else so I'll close for now hoping to hear from you soon. Sincerely, Nathaneal Bar Jonah.

P. S. Again my first name has no "I" in it. It is spelled: NATHANEAL, No "I" (EYE) in the name.

On November 1st, Bar Jonah had agreed to an on-camera interview. But he said he was not overjoyed at the prospect of "being on TV." *"The idea of everyone seeing me in an orange jumpsuit with my hands cuffed isn't exactly what I'd like people to see. Also I don't know if they will allow a face to face meeting. It may be between glass and we have to talk through a small screen which makes it hard to hear people talks unless you are right up to it. I just figured I'd warn you ahead of time."* Bar Jonah also told Mahi that, *"So far you are the only reporter I have consented to for an interview. I just turned down 2 reporters from Great Falls."*

Mahi filmed a two-minute interview with Bar Jonah clad in an orange jumpsuit behind bulletproof glass. Throughout all of the years that Bar Jonah had been entangled with the judicial system, this was the first opportunity to speak in his own voice on camera. This was an opportunity to tell of his sorrowful life, allowing others to be witnesses to his lifelong suffering. Facing Bar Jonah one-on-one, Mahi tried to mask her unseasoned youth by steeling up her voice. Her short-burst, clipped questions served as a tell for Bar Jonah to exploit her naiveté. His eyes were pitiably astringent. He was, he said, his voice becoming seductively soft, raped as a child ... with sticks and fire ... Kevin ... the eight boys ... It set him on a bad path, an angry path. Mahi asked him questions about Zach Ramsay. He gave her nothing. He got his two minutes.

Habakkuk 2:8

Bar Jonah spent the next two years waiting to be released on appeal. If Vernay and Jackson had done their jobs right in the first place, he wouldn't be sitting in prison. But now he could only pray they weren't as incompetent in making his appeal to the Montana Supreme Court. As the appeal approached, Light became increasingly nervous. Bar Jonah had slipped under the wire before; Light didn't want it to happen again, especially on his watch. The appeals and responses had been filed. It was now a matter of waiting for the Court's decision. On the morning of December 7th, 2004 a five-judge panel rejected all of Bar Jonah's appeals. These included:

1. That the initial stop of Bar Jonah dressed as a police officer was unlawful. The court said that given Bar Jonah's background of dressing like an officer, kidnapping, and strangling boys in Massachusetts, officers had reason to suspect Bar Jonah of committing a similar offense in Great Falls.
2. That officers went beyond the scope of the search warrant when they seized the photo albums, cameras, and other evidence used in the long investigation: the court said the items were "reasonably related" to the offense of impersonating an officer.

   And because the search warrants were tied to the charges against him at the time, the searches were not a mere pretext that authorities used to look for evidence linking Bar Jonah to Ramsay's disappearance, the court added. If that was a motive for the searches, it does not matter because they also had a legitimate reason, it said.

3. That the Butte trial should have been moved a second time to Billings because of pre-trial publicity: while the reports of possible cannibalism probably stirred strong feelings, the news coverage "did not go beyond the objectivity expected of the press," Justice John Warner commented for the court. He also said Bar Jonah failed to show he was prejudiced by the Butte trial and that moving the trial to Billings would not have served any useful purpose.

4. That jurors were prejudiced by seeing the photo albums packed with photos and magazine clippings of children, pamphlets of rope tying techniques, and articles about erotic asphyxiation: the court said the evidence applied because it explained how and why Bar Jonah befriended young boys, supporting the testimony of the young victims.

Jackson, upon hearing the court's decision, said the next step was to appeal to the US Supreme Court. He did acknowledge there was little chance they would even hear the case. Light said, "I'm overjoyed about it." He was finally relieved to know for certain that Bar Jonah "will never leave Montana State Prison, that he will never have a chance to hurt someone else."

Epilogue

Bar Jonah was housed in solitary at the Montana State Prison. He was never allowed to be without an escort. His cell was white cinder block with a 24x18 inch rectangular window that looked out onto the Flint Creek Mountain Range. He typically kept two tan cups sitting to the right of a small television. Usually the cups were caked with the remains of dried hot chocolate. Bar Jonah liked to stretch out on his bed and lay on his belly when he wrote to his pen pals. He would only use the electric typewriter, kept on a small table against the wall with the window, for special correspondence because the ribbons were so expensive to replace. Some of his special friends would periodically get typewritten letters on thin onion skin paper.

His toothbrush sat on the top ledge of his stainless steel sink and toilet combination. There was a bar of yellow soap for daily clean-up. He wished that someone would come in and clean his toilet but unfortunately, he said, it was up to him to keep it clean. The prisoners in solitary got a shower three times a week. That was when Bar Jonah liked to wash his underwear. On the bulletin board that he kept hanging on his wall above the television, there were dozens of photographs of family, especially Tyra, and pictures of kids. He said they were family too. In the center of the collage was a picture of Bar Jonah, taken right after he was released from jail in the Shawn Watkins case in 1995. In the photograph he is dressed in an *el Traje de Luces*, the matador's traditional suit of lights. His head is tossed back and his hanging jowls are puffed up to the brim of the *Montera* that adorns the top of his head. It was the photograph that he was most proud of. He liked to say that, "The picture shows how I can have a commanding presence even in the face of adversity. *No one* will ever break me!"

* * *

There was nothing more to do. There was no way out. The remainder of his life would be spent behind the walls of Montana State Prison. Bar Jonah became somewhat of a celebrity. Everyone it seemed wanted to take a crack at him. A well-known media psychiatrist, coming to talk to Bar Jonah, delivered a taped monologue in a limousine before his interview with Bar Jonah. He was sure he was going to get the goods on Bar Jonah. The doctor had spent time with criminals the likes of Bar Jonah many times before. Periodically during the interview, the background music would drop to a minor key, setting up the expectation of a revelation. It never came. The psychiatrist looked more like Mr. Popcorn Head being danced around in Bar Jonah's garage.

The head of an organization called the Missing Children's International Ministry was able to get an on-camera interview with Bar Jonah in July 2005. It was the usual interview with the exception of the interviewer trying to solicit $50,000 from viewers so the MCIM could continue with publishing a "coloring book," designed to help teach children the dangers of potential predators. One of the most interesting parts of the production was when the interviewer asked Bar Jonah if he had any advice for kids who are already captured. Bar Jonah sat quiet for a moment and leaned his heavy body back against the whitewashed concrete wall. Then using the occasion to act as a "pulpiteer", he looked directly at the interviewer and said, "Have you ever tried to bind a child? Even though they're bound, it doesn't mean they're totally bound. It depends on how they're bound. It all depends on how tightly they're chained." He then fanned out his arms and gestured as though he was wrapping something around his thick waist, and said, "If it's taped around here. Have you ever tried to catch a child? Kids wiggle around," (MCIM, 2005) Bar Jonah said in closing the segment. The interviewer then asked Bar Jonah if he would recommend that, "parents tie their kids up and teach them how to get out of it?" In a bizarre twist of circumstances, Bar Jonah looked incredulously at the interviewer, cocked his head dumbfounded, and said, "No, I wouldn't recommend that."

* * *

It never sat right with Wilson that the FBI cryptography lab said they couldn't break Bar Jonah's code. Zach Ramsay's body had never been found. The murder charges had been dropped and the Great Falls Police Department had closed the case. Wilson was the only special agent in the Great Falls office. He alone managed to keep an open file on the case. At least this would give him access to Bar Jonah if he was able to turn something up. In late September 1995, Wilson took a train from Havre, Montana back to Quantico to requalify as a firearms instructor. He also decided to take the train because he wanted to have some uninterrupted time to himself. Wilson was known to be a reader but on this trip he took no books. He took eight of the nine words that Bar Jonah religiously carried around with him tucked away in his wallet. When Wilson was copying down the words, he uncharacteristically overlooked the fifth word of the sequence, RAB(bit).

The eastbound train runs across the Montana High Line, just south of the Canadian border. The seats are sprawling and comfortable. In those days, the food was good too. Wilson sat toward the back of the car, his black leather brief bag unzipped in the seat beside him. In his lap lay a notebook. Across the page, the words, *HASAH, CAFORUM, MINNA, LECOURUM, PLUMIUS, DEPORUM, ALEGY, MACKDUM* stared back at him. Wilson had thought about the words many times before. He was convinced that they held the key to something. He just wasn't sure what. He had tried on several occasions to get the cryptographers' help but it always seemed to go nowhere. For several hours, Wilson just sat and concentrated on the words. Then it dawned on him. What would happen if he pulled out the vowels? Drop them down like you do when you reduce a fraction. Consider the vowels as the least common denominators. Now when the vowels were dropped out, the words looked even more odd than before, just a bunch of consonants hanging in the air. What would happen if he made a circle? A wheel with just the consonants? In his readings, he had come across something called a "slider code," where a circle is made from the consonants. You place your fingertips on the consonants that remain in the word you are trying to decipher and then shift your fingertips to the left, respective to the number of the words in the sequence. So if you have four words in a code sequence, you would begin by shifting your fingers one time for each respective word. You would have already dropped out the vowels. Then you replace the former consonant with the new "shifted" consonants and see what is spelled out. Wilson took the first word, HASAH. He dropped down the two As. Then he placed his fingers on the H S and H and moved them one position to the left. Wilson sat stunned when he looked down at the new word. He wasn't sure what to have expected or if to have expected anything. Even though he had been convinced that the words meant something, some of the world's most brilliant cryptographers hadn't been able to break the code. Why should he have any better success? As the train jostled him back and forth, Wilson now stared down at the word GARAG.

When Wilson tried the same sequencing with the second word, CAFORUM, only now shifting two positions to the left on the circle of consonants, another equally indecipherable word emerged. Wilson sat stymied. He then got the idea that since "ORUM" in several variations appeared four times in the sequence of words, that possibly they may be again like fractions. So he cancelled them out. Later on, he would say they were "Bull crap." He was left with CAF. Wilson dropped down the A. Then he shifted his fingers to the left two spaces and dropped down the consonants and there was ZAC.

MINNA proved to be more challenging. Since MINNA was the third word, Wilson should have been able to drop down the vowels, set his fingers on the consonant circle and then move them three letters to the left. When he did he got gibberish. Bar Jonah broke rules, Wilson thought. Maybe he broke the *rotational rule* also. "Okay, third word, let's try four, no not that, let's try five, what about going back the other way? Let's try two again." Then Wilson dropped down the I and the A and moved his fingers two letters to the left on the circle. The depth of his breath seemed to come spontaneously and was followed by a saddened exhale. There before him the word MINNA had now become KILLA. Wilson took the same approach with

LECOURUM that he did with CAROREM. He "cancelled" the OURUM leaving LEC. It was the fourth word in the sequence. Better to begin with what it was supposed to be then try to second guess how Bar Jonah may have tried to break the rules.

Wilson then repeated the same process as before. He dropped down the E and this time shifted his fingers four consonants to the left. The word HEX appeared. Many years later, when the consonant circle was applied to RAB, it became DAM. With RAB you had to move eleven times to the left on the consonant circle. The first nine words had now been deciphered to say, "GARAG ZAC KILLA HEX DAM." Wilson tried every combination backwards and forwards for PLUMIUS, DEPORUM, ALEGY, and MACKDUM. Nothing revealed itself. To this day, the last four remaining words have not been decoded. It is possible that they are actually key words for other coded writings that may not necessarily appear to be written in code.

Bar Jonah continued writing his pen pals throughout his incarceration at Deer Lodge. He said he had over 300. Most of them were in the former Eastern bloc states, Yugoslavia and Bulgaria. Most were men. Most had no last names on the return envelopes and were delivered to untraceable drop boxes. In 2009, Wilson transferred out of Great Falls. Once he left, the open case against Bar Jonah was officially closed.

* * *

The day after Andy Puglisi disappeared from Lawrence, Massachusetts in 1976, his little girlfriend, Melanie Perkins stood between their houses in the projects and made a promise to herself that she would do everything in her power to find Andy. Melanie grew up and went to film school. In 2008, Melanie Perkins won an EMMY for her documentary, *Have You Seen Andy*. It was a ten-year project dedicated to finding her first love, Andy Puglisi. The pool is there where Andy and Melanie were playing that day. The projects are still there too. The former detectives in the case are interviewed, as is

Andy's mother. Somewhere along the line, a bloody sock was part of the evidence collected but it was lost a long time ago. Wayne Chapman is suspected in the disappearance of Andy. Bar Jonah, then David Brown, was suspected too. Some even thought that Chapman and Brown kidnapped Andy together. In August 2009, Melanie Perkins was asked if the word "Puggy" meant anything to her. Bar Jonah had written the name, *Alonzo "Puggy"* on one of the pieces of paper recovered during the search of his apartment in December, 1999. Perkins said the name had no meaning to her but she would check with Andy's mother. When Melanie asked Andy's mother if the word "Puggy" meant anything to her, she was aghast and began to cry. "Puggy" was the pet name for Andy and his father. The day Andy disappeared, his father walked over to the pool to check on Andy. Embroidered on Andy's father's baseball jacket was the name "Puggy."

* * *

CODIS stands for the *Combined DNA Index System*. It is the national repository for DNA profiles taken from prisoners and missing or murdered children. Every time a DNA sample is obtained, it is supposed to be sent to CODIS to determine if the extracted DNA belongs to a child that has turned up missing or has been killed.

In 2009, the question was raised whether the DNA from the bone fragments found in Bar Jonah's garage in 1999 had been compared to Andy Puglisi's DNA. Through the assistance of Melanie Perkins, Jerry Nance from the National Center for Missing Children was contacted. After checking, Nance was unable to find the DNA profiles from the recovered remains. In following up, John Cameron was asked if the DNA profiles from the remains had been submitted to CODIS. Cameron responded with "Yes!" "Are you absolutely sure" was put back to Cameron. Cameron said he would check with his contact at the Montana Crime Laboratory. A short while later, an incredulous Cameron received his answer. The DNA profiles had not been submitted to CODIS. Through a series of circuitous steps, the original profiles from 2000 were obtained from Mytotyping Technologies. The profiles were then sent to B. J. Spamer, program manager of the Forensic Science Division of the University of Texas. As best as could be determined, the DNA did not match Andy. But in the process, it was discovered that the DNA profiles from Mytotyping Technologies were so incomplete that they could not be used to rule out anyone, most especially Zachary Ramsay.

In early September, Spamer voluntarily agreed to retest any remaining bone fragment, the plywood board with the stab marks, and Bar Jonah's blue nylon police jacket at no cost to the Great Falls Police Department. More than $100,000 of state-of-the-art DNA testing, including nuclear profiles, to determine the sex of the victims. They would even pay for the cost of transporting the evidence to Texas. On September 14th, 2009, a meeting was held with Brandt Light, now the assistant attorney general for Montana.

Light's new office sits on the second floor of the Justice Building in Helena, Montana. Light is noticeably thinner now than when he prosecuted Bar Jonah. He was also moving at a slower clip, having recently recovered from surgery for what was fortunately an early–detected colon cancer. "Okay what you got?" Light asked. Theisen happened to be in Helena for another meeting and decided to attend this meeting as well. As the DNA saga unfolded, Light sat in disbelief, shaking his head back and forth. He had not only believed that the profiles had been entered into CODIS but he also assumed that Mytotyping Technologies' declaration that the DNA was not a match to Zach was infallible. After the initial presentation, Spamer was conference-called into the meeting. She reviewed the specifics of her findings and also formally made the offer to completely retest any existing remains at no cost.

Light said, "Of course it had to be done." However, the case was officially closed by the GFPD and he had no direct authority to order the remains sent to Texas. The next morning Light contacted the GFPD. He said they immediately agreed to send off the remaining bone fragments, the board, and the jacket.

Time came and went and the GFPD still failed to send off the material. There were many excuses. The main one being that the detective, who was "handling the case," even though it was a closed case, had back to back homicides. He was "overwhelmed." In June 2012, almost two years after constant prodding by Light, the remaining bone fragments were finally sent off for reanalysis. The results were inconclusive due to the further deterioration of the samples. The Great Falls Police Department failed to include the plywood board or Bar Jonah's police jacket or any other material that may contain relevant DNA for analysis.

* * *

Bar Jonah's diabetes continued to worsen. The half-dollar size ulceration that had opened up on his right leg was becoming so bad that he was in danger of gangrene starting up. He said the prison doc could have treated it and relieved him of his suffering but they hadn't gotten around to it. But, just like in BWSH, Bar Jonah regularly refused his medications. Open sores continued to well up on his right leg. There was nothing more they could do. Gangrene was now threatening to spread up his torso and kill him. His leg had to come off. The day before the amputation, Bar Jonah sat on his bunk, picking and running his fingers around the suppurating, concaved abscesses. When one of the guards came by to check on him, Bar Jonah looked up and said how in the old days they would just put maggots on the lesions and let them eat the dead flesh away. The guard shook his head in disgust and walked away.

* * *

The amputation was successful. His obese, scarred leg was now no longer a part of his body. At the time of the surgery Bar Jonah weighed 370 pounds. His leg weighed thirty. With the deepness of the scar, there was probably five pounds of flesh missing from the leg. Bar Jonah was only in the hospital a few days before he was transferred back to the prison infirmary. The nurses knew that his stump care was going to be a pain in the ass and he was going to be demanding.

* * *

At six a.m. on Sunday morning, April 13th, 2008, a guard found Bar Jonah lying on his back, not breathing. The guard called for help and began to try to resuscitate him. They knew it was no use: Bar Jonah was dead. They continued to do chest compressions until the ambulance got there and rushed him to Powell County Medical Center. He was pronounced as soon as the doc on duty saw his black head come through the door. Later that morning, Bar Jonah's body was sent to the state crime lab in Missoula where it was determined that he had died of a pulmonary embolism from complications of surgery. It was noted that he had two teeth left. Both were little more than rotted slivers.

The night before Bar Jonah died, Rachel Howard had a dream that someone was strangling her. When she heard the next day that Bar Jonah had died, Rachel thought that Bar Jonah had been strangled by one of the guards for what he knew. They were all in on it, she said. They killed an innocent man.

After the autopsy, Bar Jonah's body was picked up by Garden City Funeral Home, just a block down the street from the crime lab. The morgue attendants used a sling to transfer his body to a cardboard casket. They cranked up the scissored gurney and rolled it toward the open door of the crematory retort. As Bar Jonah bounced over the metal pad rollers, one of the attendants said, "Goodbye, fat boy," as he was pushed headfirst into the oven. Eighteen hundred degrees and three hours later, Nathaneal Benjamin Levi Bar Jonah AKA David P. Brown was reduced to a large pile of bone chips and ashes. His cremains were sent back to the Jewell Funeral Home in Deer Lodge, just a few miles from the prison. Jewell called Bob to come down and pick up his brother. There was to be no wake.

* * *

The day after Bar Jonah died, Brandt Light issued an emergency warrant for the state to take possession of everything in his cell. The cops said they wanted to get a look at the letters he had written for the past six years. Cameron had retired and moved on but Bellusci by now had his gold shield back and had returned to the detective division. He told Light that he would go through them and see if anything of interest turned up. On the afternoon after Bar Jonah died, Light called Greg Jackson. "Now that he's dead can you tell me anything, just man-to-man. Let's give Rachel Howard some relief." Jackson told Light in a somewhat despondent voice that he couldn't. He would if he could but Bar Jonah hadn't told his attorneys anything either. Both men shook their heads, sighed, and cordially said goodbye. Light had always considered Jackson to be a gentleman. He had no doubt that he was being honest. Bellusci was never able to find the time to read any of the final letters that Light had confiscated from Bar Jonah's cell.

After Bar Jonah was convicted, Cameron and his wife filed for divorce. He and his ex-wife remain good friends. Bellusci continued to hold the belief that Rachel Howard killed her son. So did Corky Grove, who eventually became chief. Cameron refused to go along, saying that there was not one shred of evidence that pointed to Rachel Howard as a murderer. When Cameron retired in 2005, he was hated by the GFPD. A few months after he left the detective division, Cameron started having abdominal pains and thought he should have it checked out. He was diagnosed with colon cancer in 2006. Cameron was one of the lucky ones. Today, Cameron works privately investigating cold cases. He also plays piano and sings in a popular band in the Great Falls area. When he rides his bicycle along the corridor of the Great Missouri, Cameron is always on the lookout for bone fragments. He still hasn't stopped looking for Zach.

Brandt Light left the prosecutor's office in 2008 and became the assistant attorney general for the State of Montana. He heads up the criminal division and focuses mainly on cold cases. In 2009, Light was diagnosed with colon cancer. Like Cameron, Light was lucky too. It was caught early and he has made a full recovery. So was the lung cancer that he contracted a little more than a year after his run in with colon cancer. He has survived that fight too.

James Wilson was transferred to Dallas in 2010. He continues to remain obsessed with the Bar Jonah case.

Bellusci has retired from the GFPD.

Tim Theisen retired and is now working for the Gambling Control Division for the State of Montana. Renman is his boss. He and Laurie remain a solid couple. At Theisen's retirement party, Corky Grove came up to Light and said he was going to be glad to see Theisen go. Light retaliated and said Theisen was one of the best detectives he had ever worked with. According to Light, Grove continued to make snide comments about Theisen until Light grabbed Grove by the shirt collar and shoved him into a wall. Light pulled back his fist, ready to punch Grove but decided it would be a bad career move.

Don Vernay is now in practice in New Mexico. Greg Jackson remains in practice in Helena, Montana.

The Ladies still live in Great Falls. Darlene still gives psychic readings. Delores died in 2011. Darlene continues to help Rachel search for Zach.

Rachel continues to work daily trying to find Zach. She remains convinced that Franz kidnapped him and that currently Zach is living in Sacramento or maybe Ghana. There is also a possibility that Zach is a medical student and chess champion in the West Indies.

Franz had the courts declare Zach dead on January 26th, 2011. According to Rachel, he just wanted the $20,000 in insurance money. Rachel knew she must be getting close to something in her ongoing investigation because her phones were being tapped and she was being followed again. The night before the courts declared Zach dead, Simone had a dream that someone had killed Zach. Rachel said she understood but it couldn't be because Zach isn't dead.

NOTES

Adams, D., personal communication, July 2009
Bar Jonah, N., personal communications, January 2002–May 2002
Beljan, P., personal communications, January 2002–May 2002
Bellusci, W., personal communication, June 2009
Brown, R., personal communication, April 2002
Brown, T., personal communication, April 2002
Cameron, J., personal communications, April 2009–December 2011
Flaherty, P., personal communication, July 2009
Gustovich, D., personal communication, August 2009
Hipskind, G., personal communication, June 2009
Howard, R., personal communications, May 2009–June 2010
Howard, S., personal communication, October 2009
Kimmerle, D., personal communication, August 2009
Light, B., personal communications, April 2009–June 2012
Metzger, M., personal communication, July 2009
Patterson, R., personal communications, June 2009–August 2009
Perkins, M., personal communications, August 2010–November 2010
Richardson, M., personal communication, August 2009
Scott, L., personal communication, July 2009
Spamer, B., personal communications, August 2010–June 2012
Theisen, T., personal communications, April 2009–December 2012
Wilson, J., personal communication, June 2009

All trial related material is taken verbatim from trial transcripts or court related material in the public domain.
All poetry by Bar Jonah is a matter of the public record.

REFERENCES

Belkin, D. (2000). Cops Seek Other Child Victims in Cannibal Case/City Horrified By Alleged Cannibal Case/Boy, 5, may have been served to neighbors. *Boston Globe*, 31 December, p. 1. Available at: www.sfgate.com/news/article/Cops-Seek-Other-Child-Victims-in-Cannibal-Case-2718264.php#ixzz2HD9zrJLl.

Bruck, M. & Ceci, S. (1993). Child Witnesses: Translating Research Into Policy, *Social Policy Report*, 7(3) Fall.

Dracula Has Risen from the Grave (1968). Dir. Freddie Francis, Perf. Christopher Lee, Rupert Davies. Hammer Film Productions.

Great Falls Tribune (1991). Letter testifying to the miracles of Jesus Christ, November.

Hamblen, S. (1954). *This Ole House*, released by EMI on the His Master's Voice label as catalogue numbers B 10761 and 7M 269.

Missing Children International Ministry (2005). Interview with Bar Jonah, July.

The Texas Chain Saw Massacre (1974). Dir. Tobe Hooper, Perf. Marilyn Burns, Edwin Neal. Vortex Films.

Wesley, C. (1749). *In The Name of Jesus All Things Are Possible*. In: Hymns and Sacred Poems, Volume II. http://www.hymntime.com/tch/htm/a/l/l/allthings.htm.

ABOUT THE AUTHOR

John C. Espy, PhD, LCSW, has been practicing psychotherapy and psychoanalysis for the past thirty-five years. He was supervised by R. D. Laing for many years and conducted a weekly supervision group with Sheldon Kopp. He has worked extensively in the area of primitive and psychotic personalities and has interviewed more than twenty serial murderers and pedophiles in the United States and Europe as part of his research on the manifestation of malignant projective-identification. His current practice primarily focuses on clinical and forensic consultation and long-term treatment. He was previously a neurotoxicologist with NASA and has taught at numerous universities throughout the United States. Dr. Espy is also a long-standing member of the American Academy of Psychotherapists, the American Association for Psychoanalysis in Clinical Social Work, and northwestern United States group moderator for the International Neuropsychoanalysis Society.